Surrender
Book 3 of the Elfin Series

By USA TODAY
Bestselling Author
Quinn Loftis

Published by
Quinn Loftis

© 2015 Quinn Loftis Books LLC

Photography KKeeton Designs

Dedication

This one goes to everyone who had to put up with me while I was pregnant and writing this book. You each deserve meddles for your constant patience and ability to keep from throwing me out of a window. God bless you all.

Acknowledgments

As usual, there are so many people to thank when finally finished with a novel. Always, first and foremost I thank my Savior, Jesus Christ for loving me, blessing me and being my rock. Thank you to my husband, Bo, for being so incredibly supportive, tolerant, patient and loving, not to mention incredibly helpful. Thank you to my copy editor…who just so happens to be my husband. Your insight and ability to wade through all my crap writing is what makes it good enough to publish. Thank you so much. Thank you to my Beta readers. Your input and ideas are invaluable to me and have made this book so much better. Thank you to all of my friends and family who have constantly supported me and cheered me on. And thank you to the readers. Without each of you deciding to give my books a chance, I would not be able to do what I do. Thank you for taking your time, money and emotions and spending them on my books. Thank you for all of the messages, emails, Facebook posts, tweets and other shout outs that you all send me. Whether you know it or not, it makes a difference when the readers share their thoughts with the author so please keep it up. There really isn't enough gratitude I can express for those who have read my books and shared them with others. I am truly humbled by you all.

Other Books by Quinn Loftis

The Grey Wolves Series
Prince of Wolves
Blood Rites
Just One Drop
Out of the Dark
Beyond the Veil
Fate and Fury
Sacrifice of Love
Luna of Mine
Piercing Silence (Novella)

Dream Makers Series
Dream of Me
Dream So Dark (coming soon)

Gypsy Healers Series
Into the Fae
Wolf of Stone
Jewel of Darkness (Coming Winter 2015)

Stand Alone Works
Call Me Crazy

Prologue

**"Things are not always what they seem.
Though the world may seem like it's coming to an
end, okay, so in this instance things are exactly
what they seem. Sucks to be us." ~Elora**

*From the Diary of Elora, half dark elf extraordinaire: So I
just might die a virgin after all. That's what sucks about the end
of the world. You just don't plan for it and once it's upon you it's
too late. It's been a few weeks since I've had time to actually write
anything down, which sucks because more has happened in my life
in the past three weeks than it has in all my seventeen (soon to be
eighteen) years. So I'm going to give you a quick recap, as if my
diary is a living breathing thing and really cares. I've told you
about Trik—the dark elf assassin that Cassie, my best friend,
has fallen for. Apparently elves have these things called Chosens
and it's like their soulmate or whatever. Well Lorsan, the dark
elf king, didn't like his favorite assassin being distracted by a
human especially since said human was causing Trik to have a
conscience. It kind of puts a dent in a wicked king's plans when
his assassin stops killing the people the king wants dead. Trik
comes to realize that he doesn't want to be the dark elf assassin
anymore for a couple of reasons. First, because he has Cassie and
second, because the Forest Lords, those are the creators of the
elves, came to see Trik and reminded him of who he is—or who
he was supposed to be. Okay, so hold onto your butts because this
is going to blow your mind. Okay, maybe it won't because really
what do you care about the elf people? Trik is the one true king of
all the elves. Long story short, he got dethroned, went into exile,
and has been a douche for the past few centuries. Fast forward,
Lorsan wants Trik dead. Trik wants to reclaim his throne and
help heal the rift between the light and dark elves and Cassie is
meant to be his queen. Of course, that means Trik had to be all*

6

caveman and drag Cassie to the altar, not that she gave up much of a fight (no fight at all actually). They got hitched and meanwhile little old me found out a few other interesting things as well.

First, I am not just human. Just blew your circuits, didn't I? Turns out dear, old, departed dad was a dark elf. My mom, Lisa, totally went for the bad guy. For some reason, I'm not surprised. That means that Oakley, my brother, isn't fully human either. On top of finding out that I'm not fully human, I also found out that I'm a Chosen to a light elf warrior, who I call Cush. Why, you ask? Because his real name means butt cushion. Okay, maybe not that exact translation but you get the idea. We had a rough start because we're both as stubborn as hobbled mules, but we finally realized that not only are we destined to be together but we actually like each other. Go figure.

Basically we are on the run from Lorsan, while at the same time attempting to shut down the sale of Rapture, a liquid drug the dark elves devised to enslave the human race. If you ask me their goals are a little lofty, but then nobody asked me, and therein lies their problem. But our problems don't end there. On top of trying to get Rapture out of the human realm and taking out Lorsan, we also have to rescue Cassie's parents. Apparently there's a dark elf who is delusional and believes Cassie is his Chosen reincarnated. So naturally he thought kidnapping her parents would win her heart. Loser. What happened to love notes and flowers? Anyways, now you're caught up, roughly. The point is life is about as jacked up as it can get at the moment. I would like to be able to give some Braveheart worthy speech and say that we totally got this, but honestly, I have no idea if we can pull this off. If this turns out to be my last entry, then I have to say that at least I get to go out with a bang and a hot elf as my boy toy. Cush just asked me to write that he is not my boy toy, however, I got the hot part right (eye roll). We're off to save the world. Don't wait up for me.

P.S. I have to rub it in that Cassie's dark elf carries a quiver. My warrior carries a sword. Can you guess who got the short end of the stick (pun totally intended). Cassie, if you live and read this, I love you, but you know I can't be anything but brutally honest. Bye.

Lorsan looked down at the book he held in his hands. It had been a very, very long time since any elf had actually seen *The Book of the Elves*. It was finally his.

"How did you get it from him, my love?" he asked his Chosen who stood across from him with a smug smile on her beautiful face.

Ilyrana held her hand up and examined her nails as she spoke. Her voice was light, as though she was talking about the latest fashions of the human realm, and not an ancient, powerful book. "Tarron made the mistake of returning to his home away from home. He thought we didn't know that he had a place of his own in the human realm."

Lorsan pinched the bridge of his nose as all of the centuries of living weighed on him like bricks being stacked one on top of the other. He had lived a long life, and yet he wasn't to give up until he had all the power he deserved. "He also forgot that at one time we employed the greatest spy our race has ever seen." He looked over at her, taking his eyes off the book for the first time since she handed it to him.

"It took some convincing, but once he realized that there was no way I was letting him leave alive, he handed it over. He did seem to be in a bit of a hurry, however. When I questioned him about it, he simply handed over the book and told me he would be checking in with you later. He said he had loose ends to tie up."

"Where is a good spy when you need one," Lorsan muttered.

"Apparently, too busy attempting to gain control of our race," she answered, though she knew the question had been rhetorical.

"I hope that Tarron hasn't lost his mind and done something foolish."

Ilyrana let out a cackling laugh. "You assume that he was ever in his right mind, king of mine. You, of all people, know that Tarron is a step beyond wicked. You'd be better off hoping that he hasn't started making Rapture on his own and passing it out to the humans like candy. He hates humans more than any other elf I've ever known."

"If your mate had been human and had rejected you, then you might also harbor the tiniest bit of ill will."

"I didn't say he doesn't have a good reason for disliking the humans," she pointed out. "I'm simply saying that his hatred goes a step beyond just words. Tarron is not one to sit by and just let an insult go. It may have been centuries ago that his Chosen walked away from him, but he has not forgotten. Like any good hunter he has been patiently waiting for the opportunity to strike."

"I just hope his endeavor to exact his revenge doesn't interfere with my plans," Lorsan bit out.

His Chosen waved her hand as though batting away a fly. "I don't think you need to worry about that, my love. If there is any one he hates more than the humans, it's Triktapic. His jealousy of our former assassin runs deep. Once he has taken care of whatever plan he has fleshed out, he will be going after the self-pronounced king. Who knows, he might even solve that problem for you and kill Trik himself."

Lorsan shook his head. "We'd be better off looking for a new chemist than believing that Tarron has the power to overtake Triktapic. Even I would be a fool to underestimate him. He is sly, cunning and fearless."

"Perhaps, but he also has something he has never had before," she pointed out.

Lorsan brow dipped low as he tilted his head and looked at her. "What?"

"Something to lose."

Chapter 1

"I met the man of my dreams tonight. Well, he actually isn't a man. He is an elf. He is amazing and mesmerizing. I can't imagine my life without him but even as wonderful as he is, I can see a darkness that lives in him. I want to think that I'm enough to keep him from letting that darkness rule his heart, but I don't know if that's true."
~From the diary of Lucy Tate

He wanted to curse his wretched queen for interfering with his plans, but Tarron knew it wouldn't do any good. He didn't have the time to pick a fight with Lorsan. He had more personal things to deal with. *The Book of the Elves* wasn't going anywhere and at least he knew its whereabouts. Besides, he doubted that Lorsan would be deciphering its secrets anytime soon. He would just move on with the rest of his plans and worry about that after. His mind drifted back to those plans and a tight smile stretched across his face. Yes, he had more important dealings and it started with his prisoners.

Tarron glared at the two humans that sat bound and gagged across from him. They looked every bit like the filthy stuffed pigs they were. He didn't even like having to touch them to tie them up, but it was a necessary part of the job. They were the key to getting what he wanted, *who* he wanted.

"Your daughter is beautiful, even though she is human," Tarron sneered. "I suppose that's not her fault. Like her great-grandmother, she is a product of her DNA. I can't very well hold that against her, unless she chooses incorrectly, of course—just like Lucy did." The name was like acid on his tongue.

Even after all those years, thinking about her still hurt. Like a wound that refused to heal, he ached for her. He remembered the night he'd walked away from her like it was yesterday. Her voice was as vivid in his mind as if she was standing there before him.

"Why would you want to stay in the human realm and age until you died when you could live with me in my realm and be immortal?" Tarron asked his Chosen.

"I don't know if I can make you understand, Tarron. But there is beauty in life that is fleeting that you can't find in a life that is endless. Pain hurts worse, but the joy that comes after the pain is indescribable. Sometimes the night seems endless but then the morning comes and the beauty of the sun rising, its rays bathing the land in its warmth, makes the night worth it. Knowing that one day I will die, that I will leave this world and all that it is, makes me appreciate it more. I don't think I could feel the same way if I had an endless amount of time before me."

Tarron was trying to understand her point of view, but he just couldn't understand why anyone would choose death over an eternity with the one you were meant for.

"You are right," he admitted. "I do not understand. All I hear you saying is that you do not want me. You do not want your soul mate."

Lucy shook her head. "No, that is not what I'm saying. I'm saying that I want you to stay here with me and experience all of those things with me. Wake up with me every day and live it like it could be your last. Gaze at me as though it might be that last time you see me. Kiss me with the passion of one who will not ever taste my lips again. I am not choosing this world over you; I'm simply asking you to share our life together in this world. I want to give myself to you, but I want you to be willing to give yourself to me."

The memory faded like an aged photograph left in the sun and his mind was brought back to the present. Part of Tarron wished he had said yes, that he would have stayed with her, lived out their life together and then died with her. But he hadn't, and he couldn't have regrets. Eternal life was way too long to live with regrets. So he had walked away, turned his back on his Chosen and dealt with the pain. It had dulled some over the century, but he attributed that to the bitterness he felt toward her.

Few elves survived losing their Chosen. It wasn't an immediate death; it was far worse. Once a Chosen was taken, the soul withered, cut off from its other half. It was even worse if the bond was completed but Tarron hadn't completed their bond by mating with her. Had that happened, then the outcome might have been a little different. As it was, he simply turned all of his energy into figuring out a way to destroy humans. They were weak, fickle creatures. Lorsan had thought that Tarron worked for him. Stupid king. As if someone could control him. He hadn't let his Chosen control his destiny and he sure as hell wouldn't let a king.

After decades of study and trial and error, he'd finally come up with something as inconspicuous as a simple liquid—a drink—but it would be the downfall of the humans. Rapture, made from plants found only in the elfin realm, was as addicting to humans as their most intoxicating illegal drugs. Tarron had managed to get the drink distributed in all of the casinos owned by the dark elves. To the humans it was simply an exciting new drink. Little did they know, that with every sip, their bodies grew more and more dependent on it—most to the point of violence and desperation. The dark elves wouldn't even have to lift a weapon against the foul creatures. The humans would destroy themselves. It was a brilliant plan, if he did say so himself.

Tarron was pulled from his thoughts when he saw that the human male was trying to say something. He reached over and pulled the gag out of his mouth. "What?" he snapped.

"Whatever vendetta you have against humans, let me bear your wrath. Please let my wife go," the man pleaded, though to Tarron's surprise, it didn't come out in a groveling manner. Tarron almost respected the man for not begging like a sniveling idiot, almost. He had been a little taken aback by how easily the couple had accepted finding out that elves actually existed. Although, when Tarron traveled through the reflective surface with them, they pretty much couldn't deny that the supernatural did indeed exist. The husband, especially, had moved past the whole *I'm a dark elf* and onto *what do you want* rather quickly. It was a tad refreshing not to have to attempt to convince them of what he was. He was able to focus more on making them realize how inferior they were to his race and that it was hopeless to try and defeat him.

"Your wife is much more appealing to me than you are. Why would I let her go when I could have fun with her while we wait for sweet Cassandra? Besides, she's female. She, above all others, deserves my wrath. Deceitful, loose, fickle bitches. That's what women are." His words were laced with the venom of his hate.

It was like a living thing, swimming in his blood, and Tarron wasn't even sure he could change if he wanted to. He wouldn't *really* touch the man's wife. Such a thought made his stomach turn. But it didn't hurt to scare them both. Their terror was humorous to him because it just proved how useless they truly were. How humans had survived as long as they had was beyond him. But their time was coming to an end. Soon the dark elves would rule more than just one realm and Lorsan would not be leading them, not if Tarron had anything to say about it.

He stood abruptly and turned from the two captives. He was tired of watching the woman shake and the man glower. Instead he walked over to the window and stared out into the dark night. He pictured Cassandra's face in his mind and imagined what it would be like when she was finally in his arms. He would have to make sure she knew her place, of course. But once she realized that she was his, she would do as he told her. Then the fun could begin. It had been so long since he'd touched a woman—not since Lucy. Until he'd laid eyes on her descendant, he hadn't wanted to. But the beautiful blonde with eyes as green as the grass in his realm had captivated him and his fingers itched to become familiar with every dip and curve. His lips turned up in a wicked grin. Yes, they would have lots of fun and he would finally have what he needed and the void would be filled. Finally.

Cassie felt the gentle touch of lips against her neck

15

causing her to shiver with awareness as sleep began to fade. The sun was shining through the window of her bedroom attempting to woo her into believing it was going to be a bright, joyous day. She stared at the curtains that had hung there for as many years as she could remember. The memories of the night before and everything else came rushing in. The sun could shine all it wanted; it wouldn't change how dark the world was becoming. Her mind was flooded with images—some bad, some good, and some *very* good.

"Very good?" Trik's voice rumbled from behind her. His touch allowed him access to her mind and he wasn't shy about listening in whenever he wanted. "I would say *those* particular memories are a whole hell of a lot better than *very good*." His arm was wrapped around her bare middle; his large hand splayed across her stomach stroking her flesh in an intimate way that only a husband could.

Husband, she thought with excitement and also a small amount of shame at realizing that her parents had not been present during their exchange of vows. And that was when the pain hit. Her parents were gone. Taken by a madman—elf, whatever, and held against their will because he wanted Cassie.

"He can't have you," Trik growled. "I don't share."

"Did you get in trouble for not playing well with others on the playground?" Cassie asked dryly.

"I play just fine with you."

She trembled with desire at the suggestive tone and fought the urge to turn around and beg him to have his way with her.

"Why are you fighting it, Beautiful? We are married in the way of your people. I thought that meant all access." His voice was laced with false innocence that had her sputtering at his candid words.

"Did you seriously just say all access?"

She could hear the smile in his voice when he responded. "My, my, wife of mine. Your mind has become quite the gutter since losing your innocence."

"Okay, you have got to quit saying things like that," Cassie said breathlessly as she turned around to face him. When his eyes dropped down to her naked front she realized her mistake.

A wicked gleam filled his silver eyes as his gaze drank her in like a man who'd been deprived of liquid for far too long. His fingertips began to trace where his eyes landed, and Cassie bit back a moan that would only encourage him.

"Trik, we need to get up," she said attempting to reason with him. "There's a world to save and parents to rescue and, and—" For the life of her, she couldn't think of the other pressing emergencies that required their attention. How could she possibly think when Trik's mouth had taken the place of his fingers?

"Shh," he told her as he continued his pursuit. "If the world is going to come to an end, then this is definitely the last memory I want to have of you. I can die with a smile on my face because I had the honored pleasure of bedding my Chosen."

"You are disturbed; you know that right?"

"Hush," was his only response and even if Cassie had wanted to say something she couldn't. Her brain was effectively scrambled by Trik's unwavering, thorough attention.

A little while later there was a knock at the door. Cassie wasn't sure who it was because she hadn't bothered to move from the place she had ended up. Sprawled across the bed, warm and well loved, her faculties had not come back online at that point. Trik seemed to be much more alert. *Tricky dark elf,* she thought to herself. So she let him climb across the bed and deal with whoever was at the door. She had no idea what time it was but knew it was past time for them to have been putting a plan in place and then into action. As much as she wanted to find her parents and to save humanity, she had needed Trik. There was something found in the arms of a soul mate that couldn't be found anywhere else. The passion, comfort, and security that Trik gave her when he loved her could not be duplicated or fabricated by anything or anyone.

Trik's hand on her exposed calf drew her from her thoughts and Cassie began to force herself to move. When she sat up with the sheet wrapped around her, she was a little surprised to find Trik already dressed.

"Everyone is gathered in the living room," he told her. "Why don't you grab a quick shower and then meet me down there?" He leaned forward and pressed a tender kiss to her forehead. "Thank you," he whispered.

"For what?" Cassie asked as her brow wrinkled.

"For letting me love you this morning and for being every bit as incredible as I knew you would be."

He was out the door before she could respond. Cassie sat staring at the place her husband had just been, shell shocked once again by his boldness. She should be used to it, but she wouldn't hold her breath waiting for the day when she didn't blush when Trik made such sensual and graphic comments. He was hundreds of years old; it was a safe bet to say that he wasn't going to change. And she was okay with that.

She climbed out of the bed and headed for the shower pushing thoughts of Trik and their morning away, forcing her mind to focus on what was ahead of them. Before Trik, she had been a normal teenager worried only about school, clothes, and boys. Now she was as far from normal as she could get. Instead of school, she had a whole race of 'people' to worry about. Instead of clothes, she had weapons and war to think about, and instead of boys, she had a husband who just happened to be the Elfin King. Life would never be normal again.

Trick stood with his back against Cassie's closed door. His jaw was tight with the anger he had fought to keep from showing her after having spoken to Cush. He hadn't liked being interrupted. His times alone with his Chosen would be few and far between, and he wanted to savor any opportunities they had. But he was king and no matter how much he needed Cassie, his race needed him as well.

Cush had come bearing bad news. He had told Trik that he'd been outside checking the perimeter of the house—old habits of a warrior die hard—and he had felt something in the front yard. He said he walked toward the street and the closer he got the stronger the feeling became. It was the residue of magic, dark magic. They had had visitors recently and they hadn't even known it. It must have been Lorsan and why he left them unharmed after having caught them unaware, he didn't know. Trik did know that he had failed to protect the people in his care and he was beyond pissed with himself. "Stupid, amateur mistake," he growled to the empty hallway. He'd been so focused on Cassie and wanting to comfort her as she dealt with the fear and pain at the loss of her parents that he hadn't bothered to think that, perhaps, someone should be keeping a lookout.

He took several deep breaths. There was no point in letting his anger distract him. He needed to have every single thought focused on what he *could* do. He had promised Cassie that he would get her parents back, safe and alive. He would not let her down, not again.

Chapter 2

"Every parent both dreads and looks forward to the day their children find the one with whom they will spend the rest of their life. They dread it because it is the ending of a season of life, but they look forward to it because it brings them joy to see the ones they poured themselves into find love. They dread it because they fear that their children might experience the loss of that love in some form, but they look forward to it because when that love is fought for, when it is chosen and nurtured, it is one of the greatest gifts they will ever experience." ~Lisa Scott

Elora paced the living room. Her eyes were on the floor, watching her feet leave impressions in the thick carpet. She was chewing on her bottom lip completely unaware that she had made it bleed as her mind conjured up every horrific scenario that could happen. When they started their little journey, escaping the dark elf prison, their only concern had been the dark elf king and the Rapture that he was handing out like candy to humans. But then *The Book of the Elves* had been stolen and they had discovered that Cassie's parents had been kidnapped by a crazy dark elf determined to claim Cassie as his own. That had added a whole other list of worries to the pile.

It wasn't as if they were completely helpless. They did have the rightful elf king on their side and he had the backing of the Forest Lords. That made him pretty bad ass, right? They also had some incredible elf warriors. The thought had her eyes darting to the right to check on the warrior who had claimed her heart. Cush was temptation in its purest form. From what Elora could tell there was no such thing as an ugly elf, but Cush took the rugged handsome look to a whole new level. *Focus, Elora,* she mentally snapped at herself. There would be time to drool over his hotness later—she hoped. Now was not the time.

Just as she was making her loop around the room to head back in the other direction, a strong arm wrapped around her waist and pulled her into an equally strong chest. Warm air caressed her cheek as soft lips pressed to her ear.

"As much as I enjoy the view of your long legs in that cute skirt and those boots, your pacing is a tad nerve-racking." Cush's rich voice spoke to more than just her mind. His words reached her soul and miraculously brought her a measure of calm that nothing else could. "What has you so worried, Little Raven?"

"You were the one who discovered the left over magic out front."

"Residual magic," he corrected.

"And you are the one who said it was dark magic," she continued as if he hadn't spoken. "How can you ask me what has me worried when we know Lorsan or one of his lackeys was out there staring at the house like some sort of creeper?"

"Nothing can be done about it now. There is no sense in giving energy to worrying about it." His lips were still near her ear, still driving her crazy. The low chuckled that rumbled in his chest told her he knew exactly what effect he was having on her. Cush's hand came up and cupped her face turning her head so that she was looking up at him. He used his thumb to pull her bottom lip from the relentless abuse she'd been subjecting it to and shook his head at her. "It should be a crime for you to cause injury to lips as beautiful as yours," he murmured. His head had dropped even lower and Elora didn't have time to enjoy his words because she was too busy enjoying his lips pressed to hers. Cush's arm tightened around her waist like a steel band and pulled her more firmly against him. She wanted to turn around so she could wrap her arms around his neck, but she couldn't move within his powerful hold. Elora loved the groan that left him as he pulled back from the kiss.

"You're dangerous, Elora Scott." His light blue eyes were as clear as glass as he stared back at her with an intensity that should have her scared. Instead she was excited. She would blame that little issue on the dark elf blood that was running through her veins. Once she'd learned that her father had been a dark elf, she immediately understood why she fought certain urges that, heretofore, had been unexplained. Elora was pretty sure the attraction she felt toward Cush could get out of hand if she let her dark elf half reign. That side of her wanted Cush to kiss her roughly and not hold back all of his strength. That side of her wanted things that made even her blush.

"Either I need to stop touching you, or you need to think about little bunnies and rainbows," Cush said a little breathlessly.

Oops, Elora thought. She forgot that as long as they were touching Cush could hear her thoughts, just as she could hear his. And even if he wasn't trying to listen, if the emotion behind the thoughts was strong enough, he would hear it anyway.

"Sorry." Her voice was small as her embarrassment swept over her skin.

"You don't have to be embarrassed," Cush responded in her mind. *"You are my Chosen, and because you want it, someday very, very soon you will be my wife. It will be my honor to love you in any way that you need, and I will fulfill any pleasure your little inner dark elf requires. Believe me, no part of me will complain."*

Elora was pretty sure at that point that she would be permanently stained red from the blush his words had caused. A clearing throat from someone in the room saved her from having to respond. She reluctantly pulled her eyes from his and turned to face the room. While she'd been pacing, Oakley and Tony had been sitting on the couch talking about whatever it was guys talked about when they were killing time. When Cush had grabbed her and captured her attention, it was like the rest of the world faded away. She had totally forgotten that they had company while she was busy shoving her tongue in her man's mouth.

"I didn't mind," Cush whispered as he answered her thoughts.

"Shh." She elbowed him as Trik walked into the room.

Lisa came in from the kitchen, wiping her hands on a dish towel. She'd made breakfast for those who had bothered to come down that morning and then refused help in cleaning up. Elora knew it was her mom's way of dealing with her own worries and thoughts.

Rin, Tamsin, and Syndra filed in and Cassie was last to appear. Finally, their little hunting party was gathered and it was time to get to work. Elora could tell by the look on Trik's face that things were about to get serious.

Trik scanned the room taking in every person while his mind cataloged how they could best be useful against the dark elves. They needed to be smart in the way that they went after Cassie's parents as well as how they would attack Lorsan. There would be little room for error because making one could well mean someone's life.

"I will be honest," Trik began. "I'm still trying to decide how we will pursue our enemy and in which order. It seems that we must be entirely too strong for one foe, so fate has decided that we needed another. Of course, it could just be my punishment for centuries of wrong doing. It will take a lot to atone for my iniquity and, perhaps, saving my race as well as the race of my Chosen will be a good start on the road toward redemption."

"You are not the only one with skeletons, literal or not, in his closet," Tony spoke up. "The point is, you've made your choice and have turned from that life. We don't have to look back anymore. The only thing that is important is that we keep moving forward."

The group seemed to nod in agreement, and having their approval eased the tightness that had been building in his chest.

"Can I make a suggestion?" Cassie stepped up next to his side. He wrapped an arm around her waist and pulled her close. He felt pride at having her be at his side not just as his Chosen but as his partner. "There are going to be risks regardless of what plan of action we take. Perhaps, it would be smart to consider splitting into two groups. We can cover more ground that way. One group could go after Tarron and the other could head to Vegas to deal with Lorsan."

It was one of the plans that Trik had already been considering. But like Cassie said, there were risks. Obviously, one of those risks was that splitting up would make their forces weaker. There was strength in numbers and Trik didn't know how he could get any more light elves into the human realm if Lorsan was watching the portals. If Trik commanded his warriors to come through the portals, he might simply be sending them to their deaths before they had the opportunity to help. However, if they stayed together as one group, it would take longer to deal with both threats.

"We will support whatever decision you choose," Cush assured him, not that Trik expected anything less from them.

After several minutes of consideration, he finally came up with a decision. "We're going to split. I realize that means splitting our power, but I don't think time is a luxury that we have and staying as one group would make everything take longer. Cush" —he pointed to the warrior— "you will lead Elora, Oakley, Lisa, and Syndra. I will take Cassie, Tamsin, Rin, and Tony." Trik looked over at Tamsin. "I hate to separate you and your Chosen, but it allows us to more evenly divide our magic wielders."

"Unlike you and your female, we are able to keep our hands off of one another for longer than a few seconds," Syndra said shooting him a sweet smile that was anything but.

"What she means is that we understand and are fine with it," Tamsin reiterated.

"No," —Syndra shook her head— "that's what you meant. I meant that Trik and Cassie are incapable of being separated for any amount of time because of their need to go at it like rabbits."

Cassie let out a snort.

Syndra gave her a playful wink before turning back to Trik who didn't look bothered in the least by her ribbing.

"Cush," Trik continued as if the interlude hadn't just happened. "You and yours will head to Vegas. Do some recon. See if you can hear any talk about *The Book of the Elves*. Lorsan will no doubt have bragged to someone about it. Syndra, if you could use a little glamour magic. I know that it won't work on all the elves, but maybe we'll catch a break, and you will find something out before being seen. Then see about stopping the distribution of the Rapture. Find where they're storing it and destroy it."

"What about the portals?" Cush asked.

Trik's lips tightened. "We can't risk it. We will have to travel as humans do." He could tell that it frustrated the warriors as much as it did him because it was just one more way that Lorsan had the upper hand. "Those coming with me will head after Tarron." The dark elf's name tasted like rotten bread on his tongue not only because the worm desired his Chosen but because Trik knew the elf personally. He knew what depravity Tarron was capable of, and it sickened him even when he had been loyal to the dark elves.

"Quick question," Elora said raising her hand. "How exactly do you plan to go after Tarron without knowing where he is?"

"I've known Tarron for a long time." *Too long,* Trik thought to himself. "I have an idea of where he's taken Cassie's parents. If I'm wrong, well we'll cross that bridge when we get there."

They might cross it, Trik thought, *or they might just go crashing down with the bridge as it collapses on them all.*

Lorsan stood in the office of Iniquity, which, until recently, had belonged to the human male, Tony. The human had betrayed him. After centuries of relationship between his family and the dark elves and all the benefits that came with that relationship, he'd tossed it aside as if it were nothing. Lorsan wasn't worried. The male would get his due for his traitorous ways.

A sudden fight on the main floor erupted and took his attention away from Tony. He couldn't stop the large smile that stretched across his face as he watched two men tear into one another. They were near the bar so it no doubt had something to do with a certain drink that was becoming an addiction for the humans. His security team had the two men surrounded in a matter of seconds helping minimize the damage to his casino. Lorsan had found that to be one of the downfalls of the Rapture. The animosity the withdraw symptoms caused was wreaking havoc on the interior of Iniquity. He'd had to replace many bar stools, ashtrays, and broken glasses. Had he not been making a fortune on the Rapture, the repair expenses might have been concerning. But as it was, the Rapture was selling better than he could have predicted. It had been so easy to distribute; he already had it in multiple venues other than the casinos. He knew the violence and stupidity he had witnessed in Iniquity would soon spread outside its walls and then outside the city.

The power he felt at having so easily ensnared the humans was so heady he nearly felt drunk on it. Lorsan was beginning to realize that he didn't have to stop with just making money off of the desperate people. With a drug as addicting as Rapture, he could bring the entire human race to kneel before him.

"What wicked scheme are you working up, mate?" Ilyrana asked as she slipped into the room.

"I was just thinking." Lorsan turned his body partially away from the one-way glass so he could see his Chosen.

"A dangerous pastime," she teased.

"Imagine ruling more than just the dark elf realm." His eyes narrowed but grew unfocused as he pictured the future. "We could rule this realm as well. The humans are so easily influenced it would not take much to take over completely. Think about it, my love; we wouldn't be subject to the Forest Lords. We would be our *own* lords. And with *The Book of the Elves* in our possession, we could make our magic even more powerful—as powerful as it once was in the ancient times."

"I've always loved your ambition," she purred as she stepped closer to him, pressing her body intimately against his. "It's one of your most attractive attributes."

Lorsan's skin heated with desire but before he could act on the feelings building inside of him, the door to the office swung open with a loud thud as the knob hit the wall. He pushed Ilyrana aside and glared at the dark elf who dared to barge in on him, but the look on the male's face gave him pause.

"We have a serious problem," the elf said through clenched teeth.

"If you tell me the book is gone, I will skin you alive," Lorsan snarled and the elf paled.

"N-n-no," he stuttered. "It's not the book. It's the humans. There's been a break in."

"In the safe?" Lorsan asked.

The elf shook his head. "No, in the storeroom. Where the drinks are kept," he clarified.

Realization dawned on Lorsan as his eyes widened. "The Rapture," he whispered.

"They're stealing it," the male confirmed. "A lot of it."

Chapter 3

"Humans continue to amaze me with their 'technology.' These so called 'inventions' that they've come up with over the years are nothing more than efforts to stay connected. Deep down they know they are weak. They know they are vulnerable. Subconsciously they fear to be alone. So they continually strive to connect themselves to other humans. But those connections themselves are weaknesses. Like a virus spreads from cell to cell, so can disaster spread through the networks the technology affords. Their very ingenuity will be their downfall." ~Tamsin

"**H**ave I ever mentioned how much I loathe airports?" Elora asked no one in particular. The group that was now gathered in terminal C, Section A of Oklahoma City International airport each glanced in her direction. After surviving the long and hazardous journey across the airport, considering they had nearly been run over by one of those luggage golf carts, they'd finally reached their gate. Now they could sit and wait with a hundred other bodies crammed into the tiny little terminal.

"What about it exactly do you despise?" Oakley asked her. "Could it be the obnoxious lady on the intercom having to repeat herself because people won't pay attention? Or perhaps, it's the lovely smell that seems to be wafting off of these fabric seats that are more than likely several decades old? Better still, maybe you utterly loathe airports because they let guys that look like Cush walk through the security line without a backward glance, but then pull a seventeen-year-old female to the side to pat down because she looks too threatening."

"Yes," Elora answered to all of the questions. "And to be fair, I do sort of look like someone who likes to play with fire."

"I personally like the part where Cush made the male security guard who stepped toward Elora take several steps back causing him to trip over a guy trying to put his shoes back on. I was sure the poor man was going to start crying," Syndra laughed.

Elora noticed that Cush did not.

"He made some comment about Elora being selected for a random pat down," Cush said. His jaw was clenched so tight Elora wondered how his teeth didn't shatter. "I simply made it clear that if he touched her I would crush his hands."

"Oh is that all?" Oakley chuckled.

"Poor guy," Elora said in a voice that was forlorn, though when she looked at Cush she knew he saw the wicked gleam in her eyes. "That might have been the only action he would have had in a long time."

"Elora," Lisa admonished though not very convincingly.

"He can touch someone else's female," he said in a deathly low voice. "No one touches you."

Elora knew better than to continue to tease him when he was feeling all possessive and protective so she let it go. But she continued to watch him and he continued to seethe. Elora was a little confused as to why he was still so upset over it, and she was just about to ask him when a voice came over the intercom.

"Attention passengers of Continental Airlines flight 233, we apologize but your flight has been put on hold for some routine maintenance of the aircraft. We will attempt to move as quickly as possible to keep your wait as short as we can. Thank you."

"Routine maintenance," Elora huffed.

"It probably won't be long if it's routine," Syndra offered attempting to soothe Elora's ruffled feathers.

Elora glanced at her brother. "You'd better be the bearer of bad news. If I tell them I'll add lots of expletives and have to blame it on my dark elf half."

"What she's not saying," Oakley started as he looked from Cush to Syndra, "is that when they say routine maintenance it usually means there's a massive leak in the gas tank, or half the engine is suddenly on the ground. They don't want to cause any fear by telling us what is really going on."

"So basically the nice human just lied to us," Cush pointed out unnecessarily, his face just as tight as it had been since going through security.

"It's a form of customer service," Lisa offered. "Keep the consumer happy and ignorant and hide everything else under the rug. Welcome to the American way."

"I always said humans were weird," Syndra said as she sat back into her chair attempting to get comfortable. Elora didn't know why she was even trying. Sitting in airport chairs was about as comfortable as sitting bare-butted on a cactus. Okay, so maybe she was exaggerating, but not by much.

Elora stood up and stretched her arms above her head attempting to work the kinks out. If they were going to be stuck here for a while, she was going to have to move around and get the blood flowing to all of her extremities again. She could see Cush standing up behind her from the corner of her eye, but she didn't bother to acknowledge him. He would give her some space, but he wouldn't take his eyes off of her.

She walked over to the huge glass windows that looked out over the tarmac where the planes docked for loading and unloading. She watched as men in blue jumpsuits and yellow vests hustled about, each moving with purpose and efficiency. It made her think of an anthill with all the little worker ants scurrying here and there to get their tasks done. Her eyes were drawn to the plane that had their flight number on the side, and she attempted to find what could be wrong with it. Granted she knew there wasn't going to be a huge sign with an arrow that said 'faulty propeller.' Nothing could ever be that simple.

Elora was just about to turn away from the window when fluid movement—much too smoothly to have been made by a human—caught her attention. Her eyes narrowed as she stepped closer to the window; her nose nearly bumped into the glass. She was sure it had to be a trick of the light but then two other men seemed to materialize next to the first one. Her eyes widened. "You sneaky, sneaky elves," she muttered under her breath as she watched three dark elves working alongside the humans, only she was pretty sure they weren't attempting to help. There was no doubt in her mind that they were dark elves because she was seeing past their glamour. Elora imagined it was probably not airline policy for their employees to have long hair flowing freely whipping in all directions in the wind where it could get caught in something. She also thought that it was probably not acceptable for their employees to carry swords and daggers at their sides.

Elora turned to find Cush. She didn't have to look too hard. He was about twenty feet away leaning against a pillar, completely unaware of the affect he was having on the people around him. The men were looking at him warily as though at any moment he was going to reach out and grab one of them by the throat, and the women were looking at him like he was the juiciest steak they'd ever seen. It would have been funny if she wasn't worried about the dark elves sabotaging their plane. She motioned for him to come over and then unabashedly enjoyed the view of his large frame moving so gracefully through the crowd. People got out of his way without him ever having to say anything. Elora was sure at any moment someone was going to roll a red carpet out in front of him. She snorted to herself at the image in her mind.

"What's the smirk for?" Cush asked once he was standing in front of her. His eyes were focused only on her. She knew that he was aware of their surroundings and he constantly watched for threats, but somehow he never took his eyes off her.

"Are you completely oblivious to the reaction of people around you?" Realizing that now was not the time to boost his ego, she shook her head and waved a hand in front of him. "Scratch that. I wanted you to come over here so you could see that." She turned and pointed at what was beyond the window to where she'd seen the elves. Are you freaking kidding me?" she huffed. They were gone.

"What's wrong, Elora? What did you see?" Cush asked her in the voice he always used when he expected obedience.

"There were three dark elves out there. They were running around just like the other workers, looking as though they were helping, but I saw past their glamour. I don't know what they were doing but I would bet my big left—"

"Little Raven," Cush said in warning.

She looked up at him with wide, innocent eyes. "I was going to say my big left toe. Where exactly is your mind, oh great warrior?"

"Quit distracting me, woman," he growled as he took her hand and led her back over to where their group was still lounging.

Elora could tell that they all new immediately something was wrong just by looking at Cush. His face was hard granite as his jaw clenched and his brow lowered over his seething eyes.

"What's wrong?" Syndra asked as she stood.

"Elora saw dark elves out by the plane that we are supposed to board," Cush explained. "For some reason I don't think it's a coincidence."

Oakley pinched the bridge of his nose as he let out a frustrated sigh. "How is this guy staying one step ahead of us?"

"Trik was not Lorsan's only spy," Syndra told him. "He just happened to be his most talented."

"So what's the plan?" Lisa asked as she joined the others all now standing.

Cush looked at Syndra with narrowed eyes. "It's time you proved just how powerful you are."

Syndra's head tilted ever so slightly to the side and a crooked smile twitched her full lips. "What exactly do you have in mind, warrior?"

Tony sat in the living room of Cassie's parent's house with Rin, the light elf warrior sitting across from him. Trik and Tamsin were making some last minute plans. Cassie had disappeared from the room after telling the other group goodbye and they hadn't seen her since. After having been employed by the dark elves his whole life, he knew what they were capable of. If his parents had been taken by one of them, he'd be just as terrified as Cassie. He had thought about offering some encouraging words to her but decided against it. Male elves were weird about other men getting near their Chosen females. Though he had known Trik a long time and didn't think he'd be offended by him, people act differently in stressful situations. Having to rescue your mate's parents from the clutches of an evil dark elf was about as stressful as it got.

He'd been surprised when Trik told him that he would be staying with the elf king. Tony would have thought that since he knew Vegas, and he knew Iniquity, that he'd be an asset for the other group. But Tony knew that Trik had been a spy and an assassin for decades. Obviously the elf knew his stuff, so Tony wouldn't question his decisions.

"What made you change your mind?" Rin asked, breaking the stifling silence.

Tony looked up from the unfocused spot on the floor that he'd been staring at for nearly twenty minutes. His eyes met those of the warrior's and he didn't see mistrust in them, just curiosity.

"What do you mean?" He was pretty sure he understood the question, but when in doubt, get clarification or risk looking like a dumb ass. Words his father always said to live by.

"Your family has been in service to Lorsan for generations, correct?"

Tony nodded.

"And you have obviously been working for them up until now. So what made you change your mind and switch teams?" Rin leaned forward and laid his forearms on his knees. It was a pose that said I'm listening, I'm interested.

Tony didn't answer right away though he thought the answer should be obvious. He would have to be a truly sick, twisted bastard to have continued to work for Lorsan knowing what he was planning. Then again, he had worked for him knowing about other crimes he'd committed, and instead of speaking up or stepping out, Tony had turned a blind eye and a deaf ear. As far as he had been concerned, all of his life he knew nothing about dark elves. At least that was always his answer when the wrong people came asking questions. Finally, he spoke. "Knowing that something is going on but not really seeing it is very different from having the evidence right in front of your face. I didn't see much of Lorsan's doings before Rapture. I'm not saying it's right or okay, but it was easier for me to ignore. But Rapture was in my house so to speak. It was destroying the people who entered it and I was watching it happen. I don't know about you, but for me, if something is keeping me up at night, it's a big clue that something needs to change. I wasted so many years doing the wrong thing." Tony paused as he rubbed his eyes. He was tired—tired of hiding, tired of lying, and just plain tired of dark elves. "I needed to do something right for a change."

The warrior stared at him as if Tony was an interesting, new bug that had never before been discovered. It was disconcerting to have someone examining him so closely. Tony wasn't sure if Rin was trying to measure the honesty of his words or if he flat out didn't believe them.

After a few more awkward seconds, Rin nodded his head and sat back in his seat. "Glad to see that you came to your senses. I would have hated to kill someone with so much life ahead of them."

Tony wasn't shocked by the warrior's words. He knew they were true. Rin would have killed him without pause if he had stayed and continued to support Lorsan and his plans, and he would have deserved to die. Hell, he thought, I probably deserve to die anyway.

Cassie followed Trik and Tamsin into the living room where Rin and Tony waited. Most of the destroyed furniture had been put in the garage so that the room looked more like the one she'd grown up with. There were still a few pieces of evidence of the violence that had taken place there—scratches on the wall, a broken railing on the banister of the stairs, and a coffee table with chips taken out of the corners. Cassie tried to look past those things because they only made her think of what her parents had been through.

"Tamsin received a phone call from Cush." Trik's voice drew Cassie's attention and she turned to face him. He hadn't told her about the call. She hoped that Elora was alright. She, of course, wanted the others to be okay too, but Elora was a part of her like an arm or a leg, and she couldn't stand the idea of something happening to her especially since her parents had been taken.

"Lorsan knew they were going to be flying; he even

knew the flight they were on. Some of his minions sabotaged the plane."

Cassie sucked in a quick breath.

Trik looked at her and his eyes softened. "It wasn't while they were on the plane, Beautiful. It was before they had even boarded."

]' he felt the rapid beat of her heart begin to slow slightly with relief.

"Lorsan is resourceful. I was not his only spy and apparently he is keeping closer tabs on us than we realized. I know it will take us longer to drive, but I just don't feel safe taking a plane at this point. There's no way to defend a plane. At least in a car we are in control and can stop or change directions if we need to."

"What are Cush and his group doing?" Rin asked.

"They are going to take a cab to a car rental place and drive to Vegas. He had the same idea I did about being in control. He didn't like the fact that he had no way of knowing if the dark elves watching them would know if they booked a new flight. And he didn't want to take the risk of finding out." Trik motioned toward the door that led to the garage. "Cassie's parents' SUV is here so that's what we will take." He paused and then looked at Rin. "I don't like the fact that Lorsan has his lackeys keeping an eye on all of us. He probably has someone watching this house. I want you to stay here as sentry. I realize that's not exactly the most exciting job. But when we get Cassie's parents back and bring them here, it would give me peace of mind to know that we won't be walking into a trap set by Lorsan."

Rin bowed his head. "It is an honor to guard what is important to my queen. I won't let the enemy take root in her childhood home."

Trik saw Cassie's face blush. "You have to remember, love, that Rin is what you would call *old school*."

Rin looked up and grinned at Cassie. "I suppose in this day and age I should say something more along the lines of, no problem, I got this."

Cassie laughed. "That would sound less formal, but honestly it sounds awkward coming from you."

He nodded. "Then I shall practice your lingo while I stand sentinel. Perhaps, when I see you again I will blow your mind with my mad skills."

Cassie gave him a thumbs up. "Great. I think."

Trik chuckled as he turned back to the rest of the group.

"Where exactly are we going?" Tony spoke up.

Trik glanced at Tamsin but Cassie couldn't read the silent communication that seemed to pass between them. She could only imagine it meant his answer wasn't going to be an encouraging one.

"As you know," Trik began as he folded his arms across his chest, "dark elves are drawn to the pleasures in this world, especially the darker ones."

Cassie shivered at his words.

"There are other places in the United States like Las Vegas. Places where being self-indulgent is not frowned upon, but actually encouraged. Dark elves feed off of the depravity of the humans. Something that might not be widely known among the light elves is that dark elves can even draw certain power from places that are especially corrupt." He let out a tense breath before he continued. "I have had the misfortune of knowing Tarron a long time and know many of the dark places in this country that he likes to frequent. One of his favorite places, and a place that definitely gives the dark elves more power, is New Orleans."

Cassie squeezed her eyes closed shaking her head slowly. "I should have seen that one coming," she mumbled.

"There's more. There is a certain part of the city that most mortals don't know about and even fewer can get to. I'm talking about a place that is only findable by people that have already been there. It's not on a map and can't be found on those GPS gadgets that humans rely on so much."

"Voodoo country," Tony offered.

Trik gave a solemn nod.

"Wait." Cassie's brow drew together as she looked from Trik to Tony. "Voodoo? Real Voodoo? Like it's actually a thing?"

"Voodoo is a religion, an old religion, based in darkness. It is as real as the people who practice and believe it," Trik answered.

"You think Tarron has taken my parents to this Voodoo part of New Orleans?" she asked her mate.

Trik nodded. "It's my best educated guess. Dark places draw dark things and Tarron's soul is about as dark as they come."

"Great," Cassie huffed. "And this is the man who has my parents?"

"He won't hurt them," Tamsin told her. "They're his only bargaining chip to get you."

Cassie figured she should believe Tamsin since he seemed to know what he was talking about, but it was hard to think any positive thoughts when her parents were in the clutches of a dark elf that had surrounded himself in a place that would only make him stronger.

Trik took her hand and she hadn't even realized that he had moved. He tilted her chin up to look at him and, as usual, his beauty took her breath away. "Don't look so forlorn, my love. Don't you remember who I am?"

Cassie's lips twitched with the urge to smile. "Even if I hadn't, you would still tell me."

"True enough, but you obviously need a reminder." He leaned down and pressed his lips to hers before pulling back and whispering against them. "I am Triktapic, King of the Elvin race, most powerful of our kind, blessed by the Forest Lords, and I am mated to the most amazing woman ever created. How can you even begin to doubt that I will defeat Tarron and get your parents back?"

A single brow rose on Cassie's forehead. "How foolish of me, great King," she said dryly. "Please forgive my lapse in judgment."

Trik pressed another quick kiss to her lips and said with a wink, "I'll think about it, but I have a feeling punishing you would be more fun."

Cassie let out a groan complete with eye roll as he took her hand and led her toward the garage where the others had already loaded into the SUV.

"I'm so glad that you don't have any self-confidence issues," she told him as he pulled her behind him. "It just wouldn't do to have a King that didn't see himself as the great leader that he is."

Trik laughed. "Just admit it, Cassandra. You think my confidence is sexy."

"Okay, Quiver Boy," —she pursed her lips at him— "let's just see if you follow through with your claims, then we'll talk about who's sexy."

They climbed into the vehicle and as Trik put the car in reverse and flicked his hand using his power, and no doubt to showoff, to raise the garage door, he glanced at her from the corner of his eye. Cassie knew he was about to say something that was going to have her blushing from head to toe.

"You of all people should know that I have absolutely no problem with my follow through."

Chapter 4

"I see you, child—curious and desperate for truth. Don't be afraid to walk into the darkness if you want to see beyond the shadows to the spirit world. Where once you were powerless, you will be strong. Where once you were unsure of your destiny, you will be confident. You only need to seek the truth. But remember, child, what claims to be truth may only be a reflection of the things you simply *want* to be true." ~Voodoo priestess.

Elora attempted to sleep with her head propped up against the window. The dull noise from the tires on the road steadily lulled her into slumber. Sleep would be a welcome retreat from all the worry that was bouncing around inside her head. In addition to Cassie's parent's being missing, now they had dark-elf spies on their ass screwing up their mission to save the world. Didn't they know it was hard enough to save the world without dark elf spies, especially when the humans they were trying to save didn't even know they needed saving or want it? It's like they were attempting to do the largest intervention ever. Betty Ford better get ready for an influx of patients.

She felt a large, warm hand on her thigh and lifted her head to look over at Cush who was driving their getaway vehicle. Okay, so maybe it really wasn't a getaway vehicle since they didn't steal it. They actually rented it with Tony's credit card—all nice and legal like.

"How are you?" Cush's deep voice caressed her. It

wasn't fair that he could make her want to pant from just a simple touch. She wondered if she held any similar power over him.

"One look from you, Little Raven, that's all it takes," she heard him in her thoughts. He had been listening in again. Maybe it should bother her, but honestly she loved the intimacy that it forged between them.

"I'm sort of waiting for the other shoe to drop and crush our Yukon," she admitted wryly. "We've been driving for three hours now and nothing has happened; it makes me wonder what they're waiting for."

"Maybe we gave them the slip," Oakley offered from the backseat.

"Gave them the slip?" Elora scoffed. "What are you, a half dark elf mafia member?"

"Hey, don't hate just because I know the lingo," he shot back.

"Oakley, I love you. But you're a dork," Elora snickered.

Cush squeezed her leg to get her attention. "Be nice," he warned, though there was a playful glint in his eyes.

"Give me a break, warrior. You don't care if I'm nice. You just don't like my attention on someone else." Elora shot him a look that said she totally had his number complete with the single brow raise.

"Perhaps," he admitted as he looked back at the road. "But then I told you from the very beginning that I didn't share well." He glanced at her again. "Aren't human males possessive?"

Lisa and Elora both let out similar snorts of laughter. "Human males might have at one time been possessive, but human women have squashed them like little bugs with a shoe called the feminist movement."

"And that is?"

Elora remembered that Trik had mentioned that Cush didn't spend much time in the human world, though he tried to keep up with the times. Maybe the 60's and 70's had been decades that he hadn't bothered to keep track of. "It started out as women desiring the same rights that men had. You know—the right to vote, to run for office, to be leaders, to work and make their own money— that sort of thing. They wanted to be a man's equal."

Syndra shook her head interrupting. "Which wasn't bad, at first. But some people have taken the idea to extremes."

Cush's eyes narrowed as he thought about what Elora had said. She could tell that he had an opinion, and she was honestly curious as to what it was.

"What are you thinking, warrior?" she finally asked.

"I can understand them wanting to be able to have the same station in life as a man and be their equal in that manner simply because they are the same species. I guess because I'm not human, maybe it's different for me. There is no way I would ever consider Elora, my Chosen, as my equal."

Elora's jaw dropped and a hundred words that weren't so nice formed on her tongue.

"Let him finish," Syndra said before Elora could verbally vomit on him.

"She isn't my equal because she makes me better—a better man, a better warrior. What man can boast about the ability to bring life into the world? What man can continue to love, setting aside all other negative feelings? What man can say that he understands a compassion that puts all others before himself? Elora, a woman, can bear my children, she can love me even if she loses all respect for me, and she will show compassion even to those that I would deem unworthy. She can do these things only because she is a woman and it is how she was created. The mere sight of her makes my day better and brighter. Even when she's driving me crazy, she's still the first thing I want to see in the morning and the last thing I want to see at night. How can someone who does those things be my equal? She is so much more than me and I esteem her as much as I love her. Does that mean she's faultless?"

"Yes," Elora piped in just as Cush said, "No."

He shot her a quick smile before continuing, "No, she isn't perfect, but she's perfect for me. And don't get me started on the female form," he chuckled. "They definitely have the market when it comes to beauty in the physical sense." Cush glanced at Elora, his eyes running over her so intensely that she could practically feel it. "In fact, I would say a woman's body is reason enough to revere them."

"Whoa, hey, mother in the vehicle," Lisa called out. "You cannot say *woman's body* while looking at my daughter like she's the last beef jerky stick in any realm. It's forbidden. So stop. Like, now."

Elora rolled her eyes but the heat on her skin didn't leave even after Cush was no longer admiring her physical form. The vehicle was silent. Cush's impassioned words seemed to have rendered everyone speechless. Elora had to admit that everything he had said had taken her by surprise. She knew he cared for her, but to hear it in the way he described it was just . . . wow. She was also pretty sure he'd won some brownie points with Lisa, despite his comments about the female body and his devouring gaze. She was still looking at him, though he was once again paying attention to the road. Elora couldn't take her eyes off of him. He felt all of those things for *her*. The thought hit her like a gale force wind and knocked the breath right out of her. She bit her bottom lip to hold in the gasp as she truly began to understand exactly what Cush had said. He hadn't been talking about women in general, he had been talking about *her*, describing the way he saw *her*, and the way he felt for *her*. She wanted to say something to him, to respond to his admission, but not there with all the extra ears in the car. What she had to say would be for his ears only.

Darkness began to cloak the night sky like a blanket being laid across the earth, tucking her in for a much needed sleep. The last sign Elora noticed had welcomed them into the great state of Colorado. They had driven up into Kansas and then over from there, and when she'd asked Cush why he wasn't taking the route on the GPS, he'd told her that it would be better to lead the dark elves on a little chase. She didn't figure that chase would last very long judging by the moaning and groaning that had begun and Oakley's constant 'are we there yet' questions.

Just when she was sure she was going to have to beg Cush to call it a night, he pulled into the entrance of a motel. It wasn't anything fancy, but neither was it one of those places where bodies were hidden in one room while a one night stand took place in the room next door.

Twenty minutes later they were all dragging themselves up the stairs that lead to the two rooms Cush had acquired. Elora's steps were heavy; her shoes felt like they'd been filled with concrete as she trudged up the last few steps finally reaching the landing. Two steps to the right and they were standing in front of rooms 24 A and 24 B, apparently a connecting suite.

"Girls in A and boys in B," Syndra announced as the doors were unlocked and pushed open. The stale scent of cleaner and mothballs hit their faces. There were lights already on and as Elora stepped into the room she eyed the bed longingly. But she knew it would be at least a few minutes before she would get to crawl into the undoubtedly scratchy sheets. Her thoughts were confirmed when the door on the right hand wall, that obviously lead to the boy's room, opened and in stepped Cush.

"Let's take fifteen minutes and go over tomorrow's plans before we call it a night," he told them as Oakley stepped in behind him.

Elora took the corner of one of the beds and Lisa sat next to her. Syndra draped herself, as only a queen could, across the other bed and propped up on one elbow as she waited for Cush to continue. Oakley took the one and only chair leaving Cush to lean against the wall, not that he would have sat down even if another seat would have been available.

"We will make it to the city tomorrow," Cush began. "Once there, Syndra is going to use a little influence to help keep prying eyes from noticing us, and we are going to see if we can sniff out Lorsan. I don't think he will be hard to find. I have a feeling that now that Tony has left Iniquity Lorsan has probably taken up overseeing the casino and the distribution of Rapture."

"What are we going to do when we find him? Declare a citizen's arrest?" Elora asked.

Cush gave her a look that clearly told her he though she was absurd. She shrugged. It was a valid question.

"We just need to get the lay of the land, so to speak," he answered her and then turned his attention back to the entire group. "We need to get an idea of how many elves he has at his immediate disposal. We also need to see if we can get an idea on just how extensive the Rapture situation is."

"Do you think he's managed to get it out of Vegas?" Oakley spoke up.

Syndra nodded. "I would actually be surprised if he hadn't already distributed it to other venues."

"The important thing is to disrupt the flow of the Rapture so it can't make it to any of its destinations," Cush explained. "Once we've neutralized that process we can focus on making sure the Rapture that's already available is destroyed."

"And how exactly will we do that?" Elora frowned.

"We could phone in a recall to the FDA letting them know that any and all production of the Rapture in circulation is contaminated and needs to be destroyed immediately. I'm sure we can manage to get some of our elves into the system to oversee the process to makes sure it is all taken care of."

"It sounds so simple when you put it like that." Oakley let out a sigh. "But for some reason I have a feeling that none of this is going to go according to plan."

Cush gave him a wolfish smile. "Where would the fun in easy be?"

"You consider this fun?" Oakley's eyes widened.

Elora let out a groan as she flopped back on the bed. "UGH, don't get him started. He was raised to be a warrior; it's in his blood, blah, blah, freaking blah."

Cush chuckled. "Perhaps, hunting dark elves is an acquired taste."

"Regardless of what it is," Lisa said as she stood up, "it will require energy. So" —she waved the boys off toward their room— "off with you two and let's call it a night."

Elora didn't move from her prone position on the bed but she did open her eyes when she felt soft fingertips tracing her lips. Cush hovered over her looking at her as if she'd single-handedly saved the human race.

"What's that look for?" she asked him unable to stop herself from raising her own hand up to trace his strong jaw.

His full lips lifted ever so slightly. "It's because of you, my Chosen," he whispered. "I'm just in awe of you."

"Because I flop so gracefully on a bed when I'm whining about you and your, 'I'm a warrior hear me roar', bit?" She quirked an eyebrow at him.

"Yes, that and many, many more reasons." He leaned down as his large hand cupped her jaw. "Sleep good, Little Raven." His lips pressed against hers but were gone much too quickly. *Sweet dreams.* His voice rumbled in her mind. She grinned up at him as he gave her lips one last gentle touch and then left the room.

"I thought I was going to have to grab the fire extinguisher." Syndra's voice popped the bubbled that had enveloped Elora in her own little world with Cush.

"What?" she asked as she rolled off of the bed needing to brush her teeth before she could crawl into bed and let sweet oblivion take her to a place where she would surely dream of her warrior.

"What do you mean, what?" the light elf queen snorted. "The tension between you two is drawn as tight as my best archer's bow. Too many more times spent absorbed in each other like that and one of you is going to snap."

"And pray tell, what will happen then?" Elora watched Syndra from the mirror where she was putting the toothpaste on her toothbrush.

"I got one word for you—rabbits."

Syndra's remark had Elora spitting the mouthful of toothpaste all over the mirror in front of her. "Crap," she muttered as she wiped her mouth with the back of her hand and grabbed one of the folded towels to wipe off the mirror.

Lisa was laughing as she pulled the comforter back on the bed she would share with Elora. "She just likes to get a reaction," she told her daughter. "If you'd ignore her she'd eventually get bored."

"It's a little hard to ignore her when she's talking about Cush and me and rabbits. Doesn't that disturb you just a little, Lisa?"

"I'm learning to think of other things when you and your mate's attraction is brought up, like roadkill guts and dog vomit. Those seem to really help me avoid images that some" —she looked at Syndra— "try to suggest."

Elora climbed into the other side of the bed and pulled the covers up to her chin. She tried not to hum happily as she snuggled down. "Good to know you've worked out a system," she told her mom as her eyes drifted closed.

"I don't understand what the big deal is. I'm just saying what everyone else is thinking," Syndra muttered under her breath as she snapped her fingers, causing all of the lights to go off at the same time and plunging the room into blissful darkness.

Elora's mind drifted in a haze on the edge of sleep

as she thought about Cush. Syndra was right to a certain degree. The attraction between them was growing stronger. It was harder and harder to deny and she wondered if being in Las Vegas was going to make it even more difficult since sin city called to her dark half. It whispered to her of all the pleasures she could have if she'd only let go and give in to her desires. Even laying there in a hotel in Colorado, simply thinking of the city and all its glittering glory and promises of fulfillment had her darker half stirring. Elora truly hoped she had the strength to keep from giving in to the desires that were not necessarily good for her.

And if I'm not strong enough, I ask the Forrest Lords to please make Cush strong enough for the both of us, she thought as she finally succumbed to sleep.

Cassie stretched her arms above her head and then bent at the waist as she tried to loosen muscles and joints made stiff after having spent so long in the vehicle. Once they'd finally left her house, they'd driven for what seemed like forever and had finally reached the sign declaring that they'd entered Louisiana. It had been a few hours since their last gas stop, and Cassie had been asleep so she hadn't gotten a chance to get out and give her cramped limbs a break.

The night air was muggy and warm, causing her neck to sweat despite the lack of the sun. Crickets chirped in the fields surrounding the gas station which was the only thing giving off light for as far as she could see. A wry smile tipped her lips as she realized that it was the perfect setting for a horror flick murder scene.

On the tail end of that thought she jumped when large hands encircled her waist.

"Jumpy, Beautiful?" Trik's voice trailed over her neck like warm honey.

"I was in the middle of writing a murder scene in my head that takes place at this rather nice establishment," she said dryly and as though her heart wasn't trying to beat its way out of her chest.

"Are we talking gory, body parts flying murder scene or something more along the lines of the quiet assassin who slits his victims' throats before they ever know he's around?"

Cassie turned her head to look over her shoulder at him. One eyebrow rose slowly as she narrowed her eyes. "You were supposed to say something like, 'Don't worry, Beautiful, I won't let any scary boogeymen murder you.' "

She could tell he was trying to hide a smile when he responded. "I kind of figured it went without saying at this point. I mean" —he pointed to himself— "dark elf assassin slash king." Trik gave a shrug and said, "I even have a shirt that says, *I'm kind of a big deal.*"

That made Cassie laugh. She remembered when he had worn that shirt to her school. That seemed like years ago but it was only months. Trik saw the sudden change in her mood and pulled her tightly against him.

"Talk to me, Cass. Tell me what I can do to make this easier?" His mind was wide open to her and she could tell that he was hurting for her just as deeply as she was hurting over the capture of her parents. Cassie wished she could tell him how to fix it. He just needed to fix it, or at least that's how he saw it in his mind. But until they got her parents out of Tarron's hands, there wasn't anything anyone could do to make it easier.

She was about to say she was sorry but he cut her off. "Don't. You have nothing to apologize for. I'm the fool for thinking I could somehow make this less painful. It's been a long time since I had parents; I've forgotten what the attachment was like."

Trik tilted her chin up so that she was looking up into his silver eyes. His dark hair was unbound and framed his handsome face. He was beautiful, but masculine in only the way a dark elf could be. Even though he'd given up his dark elf ways, there was still an air of danger that surrounded him. He was powerful, deadly, and yet he looked at her as though she was the first flower of Spring. "You do make it easier," she told him.

"I should have been able to keep them safe so that you wouldn't have to be going through this at all."

"Trik," Cassie sighed. "You may be the elf king, but that doesn't make you infallible."

"Says who?" he asked in all seriousness.

She laughed.

"We're ready when you two are," Tamsin called from a few feet away.

Trik took her by the hand and started leading her back to the SUV. "I did manage to do something right," he said as she walked beside him.

"What's that?"

"Well you haven't been dismembered by the boogeyman, so," he said drawing out the last word with a shrug.

Cassie squeezed his hand. "True enough, quiver boy."

"You know you could pick a different nickname," Trik grumbled as he opened the door for her.

"Give me something better than quiver boy,"

Cassie said as she buckled her seat belt.

Before he shut the door Trik leaned in close and whispered, "I have given you plenty to work with, wife."

Cassie knew she was blushing as he walked around the front of the vehicle to climb in the driver's seat. She had walked right into that one.

"We'll be there in a couple of hours," Trik announced as he started the engine.

"What are we going to do once we get there? How will we find him?" Cassie asked.

"We won't have to find him. He will find us," Tamsin spoke from behind her.

Cassie glanced over her shoulder at him. She felt a shiver of unease slide down her spine.

"Why don't I like the sound of that?" she muttered under her breath as her eyes were drawn to the darkness beyond her window. She settled back in her seat and closed her eyes. She knew she was going to need all the sleep she could get.

Rest Beautiful, she heard Trik's voice in her mind at the same time she felt his hand wrapped around hers. *Dream of all the babies you will one day give me.*

She let out a choked laugh but didn't open her eyes. *You're awfully confident.*

She could feel his smugness as his thoughts intruded into hers. *The Trik, pun intended, is to find what you're good at, and then do it a lot. And baby,* you *are what I'm good at.*

The laugh that bubbled up out of her felt good. *Yes, quiver boy, you are.*

Tarron stood just inside the small cabin door. The shack was surrounded by swamplands. Tall trees, bathed in moss, loomed over it and murky waters full of hidden predators swayed languidly around the stilts the cabin was built on. He let the night wrap around him as his form became one with the shadows.

"What do you want this girl for?" The thick Cajun accent would have been hard for most to understand but he had known the priestess for a very long time.

Tarron's head didn't turn when the old woman stepped from the doorway onto the porch. He heard the old rocking chair creak as she eased her worn body into it. She would wait for his answer. That was the frustrating thing about the old ones. They didn't have anywhere to be that they hadn't been already so they weren't in any hurry for anything, be it conversation or action. She would wait patiently until she finally got her answer.

After several minutes of just the sounds of the swamp serenading them, Tarron finally spoke. "She is my Chosen, priestess Chamani."

The priestess clucked her tongue at him. "Come now, we both be knowing that your lady passed on a long time ago."

"We also both know that some souls don't pass on, Chamani. They simply wait for their next chance."

The rocking chair began a steady creaking as she began to rock slowly. The rhythm of the chair seemed to blend in with the sounds around them making an eerie symphony.

"This girl, she gonna be fine with being your

female?"

Tarron turned to face her. His eyes narrowed on the old woman. He wasn't trying to intimidate her. There was no point in that; she was powerful in her own right. Their magic wasn't the same but she would be able to hold her own no matter the wrinkles that lined her leathery skin.

She let out a slow breath. "I ain't judging boy, calm down."

He almost laughed at the *boy* comment. Tarron hadn't been a boy in a very, very long time. He couldn't even remember a time when he didn't shoulder the worries of a man. No, he wasn't a boy but, perhaps, to one such as Chamani, he might still be seen as such. Tarron had no idea how old the priestess was, but he could feel the power that radiated off of her and power—that kind of power—came with age and experience.

"Why do you ask, old woman?" He crossed his arms in front of his chest and leaned back against the crooked railing of the porch. He felt the wood give a little beneath him, but it didn't break under his weight.

"Spells be tricky business. They tend to have a mind of their own if in the receiver ain't to welcome on it. Not saying I can't manage it." She shrugged.

Tarron thought about Cassie's parents who were still tied up at the old Victorian house that he'd turned into a makeshift lab. No, she wasn't going to be fine with being his female, but she would do it to protect her parents. He'd thought about just getting her reacquainted with Rapture before deciding to come to the Voodoo priestess, but he had quickly come to the conclusion that he didn't want a drunken Chosen by his side.

"I have something she wants to keep safe," he told the old woman. "She will accept the magic."

Chamani continued to rock in her chair, wrapping an old, worn shawl tight around her bony shoulders. The night wasn't cool and yet she shivered. The priestess turned her head sharply to the left as if she'd heard something he did not. All of the color leached from her eyes and her body stilled. The white orbs stared at something that Tarron couldn't see. As if the swamp also sensed a presence, the steady cacophony of noises around them suddenly died down, and they were left surrounded by an unnatural silence. He didn't interrupt her, though his body tensed with the urge to know what she was seeing. There was no point in asking. She would tell him when the vision had past, or when she was good and ready.

"What you seek does not belong to you," her voice crooned out in an accent that was not her own. The usual Cajun accent was gone, replaced by a formalness that this priestess had never known. Tarron straightened and pushed away from the rail. He didn't step toward Chamani but shifted his body so he was directly facing her. And then he waited.

"She is pure and the light surrounds her. The darkness that owns you can never touch her. All that you want, you had at one time, but now you attempt to take that of another. If you continue down this path, the destruction that you cause will ripple across more than just one generation. Any offspring you bear with her will be that of an unsanctified union. They will have limitations that will make them vulnerable. They will be unwelcome in her world and seen as an abomination in yours. Yet, if you take what is not yours by force, one of your offspring will arise and have power that will rival the King. There will be nothing to stop him from destroying the world as you know it to be now." The old woman paused as her head turned slowly to face Tarron. His heart was pounding like a steel drum inside his chest, and he could feel the vibrations all the way to his bones. When the milky orbs met his, he didn't flinch away from her gaze.

"Will you continue down this path, Tarron of the dark elves? Is this your choice?" The smooth voice seemed so wrong coming out of the wrinkled and timeworn face of the priestess. And yet he knew it wasn't the priestess that he spoke with; it was one of the Voodoo gods.

If he said yes, that this was his choice, then he would one day face the wrath of the Forest Lords for his treachery, not that he and Lorsan didn't already have things to answer for when it came to their choices. But this, this was something else entirely and he knew it—deep, deep down he knew. Cassie was of his Chosen's bloodline, but she belonged to Triktapic. If he took her from the king, he would be tearing apart a union that had been blessed by their creators.

"What will become of Triktapic?" he asked the priestess.

"He still has his free will. There are many paths open to him. The female is a part of him now and to remove her would be like taking his lungs and then telling his body to continue to breathe. His path might be further into the light, or it might lead him down into a darkness that even he didn't know existed. It is not for us to say what his path will be. I ask you again. Is your choice the female that is not yours?"

"SHE IS MINE!" Tarron snarled. "She is mine. The blood of my Chosen runs through her veins. The very DNA that makes up her body is the same that made up that of the woman who should have been by my side for eternity. I am owed this!"

"You are owed only that which you have earned or that which you take," the Voodoo lord responded.

"Then, yes," Tarron growled. "This is the path I have chosen. She is mine and I will claim her. Survival of the fittest, isn't that the world we live in? She belongs with the male who is strong enough to keep her."

"So be it." The priestess's head fell forward and it looked as if the air had been sucked out of her like a deflated balloon. Tarron didn't move closer to her but waited for her to recover from the brief possession.

Her head slowly rose and her eyes were once again clear. "I have been instructed to assist you, but it will cost you."

"What do you require?"

"The blood of three generations. Your first child, your first grandchild and your first great-grandchild. Each of them must come to me at the appointed time and serve the Voodoo lords for three years. During that time, any ability they might have from your Elvin blood will be subdued until such a time as they have completed their service."

"So I will have children with Cassie?" Tarron asked.

She didn't answer right away and the look in her eyes had him narrowing his eyes on her. Her lips pursed as she met his gaze. "You will have heirs with your mate." She stood and motioned for him to follow her. "Let us begin. I assume you brought me something that belongs to her?"

Tarron entered into the small shack after the

priestess as he pulled the necklace he had taken from Cassie's dresser from his pocket. "I brought you this." He held it out to her. "It appears to have been worn quite a lot which means it was against her skin."

Chamani took it from him and examined it closely. "It will do. I need something of yours as well. A similar object works best."

Tarron pulled his medallion from beneath his shirt. He slipped the chain over his head and looked down at the worn crest. He hadn't taken it off in over a century, but he figured this was the best possible reason to remove it."

"Where did you get this?" Chamani asked him as she turned the medallion over in her hand.

"It was a gift." He didn't elaborate more. There was no reason for the priestess to know anything more.

"It holds powerful magic."

When she realized he wasn't going to respond, she shrugged and continued gathering items she deemed necessary for the spell. Tarron watched silently, his body rigid with anticipation. Was he cheating? Maybe just a bit, but hell, he was a dark elf. Surely no one expected him to be honest. Trik was no fool. He wouldn't be waiting for Tarron to come at him in a direct attack. The dark elf assassin, now restored king, would be looking for an underhanded method. He probably even knew to look for him in Voodoo country. What he didn't know was that he wouldn't just take Cassie from him, but he would also make her want him. Trik would watch as Cassie fell in love with Tarron. He had first thought he would simply kill Trik, but it would be an even worst fate to have to watch his Chosen choose another.

The rumble of thunder drew his attention back to

the priestess. There was a book that looked to be several centuries old opened in front of her. Next to it there was a shallow bowl that held the two necklaces and some other items and liquids that Tarron was happy not to know the origins of. Her eyes were closed and her lips moved though no sound came from them. The air around him began to churn an electric charge and it danced across his skin. He felt the magic reaching out for him like tendrils as it wrapped around him, binding itself to him. Tarron closed his eyes and leaned his head back soaking in the power of the spell. It would be much more effective if he opened himself to it.

"It is done." The priestess's voice had his eyes snapping open and his head lowering.

"Will she be aware that something is different?"

Chamani began to clean off the items before her. "She won't be knowing that da spell has been cast, but she'll feel strange. She might be thinking she is becoming ill and feel a need to go somewhere. What she don't realize is da spell is causing her to want to seek you out. Da full effects of the spell will happen once she be seeing you. It'll grow more powerful with contact."

"And nothing can break it?"

"Death."

"Her death?" Tarron frowned.

"Or yours."

Chapter 5

"I'm pretty sure they release something into the air in Vegas that gets the blood pumping and makes even the most frugal, conservative person want to let loose, spend money, and do something stupid that they can tell their grandchildren about." ~Elora

"How much did they take?" Lorsan asked one of the guards. He stared into the storeroom where they'd been keeping the Rapture and saw only a few cases left. His fist balled at his sides and his jaw clenched as he listened to the man recount what had happened. Apparently some very brave, or very stupid, humans had decided to help themselves to as much of the drink as they could get out before getting caught. They'd knocked out two of the men posted at the door and held a gun on another.

"Why weren't any of my men here?" Lorsan asked the human guard.

"We were otherwise detained, my liege," a cool voice said from behind him.

Lorsan turned to see Avauc, one of his top warriors, looking highly irritated. "Pray tell, what had you detained?"

"There was an altercation that the human guards weren't able to handle on their own. I took the elves that had been stationed here with me to assist."

"You couldn't handle it?" The question was insulting, but Lorsan didn't care. Avauc should have

65

known better than to leave something so important in the hands of mere humans.

The warrior's shoulders tensed. "I suppose I could have simply let them tear your casino apart. I am not a fool to let my pride keep me from doing my job. Had I attempted to handle a mob on my own I would have been overtaken. Tanked-up humans seeking their drug of choice aren't exactly reasonable."

There was no point in arguing with him. What was done, was done. But Lorsan had to get the Rapture back. His supplies were already getting low after the little explosion at the manufacturing building, and Tarron hadn't been back in touch with him to let him know if they'd begun making more. In fact, Lorsan's teeth clenched so tightly that they might have shattered. Tarron hadn't been in touch with him at all in days. *What was his unstable friend up to,* he wondered. Then again, with a mind like Tarron's, it might be better if Lorsan didn't know.

"Take two warriors with you and track the humans who stole my property. Deal with them, and bring it back," Lorsan snapped at him. "And be quick about it."

The warrior bowed his head and then turned quickly on his heels without a word. Lorsan looked at the open door and motioned for the guard to shut it. Two more of his warriors had joined him in the hall and he narrowed his gaze on them. "You are not to leave this post for any reason. I don't care if the building is on fire or humans are throwing each other from the balconies. Your feet stay planted here. Understood?"

The two warriors nodded and took up their posts, pushing the human guards out of the way.

One of the men looked at Lorsan with a slight

frown. "What would you like us to do?"

Lorsan let out a sigh. "Go guard," he waved his hand in frustration before finally huffing, "something, anything just get out of my sight."

As he walked out onto the main floor, Lorsan glanced around. He fought down the bile that rose in his throat as he stared at the pathetic humans around him. Some sat at the bar; others, at blackjack tables; and still others, in front of the slot machines. They were weak—captivated so easily by the newest fad. Suddenly he felt as though he were suffocating in their desperation. He needed to get away from them, if just for a little while.

Without a word to anyone he headed for his office and then passed through the mirror that hung on the wall. His Chosen would be irritated that he hadn't let her know where he was going but he couldn't wait. He needed to get away from the humans or he just might start killing them. He wouldn't have much of a kingdom if he killed all of his subjects.

The lights of the city shimmered like the lights on a Christmas tree. They lit up the night sky and seemed to scream 'forget all your troubles and come play with us.' Elora felt the pull stronger than ever.

"You okay?" Cush's voice filled her mind as his hand ran down her arm until he was clasping her small hand in his larger one.

She turned to look at him and knew that her eyes

were wide with wonder. "Do you think all the lights just make it worse? Maybe if we'd arrived during the day it wouldn't seem so appealing."

Cush squeezed her hand gently. "That had been the plan but after getting those glimpses of the dark elves following us I had to take some detours. I'm sorry if this made it harder on you."

She closed her eyes as she fought the siren call of sin city. Elora looked deep inside her reaching for things that represented light and goodness in her life. She wanted to push away the dark impulses and so she was going to have to focus on the things in her life that mattered more to her than her own desires. She thought of Cassie and the pain she was in as she searched for her parents. She thought of Lisa and how she'd done all she could over the years to protect her and her brother from their father's dark world. And then she thought of Cush, her light elf warrior. He had brought a new kind of light to her life, one that shined brighter than anything else. Surely these things would be enough to help fortify her from making some very bad decisions.

"I'm good," she finally said.

Cush had pulled into a parking lot across the street from the casino, Iniquity. As they climbed out of the vehicle, Elora turned and looked at the building that seemed to loom over them ominously, as though it dared them to enter and then leave untouched by its influence. She wondered if they would make it in and out alive and if they would be the same afterward. Could a person, human or elf, come face-to-face with such strong, alluring, and tempting pleasures and not be affected? She really wanted to say yes to that question, but as she watched humans stumble from the casino, their eyes glazed over with the film of alcohol and, more than likely Rapture as well, she truly doubted that they would come out unscathed.

"The sooner we go in there, the closer we will be to ending this mess," Syndra spoke up grabbing everyone's attention. She motioned for everyone to get closer to her. She made movements over each of them while muttering under her breath. One by one, their clothes shimmered and changed, converting into clothes much more appropriate for the club scene than the jeans, t-shirts, or cargo pants they'd been wearing.

Elora's eyes widened as she looked down at the outfit that the light elf queen had covered her in. She wore red high heels, black fishnet tights, a black miniskirt, and a halter top that hung off one shoulder. Her mom's outfit wasn't much better. Her eyes met Cush's and she could tell by the clenched jaw and narrowed eyes that he wasn't too happy about the clothes, or lack thereof, that she was sporting.

"Is this really all you could come up with?" Lisa asked as she motioned to the tight red pants and halter top that enveloped her body.

Syndra shrugged. "It's Vegas, might as well go big."

The guys were dressed in slacks and dark shirts that gave glimpses of their chests from the several buttons that were left undone. Elora wasn't going to complain; the view she was getting of Cush was going to be forever ingrained in her memory.

"Listen up." Syndra clapped her hands. "To each other, our faces will look the same, but to everyone around us, they will see someone else. The glamour will make the dark elves see elves, and the humans will see humans. The spell should last several hours so everyone check your phones and make sure that we all have the same time."

They all pulled phones out and did as she asked. Once everyone was on the same page, Syndra continued with her instructions. "We will meet back here in exactly three hours. Lisa and Oakley, you two will be a pair, and the lovebirds will be a pair. Being that I can hold my own, I will be on my own. We will spread out in the casino. Keep your eyes and ears open for Lorsan and his men. And for the love of not wanting to be tortured, please attempt to look inconspicuous."

Once again facing the casino, they headed toward the doors that would lead them into the world held captive by Lorsan and his will.

As soon as they entered, they were assaulted by the sounds of ringing slot machines, shouts at the roulette tables, and boisterous laughter from all directions. Elora felt as if she was a kid seeing Disney World for the first time. She wondered why it was having a strong effect on her. The first time they'd come she'd felt something, but it hadn't been nearly as strong. She felt Cush's fingers lace with hers and looked up at him.

"You good?" he asked. The concern in his voice helped her shake off some of the affects.

She nodded. "I'm good." So it might have been a little bit of a lie, but she didn't want him worrying about her when there were more important things to be doing.

She noticed that the others had already headed off in different directions. Cush began to lead her through the maze of games and people. He walked with a confidence and appeal that had heads turning. Elora was sure the clothes that encased his fine physique had a little something to do with it as well. In short, Cush looked stunning.

"What exactly are we looking for?" she asked him silently.

"In particular we're looking for Lorsan. But finding where he's keeping the Rapture would be just as important. And finding The Book of the Elves is also a must. I'm thinking where we find Lorsan is where we will find the book."

They continued their slow perusal of the casino, nonchalantly sauntering through the different gaming areas. Elora knew the moment they got near the bar. The energy seemed to ratchet up several notches and the noise with it. Loud laughter rose up around them as people crowded around tall, round tables and the long bar along the wall. In every hand Elora could see a glass filled with a shimmering red liquid.

It didn't take long for the notorious violence that came with the Rapture to make an appearance as the bartender began to cut certain people off. She watched as two large bouncers headed over to the bar where two men were beginning to demand the bartender give them what they wanted. One of the men bumped into a woman standing next to him. Then the man on the other side of her, who Elora assumed was with the recently jostled woman, confronted the man who bumped into her. From there the situation escalated very quickly.

Right before Elora's eyes, pushing and shoving commenced, and then punches began to be thrown. Even a few glasses of Rapture were snapped from one hand only to be downed by the snatcher, which didn't go over too well with the theft victims. The bouncers were attempting to get things under control, but they were simply outnumbered. She heard Cush curse low under his breath and then turn to her. "Don't get any closer and do not move from this spot." Then she watched as her warrior rushed into the fray to assist the sinking bouncers.

As Elora watched the violence before her, she once again began to feel the undeniable pull of her darker nature. The sounds of the fighting began to fade and all she could hear instead was the pulsing music that was being played throughout the casino. The beat was intoxicating. It called to her. Come dance; come play. Her feet began to move of their own accord and before she knew it she was walking away from the spot where Cush had rooted her. She didn't know where she was going and she didn't really care. She just wanted to let go. She wanted to be one with the night, to bask in the pleasures that begged for her attention.

Everything around her faded from view until all she could see was the path in front of her. Elora left the main gaming room of the casino headed in the direction of a different kind of music. As she rounded a corner, she saw lights flickering from a single door that was held open by a big, burly guy. The colors of the lights changed rhythmically with the beat of the music and a trail of fog drifted from the room. Elora took a step closer, and another, as the undulating fog beckoned to her. The closer she got, the more she wanted to be in that room.

It seemed that in the blink of an eye she was standing just inside the door engulfed in the darkness. The laser lights that flashed around the room and the fog blanketed the floor and slithered around the bodies that were moving to the pulsing music. Her head snapped around when she felt hands sliding down her arms grabbing onto her wrists and pulling her into the depths of the writhing bodies. The heat of the crowd should have been stifling, but instead it was like a warm sauna relaxing all of her muscles until she was placid and loose.

Without another thought to any of her original plans when she'd entered Iniquity, Elora let her head fall back, not even alarmed when it landed on someone's chest as hands grasped her waist and the person behind her began to move with her. She closed her eyes and let out a deep breath and surrendered to the side of her that she'd fought for so long.

The night turned into a blur as Elora danced. She didn't stay in Iniquity but followed a group of people who she suddenly become friends with. They went from casino to casino hitting all of the clubs in them along the way. Minutes turned into hours, but time was of no consequence to her. She simply wanted to soak up the night. All of her worries slipped from her mind to be replaced by a euphoric feeling that she was pretty sure she never wanted to let go of.

Elora laughed as she danced with the group she'd latched onto, letting their energy capture her. Her hands lifted into the air as her hips swayed seductively. In her mind, she heard a whisper of approval as though she were a snake charmer and her dark half was the snake being mesmerized by her movements. It was as if she was finally home. Why had she fought it so hard? This is who she was and there was no point in denying her nature. She was a part of the night, the darkness her domain, and as she reached up and pulled the clips from her hair letting the black locks free to sway around her, she gave herself over fully to the blood of her father's people.

Cush wiped the blood from his lip as the last man was finally removed from the casino. One human male had gotten in a lucky shot but only because Cush had been fighting four on one. The bouncers who'd been in the middle of it with him gave him a quick nod of thanks as they returned to their stations. Those left that had simply watched or cheered on the fighting slowly meandered away as they realized the excitement was over.

He turned to find Elora, to make sure she was alright, but instead of her scantily clad body, he found an empty spot on the floor instead. His eyes began to quickly scan the immediate area around him, and when he still didn't see her he began moving. His head swiveled from side to side as he searched face after face for his Chosen. At that moment his frustration equaled his worry. He wouldn't think the worst just yet. At the moment he was irritated with her for leaving the place he'd specifically told her not to budge from. But as his search continued with no sign of her, his irritation lessoned and his anxiety and fear increased. The ache that often accompanied the separation of a male and his Chosen began as a dull annoyance in his chest. He knew the longer they were separated, the worse it would get.

What if Lorsan had realized who she was and snatched her while he'd been helping break up the fights between the drunk humans? What if some human male had decided she was an easy target and somehow managed to drag her off to some dark corner to—he cut that thought off before it could go any further. Picturing the horrid things that could be happening to her would not help him; it would only serve to increase his anger and fear, which would hinder clear thought and purposeful action. He would be of no use to her if he flew off in a blind rage. So he stopped and took several deep breaths. But before he could take another step, a hand landed on his shoulder. He so desperately wanted it to be Elora, but he knew immediately that it was not.

"Why are you on your own?" Syndra asked as she stepped around him into his line of sight. "Where is your little troublemaker?"

Cush's chest tightened painfully as he looked down at the light elf queen. "She's gone."

"Gone?" Syndra's eyes did a quick sweep around the room. "How did she get separated from you?"

"A fight broke out among the humans and it was escalating."

"And you, being the light elf warrior that you are, intervened," she interrupted.

"I told her to stay put. She knows how dangerous the situation is. I don't think she would have wandered off of her own accord."

Syndra's lips tightened as her gaze met his. "Perhaps, that would be true if she didn't have dark elf blood running through her veins."

He took a step toward her. "What do you mean?"

"You know how she was affected the first time that we came to Las Vegas. She isn't fully dark elf, Cush, but she is half, and that part of her DNA will have an influence over her unless she is paying very close attention especially in a place such as this where the darkness rules even in the light of day."

Cush didn't want to believe what she was saying, but he knew the light elf queen was right. It didn't bother him that his Chosen had dark elf blood; he honestly couldn't care less. Her heritage didn't have to determine her future, but that didn't mean it wouldn't be something she would have to force into submission. He should have considered how difficult it would be for her to be surrounded by the pleasures of the flesh in a place saturated with self-indulgence. But he'd been too focused on finding Lorsan, the book, and dealing with the Rapture situation.

"Can you feel her?" Syndra asked. "I'm assuming that your souls have connected seeing as how you can't keep your hands off each other. Can your soul reach out to hers?"

Cush closed his eyes and let his soul search for its other half. It was as though he was looking for a light only he could see. He grew more frustrated as the minutes ticked by and still he felt nothing.

He growled, "Nothing. I can't feel a damn thing."

Syndra tapped her lips with a long slender finger as she stared at him. "I wonder if—perhaps because of what she is—that maybe you have to connect with her in another way as well."

Cush's jaw clenched. "You mean by mating?" He did not particularly want to discuss something so private with Syndra.

She shook her head. "No, at least I don't think so. I mean with her other half. You've connected with her human soul, the part of her that isn't tainted by her father's blood, but I bet you haven't connected with the dark elf in her."

His brow drew together as he crossed his arms in front of his chest. "I don't understand what you are saying. How would I connect with her dark elf?"

"Honestly, I have no clue."

Cush wanted to snarl at her, *why the hell bring up something that you don't have an answer to,* but he kept the thought to himself. He knew that if Elora had been with him that she wouldn't have approved of him snapping at the light elf queen. His gut clenched as he realized just how much of an influence she'd had on him in the short time they'd been together. When he'd first met her, he'd been shocked, but that had quickly morphed into defiance because he'd never thought he'd find his Chosen. He was a warrior; it was all he knew. How in all the realms could he possibly be a mate? But he had realized very quickly that now that he'd found her, there was no way he could let her go. She was his and he was hers, that was all there was to it. There was no Cush without Elora, and yet his biggest fear had already come to pass. He'd feared not being able to take care of her the way she would need. Now here in Sin City, he'd foolishly gone and lost her.

"Not to be a mom or anything, but where is my daughter?"

Lisa's voice broke through the turmoil raging in Cush's mind and his eyes met hers. How was he supposed to tell the mother of the woman he loved that he'd lost her? He'd rather face an army of dark elves.

"Don't freak out, Lisa," Syndra spoke up before he had a chance.

"I don't like it when someone starts a sentence with 'don't freak out, Lisa,' " she retorted turning to look at Syndra. "Usually that implies that freaking out is definitely the best course of action."

"I stepped away from her for a few minutes." Cush's voice was strained as he fought to hold his emotions in check. "I was assisting with an altercation and when I returned she was gone."

Lisa pursed her lips briefly before nodding. "Okay, so we need to find her."

Her response was not what he was expecting. Cush was sure Elora's mother was going to rip him from one end to the other, but like her daughter did so often, she surprised him.

"Lisa," he began but she held up her hand to stop him.

"I don't blame you, warrior. Elora is a big girl and you don't have eyes in the back of your head. We'll find her."

"Did you guys call a meeting and forget to invite me?" Oakley quipped as he walked up to their small circle.

"Your sister has wandered off and we have to find her," Lisa told him without preamble.

Oakley blew out a breath and rubbed his face. "Why does this not surprise me?"

"Like you said, Lisa, Elora is a big girl. She can handle herself," Syndra said confidently.

Cush agreed that Elora could handle herself, but she was still a female in a city full of hungry males that would be more than happy to make her their snack. Not to mention the fact, Lorsan was lurking somewhere like a slinking wolf waiting to devour them.

"Syndra, you and Lisa search this side of the strip. The Casinos all connect so you can walk straight through without having to leave the building. Oakley and I will go across the street and canvas that side." Cush reverted into the familiar role of leader. He was used to commanding soldiers. Now taking charge helped ease his worry for his Chosen. "We'll meet at the fountains of the Bellagio in an hour." Cush motioned for Oakley to follow him, leaving Syndra and Lisa who were already moving toward the exit. He knew that Syndra was more than capable of taking care of herself as well as anyone in her care.

He moved with confidence through the crowded casino, not bothering to walk around people because they just seemed to move out of his way. Elora had mentioned that to him once and he'd admitted that he'd never noticed it. But now as he headed for the front doors he realized she was right, and it was a good thing because he had no doubt that if they didn't get out of his way he would plow right through them.

"I don't think anyone took her," Oakley spoke up as he lengthened his stride to keep up with Cush.

"Why," Cush asked without looking at the boy.

"Because Elora wouldn't have gone quietly. If she disappeared without you realizing it, it was of her own free will."

Cush would have agreed with him except he'd told her not to move, and he knew that she understood how important it was that she obey his order. Elora could be defiant, but she wasn't stupid.

"She probably saw some chick in an awesome Goth get up and went to ask her where she got her skull tights or something."

"If she did walk away on her own, it had better be for a reason a whole hell of a lot better than wanting to know about some lady's clothes," Cush rumbled. As they crossed the lobby and stepped out into the strip, the lights of the Casinos lit up the night sky of the city like a beacon calling out for all to come and revel with her. Cush could see how humans got caught up in the false security of the bright beams because they couldn't see the shadows that hid behind them—shadows that wanted to devour them piece by piece as they gave themselves over to the self-gratification of every whim the city offered. By the time they left, they wouldn't even realize they'd given up a part of themselves, desensitized by the glamour of Sin City.

They crossed the street, dodging around taxis and other pedestrians. Cush didn't bother to check and see if Oakley was keeping up. The sound of the boy's voice was confirmation enough. "Well, don't be too surprised if that's all it was," Oakley placated. "Elora can be a tad impulsive and I imagine the influence that our dark elf nature is having on her is only making her even more impulsive."

Cush had to bite the inside of his cheek to keep from yelling out in frustration at his Chosen's brother. He felt as though he'd failed her and Oakley's words were only rubbing his face in the fact that he hadn't noticed her reaction to her environment.

"Look on the bright side," Oakley continued.

"There is no bright side," Cush said cutting him off as he pulled the door open to the first casino they'd come to. They were again bombarded with the ringing of slot machines, boisterous laughter, and the occasional booing from disgruntled gamblers. Cush's eyes scanned the room. Mounting frustration continued to grow inside of him as he realized just how difficult it would be to find Elora among the mass of bodies that seemed as numerous and similar as grains of sand.

I beg of you, Cush silently prayed to the Forest Lords, *please let me find her and let her be unharmed.* With the prayer offered up, he and Oakley moved purposefully into the room, both scanning face after face in hopes that she would somehow suddenly appear. Cush vowed silently to himself and to Elora that he would tear the city to the ground if that's what it took to find her.

Chapter 6

"When my mom told me that I was half dark elf, I thought, okay, so I have a little bit of a naughty side. Perhaps, it might have been more accurate of her to say, 'you are half dark elf and if you ever give into that nature, you won't just sort of dip your toe in it. No, if you give into that nature, you will plunge headfirst and then begin to swim deeper because you don't even realize you're drowning.' " ~ Elora

Time seemed to be flying by in a whirlwind of lights, music, and laughter as Elora dove even deeper into the bowels of the city. The group she'd been tagging along with, because it just seemed like the best idea she'd ever had, lead her into an alley. It was amazing how quickly the sights and sounds faded just a few steps off of the strip. They walked up to a wall that didn't appear to be anything more than a wall until a tall guy—she didn't know his name—knocked on it twice, then again and again, in a repeating pattern that reminded Elora of a heart beating. Suddenly with an ominous grinding, the wall slid open sideways.

Elora's eyes widened as she leaned forward to look past the tall, slender man who stood between them and whatever fun was going on behind him.

"We are keepers of the secret," the guy who knocked told the doorman.

To Elora's surprise the slender man bowed and stepped aside to allow them entry. It wasn't until she had stepped through the doorway and turned to look at the man full on that she realized he was not a man at all, well, at least not of the human variety.

A wide smile stretched across his beautiful face as long dark hair flowed around his shoulders. Like all elves she'd seen so far, he was lean, stunning, and beautiful in a way that was in no way feminine. Elora compared them, especially the dark ones, to felines—panthers maybe. They moved with a fluid like grace, confident in their own form to an extent she'd never seen in anyone else.

Chills ran up her spine as he held his hand out to her and she obediently placed her own into his. *What the crap am I doing*, she thought to herself, but the worry was pushed aside the moment the dark elf spoke.

"Welcome, little sister." The voice was a purring to her eardrums.

Oh my, Elora inwardly thought, *he's got a voice as smooth as butter and as rich as dark chocolate.*

"I've never had the pleasure of seeing you here before." His hand was still wrapped around her own and he had somehow taken a step closer without her even noticing.

"That's because I've never graced you with my presence before," Elora responded in a voice that didn't sound like her own. It was sultry and flirty in an *I want to devour you* kind of way.

"What is your name?" he asked as he took her hand and wrapped it around his arm leading her further into the room which she now saw was a club, though not like the other's she'd been to that night. This club was for those in the know. It was classy, sexy, and full of dark elves. Elora felt as if she'd just stepped into the Matrix and a small voice in the back of her mind was screaming *you should have taken the blue pill!*

He was still waiting for her answer and she nearly blurted it out but something stayed her tongue. Somewhere, she'd heard that names held power and to be careful who she gave hers out to. Elora looked up at the elf who was gliding her through the dark room and tried to figure out if he was one to whom she should trust with her name. The haze that had settled over her mind was growing thicker, and she was finding it very difficult to think beyond her immediate wants.

Finally she spoke but Elora wasn't the name she gave him. "I'm Raven."

"Just Raven?" he asked with a sly smile. She wagered that many a she-elf had fallen victim to that smile.

"Yep," she responded, popping the last letter with her lips. He seemed satisfied with her answer and continued to walk with her in silence. Elora took the chance to glance over the room. She saw a stage where there were women dancing in cages, and they were dressed in some whacked outfits that she figured were supposed to be animals, but they were missing most of the pelts. It was more like they'd taken the animal hair and only covered the essentials. At the back there was a bar with huge mirrors. Nope, she took that back, they weren't mirrors; they were glass. She could see a room that looked similar to the room she was walking in, but it seemed darker, more sinister.

"What's in there?" Elora pointed toward the glass.

"That is for those who don't just want to watch the show, but instead be a part of it."

His words seemed cryptic, which she thought should annoy her, but she seemed to just let it go as if it were the most normal thing in the world.

"What show?"

He had led her to a table where her group was already seated. Once she was seated in her own chair the dark elf slipped a finger under her chin and tilted her head back to look at her. "Do not worry, Little Raven, you will enjoy it." She blinked and he was already gone. His voice echoed in her mind. *Little Raven*, he'd called her and it sounded so wrong on his lips. She'd been called that before but she couldn't remember by who. Each time she thought she'd nearly figured it out, it just slipped away like water through her fingers. Her attention was drawn away from her thoughts as the room seemed to grow dimmer. A spotlight zeroed in on the stage and, like everyone else in the room, Elora leaned forward, scarcely breathing as she waited for the curtain to part.

The music began first. It was a haunting melody. Elora could feel the lyrics imprinting themselves on her mind and burrowing deep into her soul.

> *Close your eyes, let your worries be.*
> *Open your mind, then you will really see.*
> *There is a world, there is a place,*
> *Beyond your imagining, right in front of your face.*
>
> *And you feel it, and you know it.*
> *Can you believe it, will you receive it?*
>
> *Shut out the voices, silence the cries,*
> *There is the truth, just past the lies.*
> *Many will enter, few will depart,*
> *Is this the end, or is it the start?*
>
> *Close your eyes, let your worries be,*
> *Hear my voice, all you know is me.*

You're in my world, you're in my space,
Near my soul, gone without a trace.

And you feel it, and you know it.
Can you believe it, will you receive it?

As the song continued to fill the room, ensnaring the audience, the curtain slowly opened. Elora felt the pull, something telling her to keep her eyes on the stage. Like a whisper against her ear it enticed her not to move. She was aware that a spell was being cast over her, over everyone, and yet she could do nothing to stop it. Her eyes were glued to the stage as a tall, slender woman, beautiful even among her elvish kind, walked out. She was magnificent and terrifying at the same time. Her long hair was pitch black and shimmered as it swayed around her slender frame. It hung nearly to her waist in a cascading waterfall down her back. Her eyes were silver, large, and framed in dark, long lashes. But even her looks could not compare with the beauty of the voice that emerged from her as she sang. Elora felt as if she were floating on a sea of euphoria. She had no worries, no cares, and though she knew it wasn't reasonable, she felt as if she could just sit there in that dark room and listen to the woman on the stage sing forever. A sudden bump to her elbow by the person sitting next to her had Elora's eyes leaving the stage. The fog in her mind cleared and she blinked several times, but the clarity only lasted a few moments. The fog was replaced by an unexplainable urge to leave, but she didn't know where she was going. Elora stood and moved through the dark room, ignoring any who tried to stop her. She pushed her way through the crowd that was gathering around the entry to the room and followed the path to the door through which she'd originally entered.

As her feet hit the pavement and fresh air rushed over her, she saw with utter clarity what she had to do. Her feet led her as her mind attempted to work out the details. She needed to get to New Orleans. It was as though something very important were there, something that she couldn't live without.

Lorsan followed the light elf warrior and the male who was with him as they walked briskly through the casinos. One after another they entered, their heads turning this way and that as their eyes roamed over every person they passed. They were looking for someone. He recognized the warrior as one of Tamsin's top fighters, and he knew it was no coincidence that he was in Las Vegas. He was debating confronting them or just having his men ambush them when he felt power roll over him.

"I'd like to say it's a pleasant surprise to see you, Lorsan. But, since I would rather see your ashes scattered across a barren wasteland, I just can't bring myself to feel anything more than annoyance."

The dark elf king turned slowly. His eyes watched carefully, waiting for the light elf king to step out of the shadows. He knew if the queen was here, then Tamsin would not be far away.

"Syndra," he said her name with a false fondness as he plastered a smile on his face. Still looking for Tamsin, he noticed a human woman standing just a few feet from Syndra. The woman was watching them intently. Something about her seemed familiar but he couldn't grab on to what it was. "What brings you and your pet" —he motioned to the woman— "to my city?"

She let out a snort of laughter. "As if you didn't know, and news flash, it isn't your city. It belongs to the humans; we are their guests."

"Wrong! We are their superiors," he spat, unable to hide his disdain for the species. "We should be ruling this realm, not hiding in the shadows like vermin."

"If you feel like vermin, it isn't because you have to hide from the humans. To say that you might be closely related to the rodents wouldn't be a stretch."

Lorsan itched to smack the smile off of the light elf's face. "Where is your mate? Surely he didn't let you out to play without protection."

Suddenly everything and everyone around them, except for the female that was with Syndra, froze. Lorsan felt his chest tighten as Syndra's power filled the area around them. He felt his own power building in response.

"You seem to have forgotten who I am, Lorsan of the dark elves." Syndra's voice was not loud yet it rang with authority. Light pulsed around her and her human guise was gone. Before him stood the light elf queen in all her glory. Shadows seemed to inch away from her and heat radiated off of her skin. Lorsan knew that Syndra was powerful, but he hadn't realized just *how* powerful she was.

His fists clenched at his side and he narrowed his eyes. He was no weakling. He was a king and would not cower before the she-elf especially not in front of a human.

"You may be powerful, but you have many weaknesses—your love for the humans being one of them."

She shrugged. "What you consider weakness, I consider strength. I suppose we will know who is right when the end comes."

Lorsan was going through all of the possible outcomes of their current confrontation as he attempted to scan the area for any of his dark elves. He knew there would be a few who had followed him as if he needed a guard detail. He could capture her, give himself one less enemy to worry about, but that would surely provoke Tamsin. He had *The Book of the Elves* and, though that would give him power, he'd yet to have time to really examine it.

"You look like you're in pain over there, King," Syndra retorted.

That was enough to make his decision. Damn her mate. He wouldn't stand there and be made a fool of. He made a motion to the two dark elves he'd finally noticed and they moved in on the light elf queen.

"As fun as this little chat has been, I have other matters with which to attend. However, we do have much more to discuss, so I must insist that you and your companion stay and wait for me." Lorsan watched as his dark elves grabbed both women. He held out his hand and wrapped his own magic around them, trapping them in a bubble so they couldn't move. Syndra didn't put up a fight and the human female seemed to be following her lead. Instead she simply stood there grinning that infuriating grin that told him she knew something he did not. Lorsan didn't like it and if she was trying to get under his skin, it was working.

"Take them to the iron rooms," he told his men. He watched briefly as they carried the still grinning queen and silent human away, shielding themselves from the once again unfrozen humans. His attention was drawn back to the masses as he searched for the warrior and the other human. They'd wandered off while he'd been dealing with Syndra, which had probably been her intention. He continued forward, determined to find them again. He didn't need them snooping around or interfering with his plans.

Soon he would know the secrets of *The Book of the Elves* and he would bring the humans, the light elves, and their newly reinstated king to their knees.

Cassie, Trik, Tamsin, Rin, and Tony all stood staring at the dilapidated looking motel. They were all tired, hungry, and in need of a good night's sleep.

"Why again, can we not find a nicer place to stay?" Cassie asked as she rubbed her weary eyes.

"Because as soon as we all get some sleep, we will be heading deep into the swampland," Trik explained. "And this is the closest place to rest before we go."

Cassie understood, but that didn't make it any easier to consider the creepy, crawlies that she might have to share a bed with. She was tired, but she also wanted to get her parents back as quickly as possible, and if sleeping in the better-off-condemned building in front of her would make it faster for her to get to them, then she'd do it.

When they'd finally checked in and were entering the two rooms they'd reserved, her fears were confirmed. Cassie covered her hand over her mouth and nose to keep from gagging at the smell.

"Let's just get some sleep and then we can get out of here," Trik told them as he grabbed Cassie's hand and pulled her toward one of the empty beds. They'd divided up with Tamsin, Tony, and Rin sharing a room and she and Trik in another. She didn't know why they were bothering to give them privacy; there was no way she would be taking her clothes off anywhere in this place.

The group dispersed and to Cassie's surprise, as soon as Trik wrapped himself around her, she drifted off to sleep.

It felt like moments later when her eyes opened, only she knew immediately that she wasn't really awake—it was a dream. A very real dream. She stood on the edge of a forest, but then quickly amended in her mind that it wasn't a forest; it was most definitely a swamp. The trees were tall and thick, draped in moss and vines. Their trunks plunged down into murky water covered in a film of algae and other marshy plants. Cassie looked down at her feet, curious to see why she wasn't knee deep in water. She stood on an old stump that stuck up about two feet from the muddy mess. The stump was about two feet in diameter giving her plenty of room to stand and not feel as though she would fall off at any moment. She turned in a slow circle taking in the area around her, and, though it was gloomy, it was also strangely beautiful.

"You being in great peril, Cassandra, queen of elves."

Cassie's head snapped back around to find the origin of the voice. About a dozen feet away sat an old woman floating on a crude raft. The raft consisted of logs lashed together by vines and it appeared to be steering itself. Despite the old woman's age, she seemed quite comfortable sitting with her legs crossed on the rough vessel. Her skin was a soft, brown color and, though weathered looking, there were very few age lines. Her hair was covered with a purple scarf that she had tied in a knot at the base of her neck. Her clothes were loose, a multicolored tunic style top made out of a linen fabric and matching pants. Wrapped around her shoulders was a black shawl interwoven with various items including several small bones, a few claws that looked to be from different types of birds, and even some very small figurines—which appeared to be dolls of some sort. The shawl seemed to exude a darkness all its own, and Cassie was certain that she didn't want to ever come in contact with that particular piece of material.

"How do you know my name?" Cassie asked looking back at the woman's eyes.

"There be power in knowing de name," she answered cryptically. Her accent was thick but Cassie couldn't place it.

"Who are you?" Perhaps, she'd be kind enough to share her name. Cassie nearly laughed. *Not likely*, she thought.

"I be many things to many beings. But mostly I be a priestess—a conduit for de spirit world." Cassie had heard such speech before on many a reality televisions show, so she recognized the woman's thick Cajun accent.

Whatever the woman's accent, she didn't like the sound of her being a go between for the spirits. Cassie was convinced that once someone or something was dead, it was time to let them go. Nothing good could come from messing with spirits, and those spirits that wanted to be messed with were definitely up to no good.

"So what do you want with me?" If there entire conversation was going to continue in this manner, it was going to be a very long dream.

"There's one who is being obsessed wit you. So enthralled he be, that he willingly sought me out. There not be many who are willing to pay de price of a Voodoo priestess."

"What price is that?" She shouldn't have asked, but a sick sense of curiosity had her mouth moving before her brain could tell her to shut it.

The woman's eyes met her's and Cassie shivered at the emptiness she found there.

"Souls," the priestess answered. "We be dealing in souls now, chile."

Cassie wondered whose soul Tarron had bargained with in order to get help from the Voodoo lady. But that was not a question she was going to voice. She didn't know how she would handle the answer.

"Tarron has my parents. I can't just run and hide."

"That not be what I'm saying. Dat elf be messing with things that ought not be messed wit. There be no benefit to my lady—da Voodoo goddess—if Tarron and Lorsan rise to power. Be no balance come from it. Triktapic must not be falling again. The contract between the Voodoo goddess and Tarron be already struck. There can't be no going back. But dees goddesses be tricksy you know?"

"What does that mean?"

"Tarron of the dark elves tink he be bringing me an item that be belonging to you." She pointed a bony finger at Cassie and, for some reason, it made Cassie want to duck out-of-the-way. "But that item from another. She already be heading dis way. The spell cast will be making them want each other no matter who their destiny be meant for."

Cassie felt ice cold as the priestess's words began to sink in. She knew what she had to ask next, but the words seemed to be lodged in her throat. It took her several tries before she was finally able to speak. "Who was the girl that the item belonged to?" Her chest tightened as she waited for the woman to confirm what she already knew to be true.

"Elora Scott, half human, half dark elf, daughter of Lisa, sister of Oakley, and Chosen of Nedhudir, da one she calls Cush."

Cassie was pretty sure if she'd eaten anything recently she would have been tasting it a second time in that moment. Tarron had thought he was ensnaring Cassie, but it had been Elora instead. And now because he had Cassie's parents as well, he had them both whether he wanted them or not.

"So what can we do? How do we stop him?" Even as she voiced the question, she didn't expect an answer. But the old woman surprised her.

"You must be stopping him. Da Voodoo priestess works for the highest bidder."

"So basically," Cassie said slowly. "You will help us if we offer you something more than what Tarron has already?"

The priestess nodded.

"Will you undo the spell? And how do I know you will do what you say?"

"If Triktapic agree to my terms, da spell will be broken. A Voodoo priestess keeps her word—to da highest bidder." This seemed to amuse the old woman and she threw her head back and cackled, a sound that reminded Cassie of a murder of crows all squawking at once.

After the woman finally calmed down, Cassie's eyes narrowed. "And how do I know you won't go back to Tarron and tell him what you've done in order to see if he will give you a better offer?"

"You don't." And she once again fell into a fit of hideous laughter.

Cassie's eyes snapped open as she attempted to catch her breath, the laughter of the old woman still echoing in her head. She knew immediately that this was more than a dream. Whoever that woman had been, she was real, alive, and flesh and blood, somewhere close by. She felt Trik stir beside her and she turned her head to see him sound asleep with one arm slung over his face and the other resting possessively on her stomach. Apparently she hadn't disturbed him at all. She let out a slow breath and closed her eyes as she attempted to sort through the bizarre dream.

"What's wrong, Beautiful?" His deep voice had her eyes snapping back open.

"I thought you were asleep," she told him as she rolled over onto her side to face him.

"I was, but I could feel your anxiety." He patted her stomach to remind her that he was touching her and had access to her thoughts.

Cassie opened up her mind fully and let the dream replay for him. She felt Trik's body grow tenser as it unfolded. Finally, after several minutes of silence, he sat up and climbed out of the bed. He was in his sleep pants but that was all and for a brief moment Cassie had to appreciate the fact that her elf was seriously sexy shirtless.

"Tarron attempted a love spell on my Chosen?"

Trik asked, though she knew he wasn't really expecting an answer.

"I don't really think that's what's important at this point, Trik. He may have thought he was doing it to me, but he actually *succeeded* in doing it to Elora. The Voodoo priestess said Elora is already on her way here."

He stopped his pacing long enough to look at her, and she could tell when it finally clicked that Cassie hadn't been the one affected by the spell. She watched as he walked over to the small bedside table that had seen better days. He grabbed his cell phone and pushed a couple buttons before putting it to his ear.

"Cush," he barked into the phone. "Where's your Chosen?"

Cassie crossed her fingers, hoping that Cush would say Elora was right there by his side. But she might as well have been wishing for trees to produce cotton candy instead of leaves; it just wasn't going to happen.

"How long has she been missing?" Trik asked.

Cassie felt her pulse speed up.

"Keep looking for her. Deal with Lorsan if you have time." He set the phone back down and shut his eyes as he pinched the bridge of his nose.

"Why didn't you tell him?" Cassie's voice sounded smaller than she'd intended.

"Because the last thing I need is one of my most powerful warriors to come barreling into New Orleans ready to make heads roll and causing chaos. We can deal with Elora. Cush would better serve us by dealing with Lorsan. He and Syndra should be able to hold their own."

"He's going to be very angry with you once he finds out," she pointed out. "Think of how you would feel if it was me, and he didn't tell you where I was?"

Trik's eyebrows dropped low on his forehead and his eyes flashed a dangerous silver. "Yes, I would be beyond pissed if he kept such information from me, but I am his king and it's my call to make. I have to consider what is best for everyone involved, not Cush's emotions."

"So what do we do now?"

He turned toward the hotel door and Cassie felt as if he was trying to look straight through it. "We seek out this priestess and find out the price."

"Something tells me that it isn't going to be something as simple as a drop of blood," she muttered as Trik took her hand and pulled her toward the door.

"Your pension for thinking positive is truly astounding, Cassandra," Trik teased.

Cassie rolled her eyes. "Forgive me if I don't live in fantasy land where the good guy always wins and evil is vanquished. The movies make it look so easy."

Trik looked back at her as he knocked on the door of the other room. "You're right. The cost that comes at defeating evil is much greater than people realize. But it is always worth it, no matter how painful."

Cush felt as though Trik wasn't telling him something. Something in his voice had sounded off, but then who was he to question the king? He continued walking through the crowded casinos with Oakley at his side, and with every step a sense of foreboding grew in his chest. He kept waiting for the discomfort that should be happening because of his separation from Elora to start, but there was no pain. He wondered if she was suffering, if she was in the hands of the crazy dark elf king? He couldn't let his mind dwell on that. If all he worried about were the possibilities of her circumstances, then he wouldn't be able to concentrate on finding her.

"I would ask if you two are enjoying yourselves, but frankly I don't give a damn."

Cush stopped in midstep as Lorsan's voice broke through his thoughts of his Chosen. He turned, placing himself slightly in front of Oakley. Lorsan stood about twenty feet away, his body tense and ready for action. Though they had left Iniquity, Lorsan and his dark elves owned half of the casinos on the strip. Apparently he'd followed them as they'd searched. Was he planning on attacking them right there in plain sight? Surely he wouldn't risk such exposure.

"Perhaps, you should consider a different line of business if you aren't interested in ensuring your customers are happy," Cush responded as he took in the people walking around them and the possible exits for him and Oakley, while simultaneously not letting the dark elf king out of his sight.

"Something tells me that you two aren't customers. I think you are here looking for something other than a fun vacation." Lorsan took several step toward them.

Cush heard Oakley shift behind him but he didn't turn to see what the human was doing. He didn't trust Lorsan as far as he could throw him, and he knew that if he let his guard down for a split second the king would take advantage of it.

"What I'm looking for at the moment is of no concern to you," Cush said through clenched teeth. He didn't want Lorsan to know that he knew he might have his Chosen.

"You won't find her or her companion," Lorsan taunted.

Cush's jaw was so tight he was surprised he didn't break any teeth as he stared down Lorsan. If he honestly thought he could keep him from the woman he loved, he truly was a fool. "If you've hurt her in any way there will be no place you can hide that I won't find you."

Lorsan's brow drew together as his lips pursed. "You seem to have an unhealthy attachment to this female. Does her mate know?"

His comment had Cush feeling as though the ground had been jerked out from beneath his feet. Her mate? He was her mate. His heart sped up as the meaning of the dark elf's words sank in, and he realized that Lorsan had said *her companion*, and Elora had been alone when he'd lost her. If Lorsan wasn't talking about Elora, then he had to be talking about Syndra and Lisa. How on earth had Syndra managed to allow them to be captured? Tamsin was going to kill Cush if anything happened to his Chosen regardless of the fact that Syndra had more power in her pinky than Cush had in his entire body. Tamsin would still expect him to make sure no harm came to Syndra or to Lisa.

"Tamsin will rip the flesh from your body if you hurt either of them. You have to know that you won't get away with any of this." Cush was trying to concentrate on the conversation but it was getting more and more difficult to think about anything but Elora. If Lorsan didn't have her then where the hell was she? He felt Oakley tense beside him as he must have realized that they were speaking about his mother.

Lorsan sneered. "I'm going to let you and the human walk out of here," he told them as he crossed his arms in front of his chest. "But only because I want you to give Tamsin and Trik a message. It is a fool's errand to stand against me. I will destroy anyone who attempts to get in my way, and Tamsin will never see his Chosen again if they don't stop their pursuit. Now, unless you plan on spending some money in my casino, I suggest you leave." The dark elf king turned on his heels and walked away from them, confident that they would obey.

"He's a pleasant fellow," Oakley said from behind Cush.

"He's a sadistic, sick, deranged SOB," Cush grumbled as he turned and pushed Oakley along with him.

"Okay, so you're keeping it real, I get that. I, however, was just going for low key. But we can go with sadistic SOB."

"You forgot sick and deranged," Cush offered as they stepped out of the casino onto the busy sidewalk.

"Did you happen to catch the part about him having caught Syndra and my mom but not saying anything about my sister?" Oakley asked as Cush looked up and down both directions of the street.

It took everything in him not to roar out in frustration. Of course, he'd caught that; of course, he was now freaking out even more about his missing Chosen.

"Why are you so calm about your mom being captured by Lorsan?"

Oakley grinned. "Uh, because she's with Syndra. That she-elf has got some powerful mojo. The fact that she didn't kick Lorsan in the balls with a little magic behind it tells me that she let herself and my mom get caught."

"Sounds like something Syndra would do," Cush grumbled. "These dang women are going to be the death of our male race."

"So, not to be pushy or anything, but what are we going to do now?"

"Honestly," Cush finally said. "I don't know. Every natural instinct I have is telling me to find Elora to make sure she's safe."

"But," Oakley prompted.

"But the warrior in me is saying never leave anyone behind, especially females. It will destroy Tamsin if something happens to her."

"Even though she's not alone, I would prefer that my mom not be in the hands of a deranged SOB."

"You forgot sick," Cush interrupted.

Oakley shook his head and let out a sigh. "Fine, a sick, deranged SOB, but she has Syndra. Elora has no one. What if something happens to my sister?" the human challenged.

Cush's eyes met Oakley's and he took a step closer. His voice was a low growl as he responded. "You think this is an easy choice for me? You think I'm not dying to tear this city to the ground looking for her? She is my Chosen and to you those might be just words but for me it means she is a part of me. Her soul calls out to mine and mine to her. The emptiness I feel inside without her by my side is like a black hole threatening to swallow me from the inside out. Do not for one second presume to think that this is a decision that I make on a whim." Cush's breathing had picked up during his tirade and his voice had risen several notches. He took a step back from Oakley and attempted to gather his usually controlled emotions.

Oakley held up his hands and took his own step back. "I really didn't mean any disrespect, man. And I get it. I feel like I'm having to choose between my mom and my sister, but I know my mom will strangle me when she finds out that we stopped looking for Elora to rescue them. But, Elora trusts you, and I imagine she would be pretty ticked off with you if you left Syndra and our mom in the hands of Lorsan."

Cush nodded. "She'd have a few choice words for me, no doubt." His soul was still not at peace with his decision. He knew he couldn't leave the two females, but he didn't know if he could keep himself from looking for Elora in order to rescue the light elf queen and his Chosen's mother. He pulled out his phone but paused before dialing. Cush was about to disobey a direct order from *the* king but regardless of the consequences he knew it was what he had to do.

Tamsin picked up on the second ring. "Where is she?" he asked instead of a hello.

"Lorsan has her, as well as Lisa." The words tasted like acid on his tongue as the sting of failure pierced him. "Elora is missing," he continued. "I don't want to leave the females but—"

"I'm on my way. I'm using the mirrors. I'll fight Lorsan's minions to get through if I have to. You find your Chosen and once the females are safe we will finish this." The light elf king hung up without another word.

"Now what?" Oakley asked.

Cush shoved the phone in his back pocket and began walking. "Now we keep looking for my mate and wait for the inevitable phone call that Triktapic will no doubt be making."

"Tamsin is going to come and get Syndra and my mom?"

Cush nodded as his paced picked up. He was growing desperate with the need to see Elora and to see that she was safe and in one piece.

Fifteen minutes later his phone vibrated. He answered it without looking at the screen; he knew who it was.

"If Tamsin is coming there then I need you here." Trik's clipped voice came through the speaker.

"I have to find Elora," Cush replied with as much respect as he could muster.

"Well since she's on her way here you should have no problem with that endeavor. Don't travel through the portals with Oakley. I've already gotten you both a ticket to fly out in two hours. We don't know how Elora is traveling so you might actually beat her here if she's taking a bus."

"How do you know Elora is coming there? Have you talked to her? Is she alright?" Cush once again felt off balance as the carpet was pulled out from under him.

"I will explain it when you get here. Don't miss your flight." The line went dead.

"They found Elora?" Oakley asked as his eyes brightened.

Cush felt as if someone else was controlling his body as he nodded in response and once again slipped the phone into his pocket. "We need to catch a flight."

"Why didn't Trik tell you he knew where she was when you talked with him earlier?"

"I don't know and at the moment I don't care. I just need to see her." He held out his hand and hailed down a cab. They climbed in and he told the driver to get them to the airport. But after that there were no more words. He was too focused on the fact that he would soon see his Chosen. And after he assured himself that she was in one piece, he was going to have to figure out a way to keep from throttling her for scaring him so badly. He and his little raven were going to have a very long discussion that may or may not end up with her chained to his side.

Chapter 7

"The saying goes that pride comes before a fall. I can agree with that to a certain extent, but I honestly think it should be changed to *stupid guarantees a fall." ~ Syndra*

Tamsin stepped through the mirror of the motel bathroom and immediately felt the presence of other elves. He raised his hands, gathering power, ready to deflect any attack while at the same time picturing the room he'd stayed in the first time they all went to Vegas to confront Tony. The blast came from his right side and he felt the rush of the power before it reached him. Tamsin threw his own blast back at it, stopping the magic from hitting him. Whoever Lorsan had guarding the portals, they weren't very powerful, which meant the dark elf king was focusing his attention on other things. Just as his foot stepped out of the portal, he felt heat at his back and twisted at the waist to fire back at the dark elf he could finally see. Tamsin threw his magic over and over at the elf until he retreated, giving him time to turn and push through the mirror into the lush room.

He waited several seconds, staring back at the mirror waiting to see if the dark elf would attempt pursuit. When nothing happened he stood up from his crouched position and looked around the room. It appeared to be empty, which was lucky since he really didn't want to have to fool with humans who might have a slight problem with someone stepping out of their mirror.

Tamsin closed his eyes and allowed his soul to search for its mate, and he hoped that Lisa was with her or at least near her. He knew she was close, so that meant Lorsan hadn't taken her to the dark elf realm. He allowed all of his focus to be centered on her—Syndra's smooth skin and her bright eyes that twinkled with mischief when she looked at him. Tamsin thought of her voice, her smell, her touch, and every unique attribute that made her special and different. Finally, he felt her. The intensity of the feeling was weak, which told him that Lorsan had used iron to bind her to lessen her magic. Knowing that the evil dark elf had stripped his Chosen of some of her power made Tamsin want to crush the dark elf king. Soon enough, he would have his chance.

He moved swiftly through the suite, his steps inhumanly quiet. Stepping out into the hall, he glanced left and right, looking for any potential threat, but the hall was empty. Once again Tamsin brought his focus back to Syndra. He felt her presence below him so he headed for the exit sign at the end of the hall indicating a stairwell.

Tamsin descended the stairs several at a time, his footfalls never making a sound. It didn't matter how fast he moved, however, it still wasn't fast enough. Just before he hit the ground floor landing, the door opened and two men stepped into sight right in front of him. Tamsin registered right away that they weren't human, and he moved with hundreds of years of battle experience as his hand flew out and pushed into the chest of the closest elf. He flung a ball of power along with it and the male hit the door with a hard thud and then crumbled to the ground. With no pause in his movements, the light elf king turned his body in a quick rotation and backhanded the other man, again pushing power into the movement. The second elf crashed to the ground as well. Neither of them so much as twitched.

He moved their bodies so he could shut the door and then, without a backward glance, continued to descend the stairs. After two more flights, Tamsin felt a rush of magic flow over him, and he knew he'd just passed through some sort of glamour that hid that part of the building from humans. The scent of iron was a pungent stench to his senses. He could even taste it on his tongue as he walked further down a long hallway. Tamsin was close to losing what little composure he had as the corridor seemed to go on forever. He knew he was going the right direction because he could feel himself getting closer to his Chosen. He didn't want to call out to her in case there were guards so he just kept going.

"Were you planning on just walking past without so much as a hello?"

Her voice came out of the dark to the right of him. Tamsin's head snapped to look at the solid wall next to him.

"Syndra?" he asked tentatively.

"It seems I have found myself in a little bit of a pickle. When I gave myself up, I underestimated Lorsan's ability to keep me captured. I have been attempting to use what little power I have flowing through me to escape, but…" She let the word trail off as her still captive state explained the rest of her statement.

"I can hear you, but I can't see you. There is no door in this wall, just stone. He pressed his hand to the bricks and though he could feel the thrum of the iron, the wall he was touching was not made of iron.

"The iron is only on the inside of the cells. Turns out that louse of a king actually does have a few brain cells that work."

"You can see me?" Tamsin asked.

"That I can and I must tell you how attractive you are to me in this moment. I guess there is something to be said for wanting what you can't have."

Tamsin tried not to laugh because he truly didn't not find the situation funny, but his female had a wicked sense of humor. He knew she was doing it to distract him, to keep him calm, and it was working to an extent. "So you're saying you want me more now because I'm over here and you're over there?"

"If you really wanted to tease me, king of mine, you could start removing clothing."

Tamsin could picture the smile that would be playing on her lips and the gleam in her eyes. Yes, his mate definitely had a sharp tongue and a witty mind to go along with it. "As much as I would love to please you, I don't think now is the time for me to disrobe."

"Oh dear, you know what it does to me when you use antiquated words like disrobe. I'm practically trembling with desire." She laughed at her own words which only made him smile bigger.

"Are you going to help me get you out of there, or do you just want to stay in there and tell me all about those desires?"

Syndra let out an exasperated sigh. "It's a tough decision, but considering we still have to get *The Book of the Elves* back and kill Lorsan, I suppose the fulfillment of desires will have to wait. Perhaps, you could build us some sort of cage for a little deprivation playtime."

"I'll build you whatever you want, love. Just help me figure out how to get through this wall."

"Not to interrupt the reunion that will no doubt become embarrassing to all of us once she's out, but I just want to throw out that I'm over here and would love to be released as well and would very much prefer it if Tamsin kept his clothes on." Lisa's voice came from directly behind him which meant she too was in a cell that had no apparent door.

"I didn't forget about you, Lisa," Syndra assured. "I just had a momentary lapse in focus. I'm going to blame it on the iron."

"Probably better than admitting that your libido got the best of you. I'd hate to have to share that tidbit with Elora and Cassie," Lisa muttered under her breath though she knew the she elf would hear her.

Elora's hands fidgeted as she sat on the bus staring out of the dusty window. The air was stale in the confined space, and though she knew she was getting closer to her destination, she felt trapped. It was irrational to think that traveling on foot would be faster than the bus, but sitting still, even in a moving vehicle, was making her antsy.

She bit her lip hard. The pain seemed to give her seconds of clarity, and it was in those few seconds that she questioned what she was doing. But it wasn't long enough for her to grab a hold of the thoughts and make sense of them. She had to get to New Orleans, but why? She felt as though she was leaving something important behind but couldn't remember what it was. Though all of those things sucked, the worst of it was feeling like she was being torn in two—like her very soul was separating itself from her body because it didn't agree with what she was doing. In her mind she could picture herself attempting to grasp it, but like running water, it just slipped through her fingers.

"You've got to pull it together," Elora whispered fiercely to herself, though she was pretty sure she needed more than a good pep talk. What she really needed was to talk to Cassie. She'd already thought that several times but each time she'd gone to reach for her cell phone, she'd stop herself. Elora would like to say that she was talking herself out of calling, but her voice wasn't the one she was hearing in her head. Something or someone else was whispering these things to her. Maybe it should have scared her, but really all it did was tick her off. She wasn't one to relinquish control easily, especially if she didn't know she was doing it. But once again her brain fogged over and all she could think about was how badly she wanted to get to New Orleans—to, well, whatever the hell it was she was trying to get to.

As she leaned her head back against the seat and closed her eyes, her mind drifted in a murky haze. Through the haze a face kept staring back at her. He was handsome, but there was something sinister about the small smirk on his face. Regardless of the danger she sensed lurking beneath the surface of the face, Elora wanted nothing more than to meet the man behind that smirk. For some reason beyond her understanding, she knew that this person represented the destination to which she was headed. He was what was waiting for her in New Orleans.

Tarron pulled the door closed silencing the human male's voice. He was so very sick of listening to Cassandra's father attempting to bargain for his mate's release. He supposed he should at least respect the man for being willing to sacrifice himself for his female, but then it was very difficult for him to find anything about humans that he could respect. They were weak, and the only fate for those that were weak was destruction.

He had to duck around the hanging herbs and bottles in the priestess's small shack. She'd been insistent that he keep his prisoners there where she could ensure that no harm would come to them as they were a part of the spell. If he allowed himself to lose his temper and cause one of them harm, it could alter the spell in an unpredictable way. He didn't remember asking her to include them in the spell, but then he knew better than to be anything but precise when dealing with Voodoo magic. A priestess would take liberties where she could if the one bargaining wasn't smart enough to cover all the angles. Tarron wasn't about to name himself a fool, but, perhaps, he should have paid closer attention.

He shook his head to himself—what was done, was done. It couldn't be changed and he'd deal with whatever the consequences were as long as Cassandra was his.

"The wind be changing." The priestess's voice jarred him from his thoughts as he stepped out onto the old porch. As if on command, the breeze suddenly changed direction. Tarron didn't show her an outward reaction though on the inside he shivered. She was powerful, there was no doubt in his mind, but even a Voodoo priestess had weaknesses.

"Does that mean something?" he asked her without looking away from the dim scenery around him.

"Maybe," she answered vaguely.

"Could be that your female is on her way, or could be that there is a storm brewing. Nothing is certain in magic; it moves according to its own will."

That wasn't very comforting to the dark elf. He was growing impatient with waiting, but he refused to give up the advantage of fighting on a turf of his choice. He would just have to be patient a little while longer and take comfort in knowing that soon he would have what he should have had long ago.

"We've recovered all of the Rapture that was taken and disposed of the humans," the warrior standing in the doorway of Lorsan's office announced.

The dark elf king stared out over the casino through his one-way glass not bothering to look at the male. He wanted to growl that it was their own incompetence that had caused them the work of recovering the precious drug. But there was no point in rehashing it. It was done; the Rapture was once again in his possession. Though what he had left wouldn't last forever. He needed to get in touch with Tarron and find out where they stood on getting a new lab up to make more, but the mad scientist had up and disappeared. It wasn't unlike Tarron to go MIA occasionally, but Lorsan was annoyed that the dark elf had chosen the present moment to pull one of his disappearing acts.

"Make sure nothing happens to it again," Lorsan barked. He heard the warrior mumble something and then the door closed. Only a few seconds after the departure of the warrior, he felt the presence of his Chosen. Lorsan turned just as she stepped through the mirror on the wall across from him.

Ilyrana stepped into the room, her dark gown flowing around her. The elfin material clung to her curves and Lorsan admired her briefly before looking up at her face. "Have you made any progress?"

She walked over to him and ran a finger up the lapel of his suit jacket. Her lips turned up in a slight smile. "You are all business these days, my love. Have you forgotten how to play?"

Lorsan placed his hands on her hips and pulled her closer. He hadn't forgotten how to play, but there were more important things to do, and until those things were taken care of, everything else would have to wait. But, he knew his queen and he'd have to let her down gently or face her wrath. "You know I love to play, especially with you." He paused, staring into her eyes, letting her feel the truth in those words. "But we have important things that have to be managed first. Then, my beautiful Chosen, we can play all you want."

She let out a dramatic sigh. "Fine, but I will hold you to your words, king of mine."

Lorsan felt as if he'd dodged a bullet. With all that he had to deal with, a perturbed mate was not something he needed added to his plate. He pressed a chaste kiss to her lips. "And I will honor it."

"The book seems straightforward," she began as she stepped back from him and began to pace as she let her thoughts take form. "There is our people's history and events, but woven into the words are powerful spells. I dare not read it aloud because I have no idea what the repercussions would be. This book was written by the elders. I think only they could fully decipher the messages it contains."

"Does it tell of the future? Does it mention humans?"

"It does mention the humans, but I have no idea what it says about them," she told him as she tapped her lips with one of her long slender fingers. "It is as if the book itself is thwarting me by hiding the true meanings of the words as I read them. I begin to grasp a thought and then it's gone."

"Why haven't you sought out an elder?" Lorsan's words were sharper than he intended.

Ilyrana turned slowly and narrowed her eyes on him. "Patience is an attractive attribute, my love, and don't think me a fool. Of course, I've sought out the council of the elders. But there is a small problem,"

"What problem?" he interrupted.

His Chosen crossed her arms in front of her and tilted her head slightly to the side. Her jaw was clenched as she answered. "The elders are missing" —she paused before continuing— "all of them."

"How!" Lorsan snarled.

"Well, there is the whole *you blew up the castle* thing that might have killed them all."

Syndra pressed her hands against the inner wall exactly opposite where her mate's own hands rested on the outer wall. He couldn't see her but she could see him just fine, and she had to admit that he was quite the sight—tall, lean, and muscular like all of the males of their race. He might not be as powerful as Triktapic, but he was no weakling. He was a formidable opponent and any who underestimated him were fools. She only hoped that their combined power would be enough to set her and Lisa free.

"Ready?" he asked her, drawing her attention back to the matter at hand.

"On your count," she answered.

"One, two, three." Tamsin's voice started to shake as he began to push his magic into the wall.

Syndra closed her eyes and drew from the source inside of her allowing it to flow like a river through her body. She concentrated on her arms and hands, pushing all of that power into them and, in turn, into the wall. The iron around her was making her weak but she didn't give up. She kept pushing, all the while asking the Forest Lords to hold her up when she felt as though she was going to fall. The air grew thick with their combined magic and the wall began to shake.

"Just a little more," Tamsin told her through what sounded like gritted teeth.

She redoubled her effort and shoved her hands against the stone and let out a low growl. She felt a surge of power run through her, and the stones in front of her shattered into tiny dust particles. There was no crash or crumbling pieces around them. It was as though the rock had been sanded away until all that remained was a pile of grains.

Syndra didn't have time to think about it as Tamsin's strong arms enveloped her pulling her tightly to his chest. She could feel his trembling as he held her and his soul rose up to meet hers.

"I'm going to kill him for this," he whispered against her hair.

"Not if I kill him first."

Tamsin pulled back far enough that he could look down at her. His jaw was tense as he looked her over.

"I'm fine," she reassured him.

He cupped her face in both his hands and pressed a gentle kiss to her forehead. *"I don't ever want to lose you."* His words were spoken softly in her mind. Tamsin's presence there was as welcome as her own thoughts, and Syndra couldn't help the love that welled up inside of her for the man who held her with such tenderness.

"It's a good thing because I don't plan on going anywhere."

He kissed her one more time before stepping back. She followed his gaze over her shoulder and found Lisa standing there staring at the ground as though it held the answers to life's greatest questions.

"Something interesting written in the dust?" Syndra asked her.

Lisa looked up, raising a brow at her. "I was just attempting to give you a little privacy. But if you're done, I am more than ready to get out of here."

"There is still the matter of Elora wandering around Vegas, unless Cush has found her."

"I'm sorry, Lisa, but when I talked to Cush he said that Elora was missing. We'll get out of here and help him search for her," Tamsin assured as he took his mate's hand.

"We also have to get the book back. That book holds too much powerful knowledge. There was a reason it was guarded by the elders at one time," Syndra added.

"I don't want to keep you guys from looking for the book. I can look for Elora while you guys search for the book," Lisa said as she stepped through the opening where the rock had disintegrated.

"Why don't we find out what Cush knows once we get out of here, and then we can make plans accordingly," Tamsin said giving Lisa a reassuring smile.

Lisa let out a slow breath and nodded. "Okay." She clapped her hands together and rubbed them. "So, how do we find the book?"

"The elders," Tamsin answered. "We need to speak with the elders."

Lisa sighed and pinched the bridge of her nose. "Please tell me that they just happen to be staying oh so conveniently in a nearby hotel because they all wanted to go on vacation at the same time."

Syndra chuckled. "She's funny. Don't you think she's funny, Tam?"

"Definitely funny," he answered dryly.

"I'm taking that as a 'no'," Lisa grumbled.

"Um, actually, other than Myrin, I don't even know if any of them are alive. But if any did survive Lorsan's destruction, I know a good place to start looking.

Syndra looked up at him. "Is it in this realm?"

He nodded.

"Why do I get the feeling that I'm not going to like where this is going?"

Tamsin gave a little tug as he pulled her after him

and motioned for Lisa to join them. "Because, my love, you are most definitely not going to like going into a dark elf club."

"A what?" Lisa asked sharply.

Syndra let out a groan. "Fantastic. I'm going to have to cloak the human lest she be lured under by their magic."

"The human you are referring to is right here and wants to know what the heck you're talking about."

Syndra waved her hand nonchalantly. "It's really no big deal. There is a popular dark elf club here in Vegas. Most of the elves there aren't really loyal to Lorsan. They actually aren't loyal to anyone but themselves. They simply live for their own pleasure. But for humans, being around them can sort of enthrall them. Sometimes it doesn't turn out so well for the human."

"Oh," —Lisa laughed a tad hysterically—"is that all?"

Syndra glanced back at her. "No, but I think it's all you need to know for now."

"Why exactly would the elders be in a place like that?" Lisa asked. "Aren't they light elves?"

"Not all of them," Tamsin admitted.

"No, unfortunately, some of them were lured to Lorsan's side, but I imagine most of them have seen the error of their ways," Syndra explained. "But, this club is not one where Lorsan would wander, so it would be a good place for the elders to lay low."

"Trik has already told some of them that they are welcome to join us, but even though the elders have been somewhat split between light and dark, they still operate as a corporate group most of the time." Tamsin paused before continuing. "I'm sure all of them will be interested to know that the missing Book of the Elves has been found and is now in the hands of a madman."

"Will they be willing to help?" Lisa asked.

Syndra nodded. "Oh yes, light or dark, they both know how important it is that our history and magic be protected. I personally think the book should be destroyed, but I imagine Trik will want to speak with the Forest Lords about it."

They were quiet for a while as Tamsin lead them back down the corridor he had descended and all the way back to the room where he'd entered.

"Did that seem a little too easy?" he asked as he looked at Syndra.

"Perhaps, Lorsan is foolish enough to believe he could keep me captive."

Lisa shifted restlessly as she looked back at the door they'd just entered through without encountering a single dark elf. "Or he wanted us to escape."

As soon as they were out of the casino, Tamsin pulled out his phone and dialed Trik's number.

"Are they okay?" Trik asked without preamble.

"I have them in my care and they are both fine. Is Elora still missing?" Tamsin asked.

"We don't know exactly where she is, but we know she's headed to us— well, to the bayou anyway. Cush and Oakley are on their way here as well. If she asks, I would advise that Lisa stay with you two. I know she's worried about her daughter, but we aren't just dealing with Tarron. We have a Voodoo queen and her priestess in the mix now. Cush is going to be struggling to keep his calm. As cruel as it sounds, he doesn't need his Chosen's mother breathing down his neck."

"Understood." Tamsin disconnected the call and slipped the phone into his back pocket.

"So?" Lisa asked, her eyebrows raising as she met his gaze.

"Trik said that Elora is headed to the bayou, where they are. Cush and Oakley are on their way as well."

"Trik talked to her?"

Tamsin glanced at his Chosen who raised a single brow at him. He rubbed the back of his neck as he let out a sigh. "He didn't say that exactly. He just said, 'She was headed to them.' "

"He also said, 'He wants you to keep your happy little butt with us,' " Syndra added. When Lisa's brow furrowed at her, Syndra pointed to her ear. "Elfish hearing."

"If Cush is going to be with her soon, then I'm fine with staying with you two. Someone has to keep you both out of trouble anyway." Lisa seemed to relax a little now that she'd heard something about her daughter.

"There's nothing wrong with a little trouble," Syndra quipped.

Lisa clucked her tongue. "It's all fun and games until someone wakes up the next morning lying next to a dark elf."

"Not everyone is so easily lured by a pretty face." Syndra held up her hands. "Just sayin."

"Really? Because you're mated to that." Lisa pointed to Tamsin.

"I said not everyone. I didn't say not me."

"Are you two done?" Tamsin asked eyeing both of them.

Syndra held up a finger. "Almost." She looked back at Lisa and Tamsin saw the wicked gleam in his Chosen's eye. "Speaking of trouble and lying and next mornings, we are going to be in a dark elf club. That means there will be many male dark elves with, no doubt, pretty faces and alluring voices. Please refrain from jumping onto that train again. You've already ridden it once and look where it got you. So do me a favor and abstain."

Lisa frowned. "You make me sound like some sort of dark elf groupie. I was with a dark elf because I happened to be his soul mate, not because he had a pretty face and an alluring voice."

Syndra narrowed her eyes on Lisa and pursed her lips.

Lisa rolled her eyes. "Okay, so it might have started because he had a pretty face and an alluring voice. But just because I was with Steal doesn't mean I want to jump every dark elf male I see."

"Lisa, dear, you haven't had any action in a very, very long time. It is not unreasonable for me to be concerned about how you might react to the attention of a dark elf male. It's just good to be prepared. Admitting you have a weakness is half of the battle to beating an addiction."

Lisa smacked her forehead as she let out a long groan. "I am *not* addicted to dark elf males. And despite my lack of *action*," she said dragging out the word, "I assure you I can control myself. Somehow, someway, I will manage to keep my hands off the dark elf populace."

Tamsin grabbed his mate's hand and gave Lisa an apologetic smile. He started to pull Syndra with him and Lisa walked to his other side, probably hoping that if she was out of Syndra's line of sight then she might be forgotten. Tamsin chuckled under his breath when Syndra leaned around him to look at Lisa.

"Just to be on the safe side keep your hands in

your pockets."

"Give me a break," Lisa muttered as she shot Syndra a murderous glare.

"Oh," Syndra added. "And walk with your legs crossed."

Chapter 8

"I can feel the distance between us growing. A darkness, bleak and empty, is beginning to fill me as I struggle with the pain that is spreading from the inside out. If I'm not careful, it will debilitate me until I can only dream of finding her. That's the double sided coin of our mated pairs. We need each other and are essential to the other. It is one of our greatest strengths but it is also one of our biggest weaknesses." ~Cush

Cush tried not to break his teeth under the pressure of his clenched jaw as he sat in the cramped plane. He wanted to use the portals, but Trik had been against it, and though it was strange to be taking orders from a new king, he *was* the king, and it had been engrained in him a long time ago not to defy the king.

The humans around him shifted restlessly. Some shot him looks from the corners of their eyes. They weren't fools. They knew there was a predator in their vicinity and, like most prey, their instinct was to run and hide. He had no problem with humans, but in that moment there was only one half human that he wanted to see, and she was out of his reach. He didn't understand why she'd left or what her motivation was for going to New Orleans. Cush felt angry at her blatant disregard for his feelings, but at the same time he knew something had to be wrong for her to have done something like that. He wondered if she was beginning to hurt the way he was. Did her heartache to be near him? Did her skin burn for the need of his touch? Was her soul screaming at her to run back to him just as his was screaming at him to get to her?

Cush felt a nudge on his elbow and looked over at Oakley. He'd been quiet since they had started their journey to the airport, only speaking when he had a specific question. Cush knew he had to be worried about his sister, but he had no fake words to placate him with.

"I don't think that armrest can take much more before it cracks," he said motioning to the armrest in question.

Cush looked down to find his hand clenched around the plastic so tight that his knuckles had turned white. He quickly released it and flexed his fingers several times. "Thanks."

Oakley nodded. "Whatever her reason for doing this, it means something has to be wrong. Elora doesn't abandon those she cares for."

Cush closed his eyes briefly, picturing her face in his mind. It only made his gut clench tighter. "I know and I'm not sure if that reassures me or scares the hell out of me."

They were both quiet the rest of the flight. Cush was lost in his thoughts imagining a life without the woman he'd fallen in love with. He kept telling himself that he would die before he let that happen, but then he wouldn't force her to be with him if that was what she truly wanted. His eyes drifted closed and he attempted to get some rest, knowing it was going to be a long night and day. Cush was sure that whatever was waiting for them in New Orleans, it wasn't his Chosen with open arms and a smile. No, it was a battle and one he was not sure he could win.

Elora climbed off the bus and stepped to the side to get out of the way of the other disembarking passengers. Her body felt tight, wound up like spring just waiting to be released. She stretched her arms over her head and looked around the bus station. A large sign attached to the old brick wall in front of her announced their arrival to New Orleans and welcomed them to the historic city. Elora felt as though there was a tear beginning to rip inside of her as her soul reached in one direction and her mind in the other. She wanted to be there, was relieved she'd finally made it, and yet at the same time she wanted to turn and run in the other direction to—. She paused as she tried to grasp on to that feeling. What did she want to run to? What was it that she was missing or, rather, *who* was it that she was missing? A physical pain was beginning to build inside of her. Her heart seemed to have to work harder just to keep beating, and her muscles were fighting against her every move. She put one foot in front of the other and made her way to the other side of the bus station where she could see taxis waiting to take people to their appointed destinations.

The image of a dilapidated motel on the edge of a swamp entered her mind as though answering an unasked question. She explained what she was looking for to one of the men leaning casually up against a yellow cab.

"Sounds like you're looking for one of the witch

doctors," he said in a thick French accent. "That's the only reason folks go that direction."

"I have friends staying at the motel," Elora explained.

He waved her off. "It's not my business. I'll drive you there as long as you got the fare."

"Do you take debit cards?"

The cabbie nodded and opened the back door for her. Elora slid in and tried to still her trembling hands as the car pulled out onto the street and headed toward a destination that didn't make any sense to her, and yet it was a destination she could not deny.

Priestess Chamani walked through her swamp, a land where she'd lived for the past eighty years and the land where her ancestors before her had lived. Her people had been born, lived, and died in that swamp for as long as anyone could remember. It was rich with the blood of her people, and it spoke to her in a way that it did no others. The trees were her friends and the moss a cloak around her like a comforting blanket. She welcomed the land to her and it, in turn, welcomed her.

The bayou was an unforgiving land, full of dangers and traps waiting for the unsuspecting. Like a coiled serpent waiting for the mouse to unwittingly walk into its strike zone so was the swamp. Not only were their hidden perils such as quicksand like pits and vines that could entangle your limbs dragging you down to the marshy land but there were predators that constantly watched for the weak or stupid.

Gators, snakes, and poisonous insects were only a

few of the animals that called the swamplands home. But even these creatures had accepted Chamani as one of their own. Just as they were a part of the bayou, she too was counted among the predators. Rarely did one of them attempt to make her prey, and if they did, she simply reminded them of why her family had survived so long in the land when others had died or given up and ran.

Her feet walked unerringly on the spongy ground, but she left no prints in the soft mud. Her own magic cloaked her from the presence of other humans as she made her way to where Cassandra and her mate were currently attempting to traverse the terrain. She'd known they would come, but she would be wary of the elf king. He hadn't been deemed one of the greatest spies and assassins in the supernatural world for nothing. No, she wouldn't let her guard down, but she would hope that he would keep his word because the balance was teetering on a breaking point, and if Lorsan and Tarron were to gain control of the human realm, things were going to get bad, very, very quickly.

The trees rustled around her and the wind whispered through the leaves telling her of the intruders. She stopped and raised her arms in the air, calming the restless spirits that resided there. As she lowered her arms Chamani heard their voices. They were less than thirty feet from her and just as she saw them Trik froze and his head snapped in her direction. She felt his magic and power immediately and was shocked at the force of it. The Forest Lords had greatly blessed him and it was obvious that their protection surrounded him. She hoped she hadn't underestimated her opponent, but then even if she had it was too late to turn back.

Triktapic, Elf King, Assassin, Spy, I so name you.
Chamani reached for his mind. She couldn't control
him, he was much too powerful for that, but she was
able to speak to him silently. He didn't seem surprised.

"Speak out loud, witch." His voice boomed
through the trees bouncing off of the large trunks and
reverberated through the air.

"Careful, King," she warned. "This not be your
land. It will not be tolerating disrespect."

"Then I would ask that you not disrespect my
Queen or my people by using mind tricks. We came
based on your offer."

"No," she cut him off. "You be here because
Cassandra's parents are in the clutches of evil. Speak
truth or don't be speaking at all." The spell surged from
her without thought, and to her surprise Trik's hand
flew out in front of him and light pulsed from it. Her
spell bounced off of the light uselessly.

"Do we need to establish who is stronger? Is this
posturing really necessary?" Cassandra spoke up.

Chamani's eyebrows rose as she took in the human
who was still very young compared to the supernaturals
around her. She was bold; she would make a good
queen and it was obvious by the way Triktapic kept his
body halfway in front of hers that he was very
protective of her. That was a very good thing because
she was also very vulnerable.

"Is that not what predators be doing?" she asked
the queen. "Do not all alpha creatures establish who be
the greatest among them? It is necessary to know who
be leading and who be following."

"Or, perhaps, we could not act like animals and
instead deal with the matter at hand." Cassandra raised
her chin slightly in the air. She would make a fierce

leader one day. She still had much growing to do, but she was definitely a good match for Triktapic.

"You be remembering the dream chile?" the priestess asked her.

Cassandra nodded.

"Then you be knowing the price."

"What about Elora?"

"Her fate is not certain. I not be seeing where she will end up and that's not the goddess's concern. Triktapic must be staying on the throne. It not be just the elves who will pay the price if the dark elf be taking over."

"So I'm just supposed to just toss my friend to the side?" Cassandra's eyes narrowed.

Chamani shrugged. "We all be making tough decisions in da hours ahead. Your parents be important to you, as is your mate. It not be fair, fo sure, but then...that not be my concern."

"We want to see her parents before any deals are struck," Triktapic spoke up.

The old woman nodded. "We must be waiting first. Elora, daughter of Steele, is getting closer and she must be here. Tarron is not being a fool, but her presence will distract him once he sees her."

Cassandra did not appear happy about that, but then Chamani was not concerned with anyone's happiness save her goddess.

"We wait here," she told them, making eye contact briefly with the other human who was standing behind them. He was a young male though no longer an adolescent. There was no fear in his posture, only curiosity and courage. Triktapic was surrounding himself with comrades that he was going to need. Though Chamani wasn't sure if it was going to bode well for her, she knew it would be necessary in order for the elf king to succeed.

The cab door was eerily loud as it slammed closed behind Elora. She paid the cabdriver and then turned to face the rundown motel as the car drove away, leaving her to an uncertain fate. Her immediate thoughts were of the Bates Motel but she quickly shoved those things from her mind. Perhaps, she would need to choose different things to watch on TV lest her imagination get the best of her. Then again, her reality had become much more bizarre than any television show, so it probably wouldn't matter what she watched at that point. The fact of the matter was that she had been in Las Vegas for reasons she could no longer remember and now was standing in the swamp lands of Louisiana for reasons she did not understand. No, TV had nothing on her life.

As she began to walk, her feet didn't take her to the motel but, rather, past it instead to a dirt road that had *past murder scene* written all over it. But no matter what her rational mind was telling her to do, as in run like hell in the opposite direction, her feet continued forward.

"Cue the creepy music as the dumb blonde heads straight for her killer, all the while thinking she's being sneaky," Elora mumbled to herself as she walked deeper into the marshland. At first, she attempted to keep her feet from getting too muddy, but after half a mile she realized it was futile. Her shoes kept sinking down into the muck and pretty soon she was caked from the tip of her toe all the way up to her shins.

Unfamiliar sounds kept her constantly shifting her eyes from one direction to another. She scanned the ground in front of her for any signs of life, mostly alligators, but she was sure there were also other things living in the swamp that she'd rather not meet. As she pulled her foot from the deepening mud, the thick sucking sound of her shoe breaking free from the mire echoed off the trees around her. She once again felt that relentless stabbing in her gut. She stumbled as the pain intensified but righted herself before she could face plant into the swamp. Elora wanted to scream in frustration. But just as quickly as those feelings came, others followed just in their wake. And as a deep voice reached out to her through the sudden fog that she hadn't even realized had formed around her, Elora felt her heart speed up and her feet eager to follow.

"I wasn't expecting you," the voice rumbled. "And I don't know whether to be angry or accepting of this outcome."

"Who are you?" Elora asked.

A man, no, not a man, she amended. A dark elf, materialized out of the fog less than ten feet from her. Her gut tightened as she looked at him and feelings of electricity ran over her flesh. It was the face from her mind, the one that kept popping up every time she attempted to think of reasons she shouldn't be doing what she had been doing. She'd never met him and yet Elora wanted to throw herself into his arms.

"I am Tarron and you, lovely dark beauty, are mine."

Tarron stared at Cassandra's best friend partly in shock and partly in awe. Raw emotions were pouring through him as he drank her in. He knew the spell hadn't worked correctly—and knew he should be angry—but as his eyes roamed over the female in front of him, he found that the only emotion he could feel was need. He needed her. He *wanted* her. She wasn't the right one. She wasn't his choice and yet he couldn't bring himself to care. Tarron knew that this was the spell at work. Chamani was a powerful priestess with old magic coursing through her veins. She had worked a love spell with the blessing of her goddess and it had done its job. It just happened to have landed on the wrong person.

He took a step toward her and when she didn't back away he took another and another until he was standing a foot from her. He was close enough to touch her, close enough to smell her, and her scent was better than the sweetest, ripest fruit. Her dark hair was a beautiful contrast to her creamy, fair skin.

"Why is this happening?" Elora asked him as her eyes met his.

"It wasn't supposed to be you," he admitted. "But I can't say that I'm disappointed. I actually think you might be a better fit for me. You aren't fully human. I can feel it. I can feel the darkness in you." Tarron couldn't feel her soul. He never would be able to; it wasn't how magic worked. It couldn't make them soulmates; it could only manufacture the emotions that soulmates feel.

"Who was it supposed to be?" she asked interrupting his thoughts.

He clenched his teeth together as he considered the changes he would have to make to his plan. Triktapic wouldn't be nearly as affected as he would have been if it had been his Chosen who was taken. It wouldn't destroy the king to see Elora in Tarron's arms, not like seeing Cassandra would have. But it would certainly do some damage to Cassandra to see her best friend captivated by the dark elf.

"It doesn't matter. All that matters is that you're here with me." Tarron reached out his hand and slowly took hers. It was cool and clammy. The slight tremor in it had him pulling her closer to him. To his surprise he found himself wanting to comfort her, to reassure that he wouldn't hurt her. Was it the magic? Was it something else entirely? The better question was, did he care?

"Walk with me," he said as he threaded her fingers through his. Elora still looked very confused and unsure but she went with him without hesitance. Tarron knew that he'd have to take her back to the priestess's shack, but he wanted some time with her before he had to deal with how she would handle him holding Cassandra's parents hostage. He wanted to woo her and, perhaps, win a little bit of her heart, not just hold her because of the thrall of the spell. But that would take time.

"I honestly don't know why I felt compelled to come here," she told him as he helped her maneuver around fallen trees and soft land.

"Do you believe in such a thing as soulmates?" Tarron asked her.

Elora suddenly clutched her chest with her free hand and leaned over groaning as though she were in pain.

"What's wrong?" he asked, truly concerned.

She started shaking her head and he leaned down to see her face. Tears streamed down her cheeks, though her eyes were clenched tightly shut.

"Elora, tell me what it is."

"I can't. I don't know. It's been happening since I left Las Vegas. I just . . . this . . . this pain it grips my insides and feels as though it's going to rip my organs from my body. I can't breathe." She struggled to speak while attempting to suck in air at the same time.

Tarron knew then what it was. Anger rushed through him like hot lava running down the side of a mountain. It burned his insides as he thought of her mate. Elora was a Chosen to a warrior. Being separated from him unwillingly would cause her pain and it would only get worse. He released her hand, afraid that he would crush it in his wrath. He didn't want to share her. Elora had not been the female he had wanted, but now she was all he wanted. As he stared down at her while she was clutching her body in pain, he considered his options. Perhaps, there was a stronger spell, something that would make her soul separate from its mate. Until then he would have to intervene so that she wouldn't be in pain. He laid a hand on her head, pushing his power into her. He caught her just before she hit the ground. Tarron swung her up into his arms and clenched her tightly to his chest. She would sleep until he could figure out a way to separate her from the light elf warrior. She would be his. How had the little dark half human so thoroughly ensnared him that he was willing to give up his plans? He still wanted to see the elf king destroyed, but it was no longer his sole purpose. Holding Elora in his arms he felt an emptiness inside of him being filled, one that he hadn't even realized had been there. Whatever the priestess had done through that spell, it was much stronger than even Tarron had known it would be.

"Sleep well, Elora. Soon enough you will wake and want only me," he whispered to her as he started off in the direction of Chamani's little shack. He had work to do and he was eager to be done with it so that he could take Elora away back to his realm and a life with him. Tarron didn't want to think about why he felt such things. He would deal with the reasons later, after he figured out what bargain he would have to strike with the Voodoo goddess to make Elora forget her soul mate.

Elora wanted to scream but her voice wouldn't cooperate. She felt trapped in her own body unable to move or open her eyes. She'd heard the elf's voice, the one that called himself Tarron, but she couldn't focus on his words through the pain that was assaulting her. Elora felt as though every one of her nerve endings was being rubbed raw, as if they were being exposed to the elements. She hurt from the tips of her toes all the way to her head. Even her eyes hurt as though she'd held them open for too long staring at the sun. Never before had she felt such agony and she hoped that when it was over, if it was ever over, that she'd never have to feel it again.

Elora didn't know where Tarron was taking her, but she hoped that it was somewhere or to someone that could help her. And if there was no one that could help her then she hoped her suffering ended quickly. She was pretty sure death would be better than what she was feeling in that moment.

Elora gasped as she heard a roar in her mind. She could feel something, or someone calling to her, reaching for her—no, not her, for her soul. She felt her soul's response as it reached back in a desperation that surprised her. *You will not die.* The voice was strong, fierce, and gone just as quickly as it had come. Elora felt a level of despair that she'd never known as her soul shrunk back inside of her. It was strange to think of her soul as a separate entity from herself, and though she knew they were one in the same, she felt a distinct split between them. Her soul wanted someone that her mind did not remember, wanted him with such need that being separated from him was slowly destroying her. Elora wasn't sure how she knew that, but she was sure if she didn't reunite her soul with the one she needed it would damage her in an irreparable way.

But even as she thought of leaving Tarron to find this other person, her mind shut down, attempting to remove all desire for such things. Elora was sure she'd never again have to wonder what it was like to be schizophrenic because, in that moment, she was split completely in half. She just had to figure out which was stronger—her mind or her soul?

Chapter 9

"Sometimes in life we plan for one thing, but then, just like the wind can change directions in an instant, our plans are blown away and we are suddenly headed in the opposite direction. Then we face a new question. Is this new direction better or worse than our original plan? Regardless, can we even do anything about it?" ~Cush

Cush took the keys for the rental car from the skinny, pimple-faced boy on the other side of the counter. It had been very difficult for the warrior to keep himself from jumping over the counter and just grabbing the first set of keys he came to. The human moved entirely too slow for his liking but he managed to somehow keep his composure.

Oakley was waiting for him on the curb outside by a sign that declared the parking lot beyond as Rental Vehicles. His hands tapped restlessly against his legs to a beat only he could hear. Cush knew that his Chosen's brother was almost as eager to find her as he was.

"Ready?" Oakley asked as he turned toward the parking lot.

Cush held up the keys and pressed the door unlock button on the key fob. Amidst the rows of black, white, and silver cars and SUVs, the lights on a bright yellow Jeep Wrangler lit up the dim area.

"You have got to be kidding me," Cush muttered. Now he knew why the pimple faced boy was wearing the sly grin that Cush had thought he'd imagined as he turned to leave.

"What exactly did you tell him we needed?" Oakley asked as he choked back a laugh.

"All I said was that we were touring the swamps."

"Maybe this is their designated swamp touring vehicle."

Cush stepped off the curb toward the ridiculous yellow Jeep and motioned the human to follow. "Just shut up and get in."

Cush set the GPS to the address of the hotel, which he'd received from Trik while they had been waiting to board the plane. With the pain inside of him growing more intense, he shoved the manual transmission into first gear and headed in what he hoped was Elora's direction.

A little over an hour later, they pulled into the parking lot of the rundown motel. Oakley let out a low whistle as they climbed out of the Jeep. "Wow, they really went all out on this place. Any nicer and I'd think we were at the Ritz."

"Considering we haven't seen much of anything but swamp for miles, I don't think they had to worry too much about their competition," Cush pointed out.

"So what do we do now?"

Cush folded his arms across his broad chest and leaned his back against the grill of the Jeep. "Now we wait."

"Waiting sucks," Oakley grumbled as he mimicked the warrior's pose.

"It is the same in any century. Waiting never gets easier," Cush said as he stared out into the vast swamp. His eyes were narrowed searching for any sign of movement. Trik had mentioned in his text that they would be heading into the swamp that morning to speak with a Voodoo woman. How on earth the woman factored into Elora's whereabouts he did not know, but with the possibility that Voodoo magic was involved, the tension in him had risen to an explosive level.

Only a few minutes passed when Oakley unfolded his arms and pushed away from the Jeep. "Really, we're just going to stand here and wait on them to come back, when we don't even know *if* they will come back? Trik said they were meeting some creepy Voodoo chick, right? So how do we know that she hasn't worked some Voodoo mojo on them? How can you stand there all calm and stoic when your king and my sister's best friend might be out there being dangled over the water as gator bate in some weird Voodoo ritual?"

Cush watched the rant with a calm face, though he felt anything but calm on the inside. When Oakley finally finished he let out a long sigh. "Make no mistake boy, there is nothing calm about what I am feeling. And you're right, I can't just stand here. Not when she's out there in the hands of a mad dark elf."

A slow grin started to spread across the human's face and a glint that would surely lead to no good shone in his eyes. "Does that mean we aren't just going to stand here like two toads shooting the breeze?"

Cush shook his head as he pushed away from the vehicle. "I don't know where humans get their sayings from, but I'm thinking it's time to find a new source when you start comparing yourself to toads."

Oakley started to respond but Cush held up a hand to stop him. "We're going but you have to do everything I say. If I say jump—"

"I know, I say *how high*," Oakley interrupted.

Cush's looked at him with narrowed eyes as he tilted his head to the side. "No, I was going to say if I tell you to jump then you jump without hesitation. If you stop to ask how high, you've already disobeyed the command, and you're probably dead."

"You're right," Oakley declared. "You really don't get human sayings."

Cush didn't respond, instead he turned and started walking toward the thick, moss covered trees. He didn't look back to see if Oakley was following. He had a feeling his Chosen's brother wouldn't last long in the bayou without him and the human was well aware of it.

"So what about the alligators?" Oakley asked as he jogged to catch up.

"What about them?" From the corner of his eye, Cush saw the boy shrug.

"They sort of live in the type of swamps we are currently walking into," Oakley pointed out.

"I guess it's a good thing I have you with me."

"Why would that be?"

A slow smile spread across Cush's usually indifferent face. "I'm pretty sure I run faster than you."

Oakley's lips pursed together as he shoved his hands into his front pockets. "I hate that I never know when you're being serious or when you're joking."

"Didn't Elora tell you? Elves don't joke. She claims we have no sense of humor."

Cush led them deeper into the trees until they could no longer see the motel behind them. They were shrouded in a forest filled with secrets and shadows. Water sloshed in the bogs around them as unfamiliar sounds rang out in a chorus like a rehearsed anthem. Tree branches stretched out above their heads dripping moss like streams of green blood.

The setting itself was enough to make most turn back and run for the cover of even a dilapidated roach motel, but that wasn't why Cush had to force his feet to move forward. He could feel the evil that had no doubt lived in that swamp for decades and probably longer. On the outside it coated his skin like thick oil, but on the inside it moved like a slithering snake searching out his weaknesses to use against him. Cush felt his own magic rise up in retaliation to the intrusion and shove the presence from his body. He heard a gurgling sound from behind him and whipped around to find Oakley grabbing at his neck attempting to loosen a noose that was not there.

"It's an illusion, Oakley," Cush calmly told him as he stepped toward the struggling boy. "It isn't real. You have to tell yourself and believe it is not real."

As Oakley continued to gag, Cush realized that Elora's brother wasn't going to be able to obey that command. He was too far gone, caught in the web of whatever malevolence had taken root in the eerie swamp. Suddenly Oakley doubled over. His mouth was open in a silent scream, and his hands gripped his head as though it had splintered into pieces, and he was attempting to hold it together. His eyes had lost all recognition of reality and Cush could tell that he was trapped inside whatever it was that was holding him hostage. He rushed forward and shoved Oakley's hands away and replaced them with his own. Cush reached for the magic bestowed upon him by the Forest Lords. It was a part of who he was, and just like any elf he could wield it for good or evil. Light emanated from his hands and flowed into Oakley. He sought out the malicious presence that he had felt trying to enter his own mind and radiated the light into it. Cush broke up the bleak darkness that was attempting to take over Oakley's mind. It had found his greatest weaknesses in the deep places that only Oakley himself knew about. The presence was attempting to use those weaknesses against him, creating a level of fear in the human that was crippling.

Gradually the grip it held on him faded and was replaced by Cush's power. Oakley straightened and the light that had faded from his eyes returned and his face relaxed.

"Better?" Cush asked.

Oakley nodded but still seemed unable to speak. Cush gave him a few minutes to gather himself.

"What was that?" Oakley finally asked.

"It was whatever dark spirit that has occupied this swamp for a very long time. Apparently it doesn't like us being here."

Oakley shook his head. "That is some messed up crap."

"Welcome to the world of Voodoo."

"What? You mean like those little dolls they make to look like real people so they can stab them?"

Cush nodded. "There's actually more to it than that. Voodoo is a religion for some people. It's their way of life."

Oakley wiped his hands on his jeans. Though he was beginning to get some color back into his face he still looked a little shell shocked. "Is it all evil?"

"Well, considering the spirits that they worship are lost spirits from the underworld, yes, I would say it's all evil," Cush answered as he looked around them searching out the trees for any presence. He felt as though someone or something was watching them, like a spider eyeing a juicy fly that was getting closer and closer to its web. It was with that thought that Cush realized that staying in the parking lot to wait on Trik and the others might have been the wiser choice. But he was pretty sure that whatever was watching them wasn't about to let them leave now that they'd walked into its domain.

"We are keepers of the secret," Tamsin told the man who had revealed an opening in what appeared to be a solid wall. Syndra had only been to this particular club one other time, and she had vowed then not to return for any reason. But that was before *The Book of the Elves* had fallen into the hands of the dark elf king. The eyes of the tall doorman widened before he bowed and stepped aside.

"Welcome, King and Queen and consort," the dark elf said stiffly before ushering them in and slamming the wall back into place. "Please, enjoy yourselves."

"Not likely," breathed Syndra as the trio pushed through the crowd.

"*This* is where the elders hang out?" Lisa was staring in awe at the bright flashing lights and the beautiful writhing bodies pressing all around her. Already she was unconsciously bobbing her head to the relentless drumming beat reverberating throughout the room.

"I know you've dealt with our kind for a long time, Lisa, but there is still a lot about us you do not know," replied Tamsin. "Elders aren't just old. They embody everything elvish—beauty, grace, and wisdom, sure, but also power, excess, and greed."

"So they just hang out in clubs debasing and pleasuring themselves?"

"Some do, some don't," muttered Syndra. "They're elders. The elvish trait they embody most of all is unpredictability. You get what you get with them." Syndra's eyes shifted around the room. It was clear from her wary look that she was becoming increasingly uncomfortable.

"Are they here? Do you see any of them?"

"I don't kn—"

"Well, well, well...a full-blown human and elvish royalty...isn't this a pleasant surprise?" Syndra was interrupted by a soft purring voice as the embodiment of masculine beauty stepped up to Lisa extending his hand in greeting.

"Can it, Rezer," Syndra spat. She glanced at Lisa and whispered, "Hands in pockets, legs crossed." Then she turned back to Rezer who was giving her a quizzical look as his eyes darted between her and Lisa. "We're looking for the elders. We're not here to play any games."

"Ah, such a pity. This one looks like she needs a drink," purred the elf and from out of nowhere a small glass filled with red liquid was in his hands and he passed the drink to Lisa. Lisa, who was somewhat used to dealing with the elves, had to admit she'd never seen anything like Rezer.

"Hm, hm," Lisa muttered. She seemed to be entranced by Rezer and began to slowly reach for the glass, never taking her eyes off of the dark elf's face.

"No, Lisa!" Syndra barked, knocking the glass to the floor where it shattered sending thousands of tiny slivers across the concrete. "You, of all humans, should know better than to take anything from a dark elf, especially in a place like this. And why are your hands out?"

Lisa shook her head and the cobwebs seemed to clear. Her face tightened as she glared at Syndra. The light elf queen simply shrugged. "Pretty face, alluring voice. Back away from the train my friend, back away from the train." Syndra turned back to Rezer who was watching her and Lisa with way too much interest. Her eyes narrowed on the dark elf. "Of course. Can we just find the elders and get out of here? The quicker the better."

"Oh come on, Syndra. You're just no fun. I remember a time when you used to be much more entertaining."

Light—brilliant white light—exploded from the light elf queen's hand, instantly illuminating the club, making it as bright as high noon in Hawaii. Syndra's hand shot out like a lightning bolt, gripping Rezer's throat. Dark elves all around them shrieked and fell back covering their eyes and cowering in corners. As if on cue, the music stopped, the monotonous beating no longer drumming their senses. A hush fell over the once noisy club. Syndra didn't take her eyes off of Rezer when, from the corner of her eye, she saw her mate take a protective stance at her back. Power radiated from her body and if there were any who had wondered who she was when they entered, they now had no doubt.

"I know that your kind has no loyalty. You pay fealty to only your selfish pleasures." The light elf queen's voice vibrated with rage. "But you would be wise to not forget who it is that has ruled our people for centuries. Loyal or not, you are not human and therefore fall under the rule of your leaders. Speak carefully, dark elf, or I will remove your tongue. Then I won't have to worry about the stupid things you might decide to spew." She released his throat and took a step back. The light surrounding her didn't extinguish completely, though it did soften, allowing parts of the club to return to the darkness that the elves there preferred.

Rezer straightened his shirt collar and then bowed slightly at the waist. "How may I be of service to the former king and queen of the light elves?"

The jab didn't go unnoticed but it didn't faze Tamsin or Syndra. They had no bitter feelings over Triktapic returning to his rightful place. A small smile formed on Tamsin's face and Syndra took Lisa's wrist and pulled her slightly behind her body. She knew that look on her mate's face, and what followed could sometimes get messy.

"You are a foolish elf, Rezer, and I honestly do not know how you have survived this long. But as it seems, you are our best bet for information, so I must stay my hand from finishing what my Chosen has started. You might take time tonight to look in the mirror and be thankful your head is still attached to your body. Now, enough of this imprudence."

Syndra heard Lisa snicker behind her and jabbed her with a well-placed elbow. She had forgotten that the human woman often found humor at the most inopportune times.

"We are looking for the elders," Tamsin continued. "I know that some have been known to frequent your establishment."

The dark elf glanced around the club and it was obvious that he was regaining some of his confidence as he realized he indeed had information they wanted. He definitely should never play cards because his poker face was about as blank as the Vegas strip at midnight, Syndra thought.

"How is it that two of the most powerful beings of our kind have lost the elders?" Rezer's voice was laced with mocking humor. "I thought Lorsan kept most of them on a tight leash."

"Lorsan is occupied with other things at the moment and we didn't lose the elders. You know that they are more powerful than we are and that they go where they please. You can't lose something that has the power to keep from being found if it wishes."

"Fair enough," Rezer told the light elf king. "And how, exactly, do I benefit from disclosing this information?"

Syndra rolled her eyes and let out an exasperated huff.

"This one is dense," Lisa muttered.

Syndra nodded. "Sometimes all they are *is* a pretty face and alluring voice."

Tamsin's eyes narrowed as they zeroed in on Rezer. His lips tightened and his voice was as cold as a blizzard that chilled all the way to the bone. "I am pretty sure that we have already covered that information and I really hate repeating myself."

"Oh, fine," the dark elf drawled. We've only had one ancient visitor as of late. "And yes, he is still here. Through that door and to the end of the hall." He pointed to a door along the wall where another elf in a dark suit was standing guard. Rezer gave a hand signal and the elf shifted to his left a couple of feet, presumably leaving the door accessible to the light elves.

"Which one is it?" asked Tamsin.

"Vyshaan."

Tamsin did not miss the way his Chosen tensed. She was probably thinking the same thing he was—of all the elders, why did it have to be *that* one? Syndra had only ever discussed her history with Vyshaan once, and after that they had tucked the knowledge away in hopes that it would never surface again.

"Personally," Rezer continued, unaware of Tamsin's thoughts or his mate's reaction to the elder's name, "not my favorite. Bit of a bore, if I'm being honest, but we'll take what we can get nowadays, I guess." The dark elf airily waved his hand about.

"There now, that wasn't too difficult now was it, Rezer." Tamsin gave the dark elf a pat on the shoulder and moved past him with Syndra and Lisa in tow.

"Ah, just one more thing you might be interested in, oh gracious former king and queen..." Rezer face was a smug mask as he let his voice trail off, half turning away from the trio.

"And what is that?" growled Syndra.

"You three aren't the only strange visitors we've received this evening. It's rare we get light elves in here and humans are even rarer still. But half-elves, well, that almost never happens. And I must say" —he stared directly at Lisa— "the resemblance is uncanny."

Chapter 10

"Things stir in the far recesses of my mind. They lay in shadow, just out of my grasp. The more I try to shine a light in those dark corners, the darker they appear. Somehow I know that these are more than long ago lost memories. Pieces of my soul lay shrouded in that darkness. I know with every cell in my body that I need to remember them. I must remember them." ~ Elora

Cassie shivered as the day drew on. Fall was coming to the swamp and, even this far south, a ten degree drop in temperature didn't go unnoticed. Priestess Chamani stood motionless, staring at them. Her weathered skin covered her like the worn surface of a concrete monument. She hadn't moved an inch since her declaration that they would be waiting for Elora to arrive, and she gave no indication that she was planning on doing so any time soon. Cassie's feet ached and she wondered if the priestess also felt a similar pain. After all, Cassie was young and Chamani was, well, the complete opposite of that. Despite the temperature, threat of alligator attack, and constant buzzing of mosquitoes, neither Trik nor Tony appeared bothered in the least.

"Have you heard from Rin?" Cassie whispered to Trik. She watched as he pulled his phone from his back pocket.

"I asked him how things are going," Trik told her holding the phone so she could see the text message.

"This was his answer."

"Tell my queen that everything is chill," Cassie read Rin's answer. She laughed under her breath. It was a strange thing to hear in such a dismal place, but she silently thanked Rin for the brief moment of lightness during this gloomy time.

It was several minutes later, when Cassie spoke again, once the humor from the text had worn off and anxiety seeped back in.

"And, uh, how long will she be?" asked Cassie glancing around, as if Elora would be walking out from behind a Cyprus tree at any moment.

"No man knoweth the day nor hour, chile." At this the priestess threw back her head and let out a long hearty chuckle that reminded Cassie of a colony of bats shrieking through the night's sky. "Besides, there be plenty a good stumps round here to be resting on." And with that the old woman plopped down on a gnarled stump and placed both of her hands on her knees, leering at Cassie all the while. "And dat be givin us some more time to parlay while she be coming."

Cassie wasn't exactly in the mood to have afternoon tea with a Voodoo priestess—especially smack-dab in the middle of the Louisiana bayou with darkness quickly creeping up on and her parents still missing.

"Great idea," broke in Tony. "These old dogs could use a rest." He too found a suitable stump, which seemed to be everywhere around them, and dropped down on it, propping his feet on a fallen log. Despite the muck that splattered his suit trousers and his expensive Italian loafers, he appeared unruffled. "So tells us again, priestess…uh, what did you say your name was?"

Again the old woman cackled. "You be a clever on, chile. But you be knowing better than that. Names be having power, and I not be givin mine out for free."

"Chamani," said Trik. "Her name is Chamani, and she and her family have trafficked with dark elves for centuries."

"Ah, you be no fun, Triktaptic," the old woman croaked with mirth in her eyes.

"So tell us, Chamani," Tony continued unphased, "why exactly does your mistress want Trik to keep his throne so badly."

"Hmm, that be an interestin question right der." The old woman's eyes rolled back in her head momentarily and she sucked in a deep breath. Seconds ticked by and no one said a word as they all anxiously watched her. After a few moments, she exhaled and her eyes refocused on Tony. "It be yo lucky day, pretty boy, I can give dat information out fo free. It ain't no secret Lorsan be bad mojo, chile. And Tarron, da potions mixer, be even worse. Now by dem selves, well they be no never mind. But they has someting now, someting powerful."

"*The Book of the Elves*," said Trik quietly.

"Dat be sho nuff right, assassin king. And wit dat book they might be being too powerful. Maybe they take over de whole of de human realm. And maybe dat make dem even mo powerful dan my mistress herself. We sho can't be havin dat now, can we?"

"Who's to say I won't challenge your mistress myself when I have the book?" Trik asked her.

The priestess narrowed her eyes at the elf. "That be another interestin question right der," Chamani responded.

"A good king doesn't seek out trouble," Cassie

interrupted. "He would never needlessly put his subjects into harm's way. Lorsan doesn't understand this. He only understands power and he will sacrifice anything or anyone to get it. That is why he isn't fit to be king. A good king picks his battles and puts his people's safety above his own." She reached out to Trik and put her hand in his.

"Well spoken, chile," the old woman said.

An uneasy silence fell over the group. Chamani stared at the sky, seemingly in another world. Trik and Cassie took turns glancing at each other and glancing at their surroundings, communicating without spoken words. After a few minutes, Tony, eyes closed and head slumped forward, began to snore.

"Some help he is," Cassie said, nudging Trik in the ribs. Trik was just about to go and warn about him staying alert when they heard noises coming through the bushes. Tony snapped up and every head turned to investigate. They could clearly hear someone lumbering through the trees, breathing heavily, with footsteps making squelching noises in the mud.

"Here be our girl now," said Chamani, a serene grin plastered to her face.

With the exception of the priestess, they each stood, alert, facing the direction of the oncoming noise. After a few moments, Elora broke through the trees, but hers weren't the footsteps that had caused the sounds. In fact, she wasn't walking at all. Rather, she was being carried by one stunned looking dark elf who had seemingly been so startled by happening upon this group that he froze in his tracks. Trik, however, was anything but frozen.

"You," he gritted out through clenched teeth, all the while stalking toward Tarron who still held Elora in his arms. Trik reached his hand back, balled up a fist that was white hot with magical power, apparently ready to unleash his full fury on the dark elf.

"Wait!" cried Cassie. "You'll hit Elora."

Trik froze and sucked in a breath. He lowered his arm as the light faded from his hand.

"That's right," hissed Tarron, who took a few steps backward away from the elf king. "Don't want to go spoiling this beautiful creature's face."

"What have you done?" Trik growled.

"What have I done? What have I done?" Tarron repeated, his voice rising to a maniacal pitch. "I've found my Chosen at long last. Just like you, Trik."

"She's not your Chosen and you know it."

"Oh isn't she?" the mad chemist responded. "If she were awake right now, I think this little raven would say differently. Wouldn't she, priestess?"

"A deal be a deal, dark elf. Da spell be working as intended. Now you be going ya own way."

"Wait a second," broke in Cassie. "You can't just let him leave with Elora. She's my friend."

"Don't ya be tellin da mistress Chamani what she can and can't be doin, chile. Da mistress always keeps her word. She not be interfering with something that not be her concern."

"Trik, stop him," wailed Cassie.

"Stop right there, assassin," barked Tarron as he took another step away from Trik. "You don't want to do that. This girl and I are linked now. The Voodoo magic courses through both of our veins. If you kill me, then she dies too. Right here, right now."

Trik stood motionless, clenching and unclenching his fists. He wasn't sure if Tarron was bluffing, but he couldn't take the chance. "I'll find you," he said at last.

"No, no you won't. You'll leave me alone if your little Chosen ever wants to see her parents again. Once I'm far, far away, I'll send you a message letting you know where I've hidden them. Until then, if I even suspect you might be following me, they're dead." With that the dark elf turned and shifted Elora onto his shoulders. "I mean it, blondie. Make sure your big bad assassin doesn't follow me." With a quick glance back at Cassie, he awkwardly bolted into the cover of the trees.

"Well, that didn't go anything like I had pictured in my head," Tony said into the silence that had dropped over them.

"What did you picture?" Cassie asked as she continued to stare in the direction to which Tarron had just vanished.

"A lot less talking and a lot more ass kicking."

Trik's eyes narrowed as he continued to watch Tarron run, his superior elf vision allowing him to see what the humans could not. "Don't worry, Tony, that picture is coming, very soon."

Cush continued to stare around at their surroundings. Though he still sensed an evil presence, he couldn't get see or hear anything tangible close by.

"Oakley, have you ever heard the saying, *discretion is the better part of valor?*"

"Oh, don't tell me you're giving up already. I'm alright, man. One little imaginary noose isn't going to slow me down."

"I appreciate your concern for Elora, I really do.

But the spirits that are inhabiting this swamp may be more than I can handle. I have to find my Chosen, but it won't do her any good if we both end up dead in the bottom of a bog."

Truthfully, Cush knew that he could probably survive the swamp just fine on his own. But he wasn't sure he could do that and protect Oakley. And he knew that Elora wouldn't be too pleased with him if he showed up without her brother because the weaker half-elf had been killed by some Voodoo swamp magic. Cush was nearing his breaking point. He knew, instinctively, that Elora was somewhere nearby. But he didn't know how to find her. With each passing second he became more and more confused. Why had she come here of all places? Every second away from her was tearing him apart. He could only figure that Trik had some answers. How Trik had known that she was here, Cush couldn't say and right now he didn't care. He only cared about getting Elora back. If anyone could help him do that, it was Trik.

"Ugh, this sucks," said Oakley. "I'm a half-elf. Why can't I do all the cool juju that you and Trik and the others do? You shouldn't have to babysit me? What is the point of being half-elf and not having any powers?"

"Doesn't work that way. Half-elves always have more in common with humans than with elves, at least the ones I have met anyway. Half-elves are very rare and most that exist don't even know they have an elvish side."

"Great," huffed Oakley.

"Being an elf isn't all it's cracked up to be anyway," Cush continued.

"I can see you are really struggling to get by. Must be terrible walking around looking like you do and, oh by the way, shooting freaking beams of light from your hands."

"Don't whine," Cush chuckled. "We can continue this man crush pity party thing you have going on later. We've got to get out of here." And with that he started tromping back the way they came. Oakley had no choice but to follow.

It only took a few minutes for Cush to realize they were in serious trouble. Like most light elves, Cush was uniquely attuned to his natural surroundings. Which is why he was able to note every tree, rock, bush, and stump that they passed, marking them in his memory. After he passed a familiar looking gnarled cypress tree a second time, even though he knew that he and Oakley had been walking in roughly the same direction, he thought it must be a coincidence. But when he passed the tree a third time, he knew without doubt that they were somehow going in circles.

"Stop," Cush whispered, coming to a halt so suddenly that Oakley almost ran into his back.

"What now?" Oakley whined.

"Hush," the elf responded, slowly crouching and staring intently around. Without knowing why Oakley copied his movements. "Does it feel like we've been going in circles?" he asked.

"I don't know, man. I've been following you. I didn't really stop to check the cross streets."

As he said this, all noise in the swamp seemed to shut off like a light switch. The crickets ceased their chirping and the frogs quit their croaking. Oakley hadn't realized how loud the surroundings had been. After so long wandering around, he had unwittingly become accustomed to the sounds. Now their absence went straight past ominous, all the way to creepy.

"Be very still," Cush whispered.

A murder of crows exploded from a tree behind them, cawing and flapping, swooping down at the pair.

"Stay down," yelled Cush. He threw his body over Oakley. "They can't hurt us," the elf ground out at he put his hands over his head hopefully protecting the tender parts from the beaks and claws. A second later the crows didn't so much as fly off, they just vanished.

"An illusion," the elf said calmly as he stood up, his eyes searching their surroundings. For what, Oakley did not know. "Just like the noose. You mustn't let her fool your mind."

"Easy for you to say," Oakley responded, rising to his feet. "What about this?" He pointed to the top of his ear, which was now dripping blood onto his shoulder. Apparently one of the bird's beaks had found a target.

"Voodoo magic," Cush said as if this explained everything.

"What's that supposed to mean? And what did you mean by *her?*"

"The crows were an illusion, but that doesn't mean they can't still cause damage. Just like the person who feels the "real" stab when the doll gets pricked, so can the Voodoo priestess cause damage from afar. She's toying with us."

"Toying with me is more like it," responded the young man. "Okay, I'm convinced. We should have waited for the others. How are we going to get outta here?"

"I only wish I knew," said Cush.

Lisa took a step forward, attempting to maneuver around Syndra. The light elf queen held out an arm, preventing her human friend from getting any closer to the dark elf, and Tamsin stepped around his Chosen to protect both females. Rezer had tossed out the information to see if the half elf meant anything to them. Tamsin knew that he was attempting to see if he had any leverage over them with the knowledge he possessed, and Lisa had handed him his answer on a silver platter.

"Did she tell you her name?" Lisa asked as she struggled against Syndra's arm.

Tamsin turned and placed a hand on Lisa's shoulder and whispered under his breath. Later, once things had calmed down, Tamsin knew that he would pay for his actions but it was for her own good. Lisa stilled, unable to take another step forward, as though her feet had been encased in concrete. She could still move her arms and speak, but Tamsin's magic held her legs in place.

Lisa shot him a glare that would have had lesser men backing up. But Tamsin was not a man and, other than feeling bad because the human was his Chosen's favorite friend, he was not bothered by her ire.

Tamsin looked back at the dark elf and did not like the interest with which Rezer watched Lisa. He could practically see the ideas forming in his mind, and the light elf king had a feeling he wasn't going to like the conclusion Rezer came to.

"Something about you seems very familiar," the dark elf murmured. He tilted his head slowly, examining Lisa as though she was a new toy that he was all too eager to play with. "Have I met you before?"

"She's not from this city. There's no way you could have ever met her." Syndra scoffed. "Not to mention, she's human."

"Not entirely." His eyes zeroed in on Lisa like a hawk sighting its prey. Rezer clucked his tongue and moved his finger back and forth like a pendulum at the light elf queen. "You've been a naughty girl, dearest queen. What spell is it you have cast on this one to prolong her life so?"

Tamsin felt Syndra tense next to him and when he looked back at her, he saw that Lisa's eyes had become large round saucers, and if her mouth opened any wider, her jaw would be resting on the club floor. He reached over and took his Chosen's hand and reached for her mind.

"I was not aware that Rezer was that powerful." Tamsin didn't have to point out to his Chosen just how odd it was to find a dark elf hiding away in the human realm with enough power to sense hidden spells. Then again, Rezer's power might be why he was hiding away in the first place. Lorsan did not take kindly to other dark elves having enough magic to challenge him. It would not have been surprising, had Rezer stayed in the dark elf realm, to find that the elf had mysteriously come up missing.

Tamsin's voice in Syndra's mind seemed to shake her from her shock. She relaxed her shoulders and raised her chin just a notch. Though her attention was on the dark elf, her words were for Tamsin.

"Had I known, I would have asked you to figure out a different way to find an elder."

Rezer returned their stare unerringly, obviously waiting for some sort of explanation. He would just have to deal with the disappointment because there was no way any of them were going to admit to the accusation.

"I suppose it is rude of me to ask," Rezer said as his gaze perused the club. "But you must understand my curiosity. A female half dark elf visits my club, which in and of itself is rare, and then within the same twenty-four hours, a human who has been bespelled by royalty and looks so very much like aforementioned female visits me as well. Come now, tell me you wouldn't be the least bit curious?"

Syndra folded her arms across her chest. Tamsin knew that look well and he nearly grinned at her. His Chosen was fierce and the Forest Lords help any who would stand against her.

"I can understand your curiosity," she began. "But since I do not care about quenching your need for answers, you can take your curiosity and choke on it." She took a step forward and once again her power began to grow. "You will lead us to Vyshaan and you will not ask any more questions. You may be powerful, Rezer, but you still are no match for us."

Rezer raised his hands in surrender and bowed his head. "Forgive me, my lady. I meant no disrespect. I simply couldn't help but ask. It has been so very long since anything interesting has happened. As you both," —he paused and glanced at Lisa— "excuse me, as you all three know, a long life is a blessing and a curse. Boredom can cause eternity to seem like a form of purgatory."

"Could we please get back to the part where you met a female half dark elf?" Lisa asked, her jaw clenching and unclenching as her patience began to wear thin. "Did she give you her name?"

"She called herself Raven," —Rezer waved a hand dismissively— "though I know that was not her real name. She obviously had knowledge of our kind if she knew not to speak her given name."

Tamsin glanced at Lisa and Syndra as they all drew the same conclusion. Cush called Elora Little Raven as a pet name. It couldn't be a coincidence that a female half dark elf, who they knew had been missing, called herself Raven and it not be Elora.

"Now before you do any more threatening of bodily harm, allow me to assure you that I do not know where she disappeared to once she left my club."

"How long was she here?" Tamsin asked.

Rezer glanced at the ceiling as though he needed to think about his answer. "No longer than an hour. She sat and watched the show and then left."

"You tried to cast a glamour over her?" Syndra snarled. "What exactly was your plan if it worked? Did you think to play with her because she was a shiny new toy?"

"Come now, you can't possibly think me so low as to do such a thing. She was beautiful to be sure, and I will admit that she caught my attention because her dark side is untouched. She is so innocent that she hasn't given in to any of her, what we would call, natural instincts."

"Yes," Lisa answered before Syndra could. "Yes, I definitely think you could be so low. Your kind only thinks of yourself first. There are very few dark elves that choose to deny their natural instincts." She spit out the words as though they tasted bad in her mouth.

A snakelike smile appeared on Rezer's face as his silver eyes swirled with awareness. "For a human, you are well informed about our kind. Am I to deduce that since this Raven beauty looks so much like you, that you are the female's mother? And if that is the case, you must have been the consort of one such as myself in order to produce such an offspring. You lot are a wicked group indeed."

Tamsin was sure that at any moment the dark elf was going to start rubbing his hands together and licking his lips over the juicy information he was gaining, without them even saying a word. It was time to end the encounter before Rezer got any ideas about using such information against them.

"As fun as this has been," the light elf king said dryly, "we have more important things to do than assuage your boredom." He pointed to the back part of the club where Rezer had claimed the elder to be. "Vyshaan, now."

"Fine," Rezer relented. "But please do not be strangers." He glanced at Lisa. "And by all means, you are more than welcome anytime."

Lisa looked as if she was going to be sick.

Rezer turned and began walking through the throngs of people before Tamsin could chastise the dark elf for his flirting. He turned to Lisa and touched her arm lightly releasing her of the spell that had held her in place.

Her head snapped around to look at him and daggers piercing him could not have been any sharper. "Don't think I will easily forget that."

He bowed his head and laid a hand across his heart. "Forgive me, Lisa, I meant no insolence. I simply wanted to protect you."

"Well next time figure out a different way like maybe saying, 'Hey Lisa, don't move any closer to the dangerous dark elf.' I'm not an idiot, I would have listened."

"No you wouldn't have," Syndra argued. "He had information about your missing daughter. You weren't thinking about the fact that you are a mere human. Maybe a human with long life, but still only a human. All you could see was him standing between you and the possible knowledge of where your daughter was."

Lisa turned her head slowly to look at her longtime friend. "Gee, Syndra, tell me how you really feel."

"I just did."

Tamsin glanced in the direction Rezer had gone and saw that the dark elf was waiting on them about thirty feet away. "You two can bicker later. We have an elder that we need to beat information out of." He started after Rezer.

"He's joking right?" Lisa asked as she and Syndra followed.

"Who knows," Syndra quipped. "Being around Trik has sort of brought out the beast in my male. It's quite yummy."

"Stop," Lisa said shaking her head. "I heard enough of your desires for your male when he was rescuing us. My ears are scarred for life and my brain needs to be run through a car wash to remove all the mental images you two gave me."

"You could have stopped at, *I've heard enough.*"

Syndra reached her mate with Lisa in tow and stood shoulder to shoulder with him. Rezer was standing in front of an unmarked door. There were no windows into the room and, based on the keypad above the doorknob, it was not a room just anyone could enter.

"If the elder asks how you found him, my name is

not to be mentioned," Rezer warned, as though he could do anything if they did disclose the knowledge to Vyshaan.

"Fine," Tamsin agreed.

They waited while Rezer stared at them, seeming to attempt to decipher whether or not Tamsin spoke truth. He could stare for eternity, thought Syndra, but he would never be able to read her mate's intentions.

After several minutes Rezer seemed to agree with Syndra's unspoken thought and held his hand in front of the keypad. The lock clicked open without him ever touching the numbers on the pad. What was the point of the special locking mechanism if they didn't even have to use it? On the tail end of that thought, Syndra realized that the keypad was simply a distraction. An intruder would assume that to enter the room they had to know the code; when in reality they needed to know the magic and be able to wield it. Clever, she chuckled to herself.

Before the door could open all of the way, Rezer disappeared at a speed the human eye would not have been able to track. Syndra glanced at Tamsin who was looking in the direction to where the dark elf had vanished. When their eyes met she knew they were thinking the same thing, Rezer was lucky to have stayed off of Lorsan's radar all those centuries. He was powerful indeed and she couldn't help thinking that he might be a very good ally to have on their side when it was all said and done.

Tamsin led them into the room beyond the door. Lisa was in between them because Syndra hadn't missed all the subtle glances Rezer had been shooting at the human female. He was definitely interested in her friend, and until Syndra knew exactly what that interest entailed, he wasn't letting him near Lisa.

The room was lit by candlelight. Sconces along the walls held the dancing flames that serenaded the shadows cast by the bodies that filled the space. Once they were inside, Syndra realized that the room was spelled to be larger than the space that it occupied. In fact, it was larger than the club on the other side of the door they'd just passed through. She and Lisa followed Tamsin as he maneuvered the crowded space effortlessly. Once she'd quit looking around, she realized that her mate was able to walk so easily because the elves in the room had no doubt who he was and in turn who she was. Some bowed their heads as they walked by; others attempted to look away, either to go unnoticed or to openly snub light elf royalty. As they reached the far corner of the room, Tamsin came to a halt. Syndra maneuvered Lisa so that she was standing next to her mate and Syndra was beside her. A male elf stood across from them, leaning against the wall with a devil-may-care air. He was tall and slim with silvery, white hair that hung down over his shoulders and past his waist. His arms were folded across his chest and Syndra noticed that the nails on his hands were long and sharp. When she looked back up at his face, she saw that his eyes were shiny black, not just the pupil but the entire thing. There was no white in them and when the candlelight hit them just right they seemed to glow. There was an ancient knowledge in those eyes that revealed the true age of the male, who appeared to be no older than thirty standard human years. This was Vyshaan, and though Syndra had met him before, it had been a very, very long time since they'd seen him. He didn't look any older, and yet he seemed older than any of the elves she'd seen, even Triktapic.

Tamsin stepped forward and placed his right hand over his chest and bowed slightly at the waist. It was a show of respect, but not one of submission. The elder might be older than Tamsin, but he had chosen to run and hide in the face of war while Tamsin had picked a side and chosen to fight. To the light elves, running was tantamount to lowering oneself into a position of subservience. Until Vyshaan could prove himself worthy of his station, not many elves would even give him the respect of a slight bow as Tamsin had done.

"To what do I owe the pleasure of your company, great elf king?" Vyshaan's voice was silky smooth with a hint of persuasive magic woven into it.

"Keep your magic to yourself, elder," Tamsin warned, though he didn't sound angry.

The elder's lips turned up into what Syndra figured was supposed to be a smile but instead looked more like a grimace. It was as though he hadn't smiled in a very long time and no longer remembered how.

"You cannot blame me for trying. It is not every day that the light elf king bothers to find one who does not want to be found."

"Why is it that you do not want to be found?" Syndra asked. She knew the answer, but she wanted him to admit it.

Vyshaan's black eyes landed on hers and memories flashed through her mind, memories that she had buried and had intended to keep buried. Yes, she had met Vyshaan before and since then Syndra had diligently been avoiding him and would have gladly avoided him for the rest of eternity.

"It has been a long time, Syndra," Vyshaan purred.

"Chosen of Tamsin," her mate growled.

Vyshaan raised a brow at him.

"If you are going to name my mate then you will name her correctly. Syndra is *my* Chosen and you will respect her and me enough to address her appropriately." Tamsin's words were sharp and relentless. On this matter he would not bend.

Syndra reached over and linked her fingers with her mate's and gave a gentle squeeze. It wasn't often that he felt the need to express his claim over her, but she had to admit that when he did it was nice to know that he wanted others to know that she was his, and that he still desired her after all the time they'd been together.

The elder shrugged. "If it means that much to you." He looked back over at Syndra and just as her mate had done, he placed his right hand over his heart but instead of the slight head bow, Vyshaan bowed fully at the waist. "Syndra, Chosen of Tamsin, once queen of the light elves, it is a pleasure to see you again after all the time that has past." He straightened and his eyes shot to Lisa. They flashed with recognition and returned to Syndra. "Perhaps, we can reminisce of our shared history."

Syndra's stomach clenched with dread at his words.

"You have nothing to be ashamed of," Tamsin reassured her through their bond.

"You know that isn't true. However, I don't regret it."

"I think we can arrange something," Syndra agreed with a sly smile. "However, we have other things to discuss."

Vyshaan's interest had been piqued. He pushed away from the wall to his full height which was about the same as Tamsin's. "What could you possibly have to discuss with me?"

Syndra shouldn't have felt so satisfied at answering

the question, but after his taunting she wished she had a butter knife to shove in his gut and twist at the same time that she spoke. Perhaps, that was too wicked of a thought for a light elf, but then Syndra had some darkness in her past that proved she was adaptable and rose to whatever the situation demanded, even if her response was greatly frowned upon. Then again maybe frowned upon wasn't an accurate description of what she'd done in her past—against the laws of her people was a tad bit more truthful.

"Just a little thing, a trifle really," she answered with a dismissive wave. Syndra waited until she knew he wanted to snap at her to get on with it before she finally answered. "Vyshaan, one time elder of the Elfin race, turned dark elf elder, turned deserter. Tamsin, former light elf king and myself, former light elf queen, seek your help in finding *The Book of the Elves.*" She paused and watched as his black eyes grew ever wider. "Okay, so seeking your help is really a load of crap. We aren't asking, we are telling you that you are going to help us find the book. You have no choice. You will not refuse us this or I will go to Triktapic, reinstated king of our race, and reveal to him our past history."

"You wouldn't," Vyshaan snarled. "You have just as much to lose as I do."

Syndra let out a sigh. "Maybe, but then I did not serve the dark elf king, nor did I desert my people in their time of need. Even if my fate is the same as yours, I can stand before my king without shame. Can you say the same?"

Clapping hands from behind them had the three turning around, and Vyshaan's head snapped up to look past the group.

"What a fantastic speech. I have to admit I am

impressed by your attempt at blackmail. Who knew that the light elf queen would stoop to such levels?" Ilyrana stepped from the shadows, her hands clasped together in a steeple with her fingertips pressed beneath her chin looking like a proud parent.

Syndra stayed her hand from reaching out and smacking Lorsan's Chosen across her smiling face. She figured that wouldn't be very queen like. Then again, she wasn't a queen any longer so really there shouldn't have been anything stopping her from dropping the evil witch and watching her kiss the floor. Instead she did the diplomatic thing and attempted to hold a conversation. Who knew, they might actually be civilized and come to some sort of arrangement, and maybe animals would start crapping Skittles, and Cush would actually smile without looking like he was in pain. Really, if Ilyrana could be civilized then anything was possible. HA! That was laughable. On the tail end of that thought, Syndra realized she'd been hanging around Elora way too much.

"Why are you here?" Syndra asked. Okay, so maybe that wasn't as diplomatic as she could have been.

"Come now, Syndra, we have known each other a long time. We're like old friends really."

"Um hm, sure old friends," Syndra muttered. "So, old friend, why are you here?"

"To thank you. After all, you and your mate and" —she glanced at Lisa and her face tightened as though there was a pungent odor wafting about— "this human, lead me to an elder. They all seemed to have disappeared after—,"

"Your mate blew up his own castle?" Tamsin finished for her.

Ilyrana's eyes narrowed briefly before her pleasant

mask returned. "A rash decision, I will admit. But then, my king has always loved to make a statement."

"Still haven't really answered my question. Why are you here?"

She snapped her fingers and they were all suddenly surrounded by a legion of dark elves. "You didn't really think that escaping would be so easy, did you?"

Lisa smacked her forehead. "I knew it was too easy. Didn't I say it was too easy?"

Ilyrana barely gave her a glance before turning back to Tamsin and Syndra. "The point is, I allowed you to escape."

"You've been following us," Syndra deduced.

"You found what I have not been able to." She glanced at Vyshaan behind them and waved her fingers at him. "So good to see you again, Vyshaan. I'm glad to see that you weren't blown to bits."

Syndra glanced back at the elder and saw that Vyshaan's face remained still as stone as he stared back at the dark elf queen. Apparently, there was no love lost there.

"As much as I love idle chitchat, I have a certain book that needs to be deciphered. Gather them up," she said to the dark elves around her.

"You can't think we will just go quietly." Tamsin's voice was low and very deadly.

More dark elves seemed to appear out of thin air as the others began to converge on them. "You can be as loud as you like, former king. Either way you will be coming with me." Ilyrana's hand shot out at the same moment's Syndra's own hand extended and the room was lit with a light so bright that everyone had to close their eyes. But just as fast as the light had appeared, the room was plunged into darkness.

Chapter 11

"We see you, though you may not want us to, and though you may attempt to hide. We know you, even if you don't want to know us. We created you, even though you do not see us as your creator. We love you, even when you toss that love aside as though it were nothing more than a trinket you no longer need. There is nothing that you could do that will ever take you so far from us that we can't welcome you back." ~The Forest Lords

Lorsan burst back into his office, gasping. Damn that Tarron and little disappearing act. The casino's final stores of Rapture had finally been exhausted, and the humans were not coping well. The worst of those that had been completely enslaved were now going through terrible withdrawals, and Lorsan had nothing with which to appease them. The riots had begun in earnest last night. Almost half of the people in the casino practically tore his main bar, and both clubs located in Iniquity, apart trying to find more of the drink. His own dark elf security staff had been inadequate to deal with them all. He'd had to go down and deal with most of the rioters himself. But in the end, even his power was no match for their numbers, for their sheer ferocity and disregard for their own safety, when they were in the throes of the drug's grip. His chief of security had been forced to call the human police force. It had been years since he'd involved humans in the security of his casino. This was completely unacceptable. He had to find Tarron—and fast. But he didn't have the remotest idea where to begin to look. Few elves were craftier than Tarron, and he had disappeared without a trace. Even though Lorsan had been monitoring the mirrors, Tarron was still nowhere to be found. But Lorsan had an idea of how he might locate the rogue dark elf—*The Book of the Elves*.

The Book rested upon the conference table in his office, where Ilyrana had left it to go find an elder—any elder—who could help translate it. Lorsan walked over to the table and slowly opened the book. Though he was powerful, knowledge of his people's lore had never been his strong suit. That was why Ilyrana complemented him so well. She was always so adept at puzzling out the secret long lost history of their people. She had more knowledge of their history in her little finger than most elves had in their entire bodies. Surely, if she couldn't deciphered the fabled book, no one could. But he must try. Not only did he need the book's power to defeat Trik but he also needed it to save his casinos. Another day or so without Rapture and the humans might tear his empire to the ground.

He gazed down at the worn pages, stained and brittle after so many millennia. How a mere human had kept this book hidden for so long was beyond him. The words seemed easy enough to read and understand. The stories within told of influential elves of the past, of long ago wars and battles both within the elvish realm and against other realms, and finally of the creation of the elves by the Forest Lords. But he didn't need stories. He needed the power contained in those stories. Those with the proper understanding could decipher the hidden meanings beneath the stories. They could unlock the power within and increase their own power a hundredfold. With this knowledge, he could strike down Trik with a wave of his hand. He could scry Tarron and bring him back, groveling, with just a word. But how?

He turned to a random page. It landed on the story of Mivertheron, the first elf to ever tame a Tirith—the intelligent tiger-like creatures of the elvish realm. As Lorsan read about the ancient elf's exploits, he grew more frustrated. What does this mean? Why would the Forest Lords choose to put such a story in their book? He could almost feel a hidden power, some deeper meaning beneath the story that was lying dormant, just waiting for the right elf to come along and unlock its secrets. But the power eluded him.

"Curse you, Forest Lords," he ground out, pounding his fists repeatedly on the table.

"It isn't smart to curse your creators." Lorsan felt the voice more than he heard it. Immediately he was forced to his knees. He could feel the power of the Forest Lords filling up the room. It was almost palpable, almost robbing him of his ability to breath.

"I, uh—"

"Silence elf." The words were spoken softly, almost whispered, but Lorsan immediatcly found that he couldn't have spoken if he had wanted to scream at the top of his lungs. He sat on his knees, his face plastered to the floor. After a few seconds he was able to look up and he saw the three men—as tall as the ceiling with emerald eyes and earth-brown hair flowing down their backs— standing around him. "Your reign as king is coming to an end." He felt the power in the voice wash over him, though whether the voice was coming from one of the figures, or from all of them, he couldn't tell. "How dare you think that you could use for evil the book that we created for good? Do you not understand, dark elf? The book can only be deciphered by one who is pure of heart, one who would use the book for good, not evil. You could sit and study that book for a century and you would be no closer to deciphering its hidden meanings."

A hollow sound rattled from Lorsan's chest. He was trying his best to stand, to rail against the Forest Lords, but he could do nothing but lay there. He could no more raise a hand against them as an ant could raise a hand against an eagle. And that is what the Forest Lords were; they were wild and powerful and flew above their elves—observing, waiting, and hoping that their creation would call out to them. They would not take their free will no matter how much they turned away from their creators. But they would hurt with them, mourn with them, cry with them, and be there to brush them off and lift them up once they had fallen and realized they couldn't do it on their own. The dark and light elves had been divided for too long, and it was because of those like Lorsan that they remained divided. No, they would not take their free will, but neither would they stand by and let evil tear their children apart again.

"Do not think your insolence has gone unnoticed by us, elf. You have stolen what doesn't belong to you. Long ago, we created the secret ways through the elvish realms, the mirror pathways, so that all of our people could move freely though this world and our own. And now you think you can control these pathways, blocking them from use by your light elf brethren? Once again you seek to use for evil something we created for good. No longer!" The closest Forest Lord touched the mirror hanging in Lorsan's office. There was pop and Lorsan felt his control over the portals evaporate. For some reason, Lorsan felt that his commandeering of the portals somehow angered the Forest Lords worse than his attempted use of *The Book of the Elves.*

"Please, please don't kill me." The once proud dark elf king was finally able to squeak out.

"Kill you?" The three voices seemed to ask in unison. "We aren't here to kill you, Lorsan, but to warn you. That is your problem and always has been. You don't understand your Creators. When have we ever interfered where we were not welcomed? When have we involved ourselves in the affairs of the elves but to warn them or comfort them? We allow you to make your own choices. But you refuse to see us. Understanding your creators is the key to understanding the whole of the elvish realm. That is why you have been such an ineffective leader all these many years. You were too concerned with your own power to think that there might be something bigger than yourself, that there might be higher purposes than your own selfish desires.

You've made your choices and those choices will be the end of you, not anything that we do. Your fate is set, there is nothing you can do to change it. Farewell, Lorsan."

And then, like a vacuum, the stifling power was sucked from the room. Lorsan wasn't sure how long he lay on the floor after the Forest Lords were gone. But once he came to his senses, he knew what he had to do. He jumped to his feet and began scrambling around searching for only the more essential items. He could clearly see the writing on the wall. The Forest Lords had basically just told him he was going to die, and soon. The humans outside would soon overtake his casino and he sure as hell wasn't going out at the hands of worthless humans. He couldn't be around when they finally made it through. He grabbed his belongings and *The Book of the Elves* and bolted for the door.

Cush and Oakley had finally decided to rest after hours of wandering around in a swamp that seemed hellbent on keeping them lost. Of course, Cush knew it wasn't actually the swamp itself, but the evil that inhabited it—which had lived in this place for a very long time. The frustration of knowing that his Chosen was somewhere nearby and being unable to get to her was beginning to whittle away at his sanity, or what was left of it.

As he sat on the ground, which was rapidly cooling as darkness chased away the heat from the long day, he looked up at the sky only to find that he couldn't see it at all. There was no view of the stars that filled the vast darkness, no moon that glowed like a large night-light. The only thing he could see was tree branches and more tree branches. It was as though the outside world didn't exist. Cush felt as though the forest around them was closing in on them, slowly suffocating them. He needed a distraction. And, as if he had heard his thoughts, Oakley came to the rescue.

"Okay, so this place is freaking me out. I'm thinking this is as good a time as any for the brother of your girlfriend to get to know you. It is my job after all to make sure you're good enough for her. I'm supposed to give you the *I'll kick your ass if you hurt her* speech. But that just seems pointless since you could probably kill me with your pinky."

Cush let out a huff of laughter. He had to admit that the human was growing on him, like an unidentifiable fungus, but growing on him nonetheless. "I've never done the *prove myself to the man of the house* thing. So maybe you should start."

Oakley nodded as he leaned back against a fallen log. He brushed the dirt from his hands and folded them on his chest getting comfortable as though he was in his favorite recliner and not the dirty floor of the bayou. "So aside from the fact that there is this supernatural connection between you two, why did you pick Elora? She's not exactly your typical female even in the human race. She's contrary, relentless when she wants something, bossy, and usually finds hilarious things others find repulsive."

Cush smiled at his description of his Chosen. He was right. Elora could be a tad difficult to get along with. But she was worth it. "Elora and I had a conversation similar to that, although there was a lot more shouting and her telling me what she thought I thought. She believed that I couldn't want her on my own, that it was only because of the soulmate bond." He paused remembering the discussion, more like yelling match, that they'd had.

"You think that I would rather go into battle than be with my Chosen?"

"That's just it, Cush. I may be your Chosen, but you didn't choose me. You feel what you feel because you have to. You don't have a choice and that's not good enough for me. Not when it means that you might just throw away something that you love

doing, something that you actually chose to do." Her face was so full of pain because she truly believed those words.

"You think that I chose to be a warrior? You think that this life wasn't forced on me? We aren't human, Elora. We don't live in a society where we go to school and get to be whatever our little hearts' desire. As a male of my race, the first thing they evaluate us for, before we are even a handful of years old, is our battle skills. Do we defend ourselves or do we hide? Do we protect others first or do we think of our own safety first? I was chosen by my king before I turned four summers. I was singled out to be a warrior long before I even had aspirations or dreams. Don't think for a minute that I ever chose *this life. It was chosen for me. I was predestined for it—just as you were predestined for me."*

"You see that's my point. You have never been given a choice in your life and I'm not going to do the same thing to you. Okay, I get it. We're soul mates. I totally believe that. But I'm not going to tell you that you have to be with me just because we were made for each other. That's not fair to you," she paused and then finished with, "or me."

Cush was pulled from the memory as Oakley's voice broke the silence of the night air.

"So what did you tell her?"

"I told her that if the only thing between us had been the Chosen bond then it wouldn't have been reason enough for me to ask her to walk away from all she'd ever known and spend eternity with me. Then I asked her to tell me she didn't love me."

"Dude, you didn't," Oakley said as his eyes widened.

Cush nodded. "I did. I also told her if she was going to lie then she better make it convincing."

"You're totally my hero. Did she lie to you?"

"Surprisingly, no. But she didn't answer the question until I'd asked her several times and admitted my love for her. Only then did she tell me how she felt." He ducked his head and ran his hand through his hair brushing it away from his face. "I thought I was going to lose her. She was ready to walk away because she thought it was what was best for me."

Oakley sighed. "She can be quite obstinate when she wants to be."

"Yes, she definitely can," Cush agreed as a smile tugged at his lips. His little raven was fierce and she was willing to hurt in order to take care of those she loved. That was only one of the many reasons that he loved her.

"Are you going to make an honest woman out of her?" his Chosen's brother asked.

Cush looked over at him and with a wolfish smile said, "I pretty much told her that when all this was settled, she was going to marry me."

"If I wasn't too tired to move I would totally give you a fist bump complete with explosion. You are going to be good for her."

"Perhaps," he agreed, but then whispered more for himself, "but she is going to be even better for me." Cush leaned his head back against the hard tree and closed his eyes. All their talk about his mate had the pain in him only growing stronger. The sweat on his forehead dripped down into his eyes causing him to squeeze them tighter. He didn't realize he'd drifted off until a voice he didn't recognize filled his mind.

"You have much to do, warrior, but for now I will let you rest. You have been lost in my land because I have a purpose for you here. You must be ready. If you want her back, you must be strong. She will not know you at first. The spell my priestess cast is a powerful one but the bond between you two is also powerful. Her soul is searching for you, let yours seek her while your mind

is not burdened with turmoil."

"Who are you?" Cush asked, his unconscious mind still alert though the man slept.

"I am the ancient one who answers those who call. They are seeking their own desires and for a price I grant them. Those who come to me are ready to give up much, but they don't fully understand the cost until the deal is done. Many believe that Voodoo is just an old religion that there is no truth to it anymore, but then there are some who are still loyal and they keep me strong."

"You know where my Chosen is?"

"You know she is close, warrior. Her soul is calling out to you. All you need to do is listen." The voice faded and though Cush remained asleep he was aware that he was once again alone in his own mind.

The Voodoo queen had said that Elora's soul was reaching out to him and he needed to listen. He wasn't sure how to do that, but he would try just about anything in order to hear from her. He relaxed even further and allowed his own soul to rise up in him as it did any time he was touching her. It was like two consciousness in one body, though one lived only for its other half.

Cush could hear his soul calling out her name, searching for the magic tie that bound them together. *Elora!* He waited and when there was nothing, he called out again. *Elora, answer me.*

The desperation he heard in his soul matched the same desperation that he felt deep in his gut. It felt as though it had been an eternity since he'd seen her, heard her voice, or touched her skin. He needed to know she was alright, unharmed, and whole. The words of the Voodoo queen hit him like a ton of bricks, *she will not know you at first.* Did that mean she wasn't whole?

If her mind was not intact, if she wouldn't remember him, what had been done to her? The queen had also spoken of a spell; she'd said it was powerful. Who had bargained with the Voodoo queen to cast a spell on his Chosen? Who would be that foolish?

They will die. His soul told him in a completely different voice than the one that had called out to his Chosen.

Yes, Cush agreed. They will most definitely die, but they might suffer first. Whoever it was obviously did not care much for their own existence or welfare. The anger he had first felt at the idea of Elora leaving him in Las Vegas was but a small flame compared to the raging fire that was now burning out of control inside of him. He wanted to wake so he could start looking for her but his soul stopped him. *Listen*, he told him. They both stilled and after several minutes they heard it.

"Cush." It was the sweetest sound he'd ever heard.

Tarron paused after a few miles of alternating between walking, running, and jogging, but mostly slogging, through the thick swamp. It had been almost an hour since he'd left Trik and the others behind. Like all elves, Tarron was blessed with a super-human physique. And while he may not be an Adonis among his own people, he could run faster, farther, and longer than even the fittest human. But the boggy terrain, stifling humidity, and continuous hidden obstacles of the swamp had a way of sucking the energy out of even a supernatural creature such as himself. Try as he might, he wasn't going to be able to carry Elora through this marshy terrain forever. He was heading out of the swamp, but to where he wasn't sure. He wasn't without options. Over the years Tarron had set up many safe houses throughout both the U.S. and in Europe—places where he could be alone, where he could think, and concentrate on his experiments. Sometimes he needed to be away from the prying eyes and ears and ceaseless questions of Lorsan and the other elves. But to get to any of these, he needed to find a reflective surface. All of the water in the swamp was so murky that when he looked at it only muddy water stared back at him. He knew that there was a mirror back at Chamani's shack, but he couldn't risk going back there. That was where Cassie's mother and father were. Trik might even be extorting the location of his Chosen's parents from Chamani.

Tarron paused and dropped the unconscious Elora, propping her back up against a fallen tree. He took in a few deep breaths, thinking hard about his next move. The sight of Trik had unnerved him, and he'd done the only thing he could think of at the time—run. Tarron was no fool; he knew that his own power was no match for Trik's. No, Tarron was much more dangerous when he was on familiar turf, when he'd had a chance to even the playing field beforehand. Here, he'd been completely caught off guard.

Suddenly, an extremely disturbing thought occurred to the dark elf. Why had Cassie and Trik been waiting for him with Chamani? Surely, they hadn't just bumped into each other in the middle of the swamp. No, they'd been waiting for him specifically, to deliberately catch him by surprise. The old woman knew that he'd be trying to get back to her shack with his new found Chosen. She had planned that meeting from the beginning. He'd been betrayed.

That treacherous Voodoo witch! Tarron spat on the ground, cursing the old woman. Why had she done this? Try as he might, he could not think of a reason. Well it wouldn't do to dwell on it now. He needed to focus on a way to get out of this swamp. Then he needed to get *The Book of the Elves* back from Lorsan. After that he could figure out a way to repay the old woman's treachery.

Just then he heard Elora moaning from her spot on the ground.

"Shh, easy, little one," he cooed as he kneeled down beside her. We will be safely away from these traitors soon enough. "We mustn't let them catch us."

Tarron knew that his bluff back at the clearing would only buy him so much time. As soon as Chamani told Trik where the Tates were stashed, Trik would be after him. After all, he had Cassie's best friend. He doubted Trik would let such an act go unpunished. He felt like a rat trapped in a maze.

But all was not lost, he thought, as he stared at his Chosen, lying on the ground, the one throughout all of history designed specifically for him. Finally, after all these long year, she was his again. He could still picture her vividly in his mind, his Lucy, the perfect mate, so loving, so kind. Surely, this new Lucy would be just as gracious.

"We must go, beloved," he whispered as he scooped her up again. She wasn't really such a burden. Her small form was quite light to one such as him. A renewed vigor shot through him at her touch. "I shall carry you as far as I need so that we can be together," he told her and began running again."

After a second hour of moving through the

swamp, Tarron's newly found strength had more than faded. He was exhausted and he didn't know why. Unnaturally, his limbs felt like they were made of lead. The muddy trail seemed to have grown hands that rose up to grab his ankles with each and every step. Somehow, even though the sun was well and truly down now, the swamped felt hotter and muggier than it had earlier. The branches of the trees reached out and grabbed him as he ran past. The moss from the branches clung to his hands, face, and body. It was almost as if the swamp itself was purposefully trying to impede his progress. And worst of all, very very worst of all, was that he was completely and utterly lost.

It wasn't that he was stumbling blindly in the dark. Dark elves could see perfectly fine at night. No, it seemed that every path he took led him further and further into the swamp, rather than out of it. All he needed to do was find a road, any road, and he could flag down a passing motorist. One glance in their rearview mirror and he and his chosen would be far, far away, leaving them bewildered and thinking they had had a chance encounter with a ghost. But no matter which way he turned, it seemed he was carrying his beloved in circles.

To make matters worse, Elora was no longer held in her peaceful slumber. Though she hadn't regained consciousness, she was babbling in her sleep more and more, sometimes even crying out in pain. Tarron tried to recast the sleep spell, but it was having no effect. He couldn't get through to her. The dark elf was growing more and more frustrated, and his frustration was turning into panic.

The elf stopped again to collect his thoughts. Again he deposited Elora upon the ground, trying to find a comfortable place to prop her head. Tarron, exhausted and worn, sat down, glancing all around him at his surroundings. The nocturnal swamp creatures were out in force now, and they didn't appreciate intruders in their realm. Already he'd killed about a dozen snakes and a mile or so back he'd spotted an alligator gazing at them from the weeds. He'd kept moving and, thankfully, the hungry reptile did not give chase.

Why is this happening? thought Tarron. Why can't I escape this infernal swamp? And then he knew. In a moment of complete clarity, he knew. Like a light bulb coming on, a name popped into his head—Chamani. It was her. It has always been her. That Voodoo bitch was using the swamp against him. She was using her power to keep him trapped here forever. Again he asked why she had betrayed him and again he had no answer.

The elf's resolve started to break. Panic was beginning to set in. He had no way out, no way to be free with his Chosen. They would both die out here in this forsaken swamp.

"Oh, Lucy, er I mean Elora," the elf practically whimpered. He sat down on the ground next to her, cradling her head in his arms. "You were so beautiful, my love. You were everything and I gave you up. And for what? Power, immortality." He sucked in a deep breath. All of a sudden Tarron's face grew dark and his voice lowered, becoming almost gravelly. "But I've got you back now. As I knew I always would. You were wrong, my love. You were wrong. Power *is* everything! You humans just can't understand this," he hissed.

"But my sweet love, what have you done to yourself?" Now his voice had become soft, almost serene. "Your beautiful golden locks, why have you dyed them, my love? My Lucy, you know that I love your lovely blonde hair." Softly, gently, he stroked her long black hair and then pressed his lips to hers.

Just then her eyes popped open. "Tarron?" she questioned, her voice breathless and desperate.

"Shh, I've got you," he cooed to her.

Elora shivered in his arms and he thought it a good sign that she wasn't pulling away from him. Why would she pull away from him? he argued with himself. She's my Chosen. Of course, she would want me to hold her.

"Where are we?" she asked.

"There's been a slight set back in my plans," he admitted. He noticed her rubbing her chest as her face tightened in a grimace. "Are you alright?" To his surprise he saw a tear drop from her eye and streak down her cheek.

"I feel like I'm supposed to be with you. But something is missing, Tarron. Something very important is gone and I feel like I'm going to die without it."

"He is close," a cool voice said entering his mind. Tarron suddenly felt very cold as the chill of the voice settled over him.

"You didn't think that you could really take another male's mate and not suffer the consequences did you? And did you think that you could come into my lands and make demands of my priestess and not pay dearly for your insolence?"

"You made a deal with me," Tarron argued not bothering to speak out loud. He knew that who he was dealing with could hear him verbally or otherwise.

"Fool!" The voice who he knew to be the Voodoo Queen boomed. *"The deal changed. You cannot be allowed to carry on Tarron of the dark elves. There is only so much room for darkness in this world and you and your king are tipping the*

186

balance. The only way you will leave my swamp is if you defeat the warrior."

Tarron would not admit that he was scared. Fear had no place in a dark elf. He, after all, was a monster, and therefore other monsters should not cause him to tremble. And yet when he looked down at the hand that was holding Elora's, he saw that it was shaking. He ground his teeth together as he attempted to rid himself of the Voodoo queen's declaration. She was bluffing. There was no way that the warrior she spoke of was there in that very swamp with them. He would find a way out and he would be taking the female he'd claimed with him. The only way he would give her up was if they pried her from his cold dead hands.

His mind filled with her voice once again and her words had bile rising up in his throat.

"He is coming. He wants what was taken from him back and there is nothing he won't do to get her."

Chapter 12

"Everyting comes wit a price. There not be anyting tat is truly free. Sometimes the price be greater and sometime tat be worth it. If you come to the land of my queen, you must be ready to pay a high price and you must understand tat da deal you be makin can change. So tink carefully afore you make da deal. Tere be no goin back once it be struck." ~Chamani

"Trik, we can't just let them get away," Cassie said shakily as she watched Tarron trample off with Elora over his shoulder.

"I know, Beautiful, but I cannot risk your parents. We have to get them back. I won't risk their safety, not even for Elora."

Cassie was broken. This had all been too much. First, her parents had been kidnapped by a psychopathic dark elf, and now he'd gotten her best friend. She needed Elora now more than ever, but her friend was beyond reach. Cassie couldn't bear to watch her carried off by such an evil creature. Now, if Trik went after Tarron to get Elora back, she might never find her parents. She fell to ground, great sobs racking her body.

"Stay with me, Cassandra." Trik knelt down in front of Cassie; his knees plopped into the muck and sank just a bit as the mushy ground gave way. He put his arms around her and pulled her close. "You must be strong. Be the queen I saw when we stormed Lorsan's castle. Be the queen who stood before our warriors and delivered that amazing speech that so inspired them. That is who you are, beloved, and you have to remember that, especially, when things seem to be falling apart."

"I can't, Trik. I've never felt so incredibly helpless," she said between sobs. Her whole body shook in his strong arms. She let him hold her. Truth be told, had he not been propping her up, she probably would have fallen face down in the sludge of the swamp that surrounded them. She didn't seem to have the strength to even hold her head up any longer.

Trik used their connection. She felt him pour everything he had into her. He poured all of his love, all of the light and all of the goodness that she had brought into this life, back into her. He continued to send her wave after wave of unconditional love. He would die for her, she knew. And he would die to get her parents back as well if it came to that. She knew that he would search unto the very ends of the earth to get them back if that is what it took. Trik's selflessness gave her strength. This dark elf, this assassin, who had long ago given up hope of finding any goodness in this world, had been redeemed by her love. And now he was doing the same for her. She took comfort from his touch, and strength began to slowly ebb back into her body.

"But where do we even start to look?" she asked him out loud, her voice still weak from the brink of despair she'd been teetering on.

"I tink I might be able to help wit dat one." The raspy voice of the Voodoo priestess, whom Cassie had completely forgotten was there, answered instead. Cassie and Trik both turned and looked at her expectantly.

"Where? And why are you willing to help us now?" Cassie clamored to her feet while Trik stood gracefully while also assisting her. His hands on her waist kept her from tipping over in her haste to stand.

"Mayhap I be bored, or I not be havin anyting else to be doin. Follow me, chile," Chamani responded and started off opposite the direction Tarron had gone. Cassie and Trik hurried to catch the old woman, who, despite her advanced age, seemed to have no trouble traversing the marshy terrain. Tony, who had been quiet giving Trik and Cassie time to sort out the situation, followed after them.

"Do you know where they are?" Cassie asked desperately as they walked.

"All in good time, chile. Patience be a virtue." And the priestess would say no more.

Cassie was in no mood to be patient. But Chamani had already proven herself to them. She had known that Elora would be coming to an exact spot in the swamp where she'd had them wait. Granted, she hadn't said anything about Tarron carrying Elora through the swamp, but no one had specifically asked *how* Elora would be coming. Cassie decided she would trust the priestess for now. After all, what choice did she have? If Chamani had any knowledge as to the whereabouts of her parents, Cassie had to find out what it was. She just hoped this wasn't another one of the priestess' devilish tricks.

After about an hour of hiking, of which each agonizing step was taken by Cassie with extreme anxiety and anticipation, they came to a small shack resting on crooked stilts.

"Okay, so that's not creepy at all," Tony muttered.

Instantly a darkness that chilled to her bones sunk into Cassie. The evil surrounding the building was thick enough to taste on her tongue. Surely her parents weren't in there. The whole front of the house was adorned by a dilapidated covered porch that threatened to fall into the swamp at the slightest breeze. Two chickens squawked at them from their places in small wire cages resting on top of each other on the far end of the porch. A human skull, old and weatherworn, sat on the handrail while moss hung from the porch's ceiling. The gentle breeze blew the moss so that it was brushing over the top of the skull as though gently caressing it. Cassie was sure this was the scariest place she had ever laid eyes on, and she couldn't possibly believe that anything the priestess would say would get her to go inside.

"Home sweet home," Chamani said and her voice erupted with her now all too familiar cackle.

"Why did you bring us here, witch?" Trik asked. The growl in his voice left no doubt that he was obviously growing tired of the Voodoo priestess' games.

"Come now, Elf King. We be partners now, remember? No need to be taking dat tone wit me. Come on inside, make yo selves comfortable."

"Just because we have a shared enemy, doesn't make us partners," said Trik. "And it doesn't mean that I trust you either. I am not stupid, Chamani. We are not going to walk blindly into your place of power."

"Oh, don't be such a stick in the da mud," the old woman chided. "Besides, I have houseguests. Couple ah lovely people here I tink you two should meet. From up around Oklahoma City, I believe they be from."

Cassie had been wrong. Chamani had said the one

thing that not only wanted to make her go into that shack but run into it. She bolted up the stairs and past Chamani grabbing at the door.

"Cassie, wait!" Trik, with his inhuman speed, grabbed her wrist inches from the doorknob.

"Trik, my parents," she pleaded, desperately trying to pull her arm away and get inside.

"Remember what our gracious host has said, *patience is a virtue*. Let's let her go inside first, just in case she might have inadvertently left any surprises in store for unwanted visitors."

"Hehe, you be too suspicious, elf. Must be yo dark nature," Chamani responded as she stepped lightly into the shack. Cassie and Trik followed on her heels. To Cassie's surprise, they stepped into what looked like a quaint cottage on the inside. A simple wooden dining table and chairs occupied the majority of the one room shack. A cast iron cookstove sat in one corner, a small comfortable bed in another, and finally, a worn wooden rocking chair in another. In stark contrast to this goldilocks' setting, however, were two bound and gagged individuals, sitting with their hands tied behind their backs in two of the aforementioned dining room chairs.

With eyes so wide they threatened to pop right out of their heads, Mr. and Mrs. Tate stared at the newcomers. But then recognition dawned on their faces as they spotted their only daughter and their eyes went even wider still. They each began straining against their bonds, muffled cries coming from their mouths. Cassie's eyes were so filled with tears that she was barely able to see straight as she ran to them practically knocking her mother backward over her chair as Cassie hugged her tightly.

"Mom! Dad! Thank God. I was so scared I'd never see you again," she said. Her body shook with the force of her sobs as she pulled her mother's gag from her mouth. Trik stepped up beside Cassie doing the same for her father.

"What? Who?" Mr. Tate gasped, his voice gravelly, as he stared at Trik.

"I know things must seem very hazy right now, but don't worry, Mr. Tate, Cassie will explain everything," said Trik as he moved around behind Mr. Tate's chair and began undoing the bindings holding his wrists behind his back.

"What are you doing here, Cassie? You shouldn't be here," Mrs. Tate pleaded to Cassie, her brow furrowed though her eyes hadn't lost their deer in headlights appearance.

"Don't worry. It's all going to be okay now, Mom." Shaking, Cassie finally released her mother and turned to her dad, giving him a similar tear filled hug. Mr. Tate, free from his restraints, returned the hug, his arms wrapping around her tightly and pulling her close as though he could keep out all of the bad things. Trik moved to Mrs. Tate, undoing her bindings as well, and he didn't miss the way she rubbed at her raw wrists.

"We've got to get out of here," Cassie's father said, as he pulled back from Cassie. "Hurry, he'll be back any second." And then, as if just realizing she was there, Mr. Tate spotted Chamani, who had deposited herself in the wooden rocking chair in the corner and was busily winding some twine into a ball as if she didn't have a care in the world. "You!" Mr. Tate snarled. "You let him do this to us." He moved to take a step toward her, but his legs were stiff and unresponsive from having sat, tied in the same position for several days.

193

He stumbled and grabbed the table for support, his breath coming out in angry pants. Cassie worried for the first time in her life that her health conscious father might have a heart attack.

"Hold!" Trik's voice broke in. "Calm down, Mr. Tate. She's not our enemy, at least not for the moment."

"*And* you?" Mr. Tate asked, seeming to fully take Trik in the first time. His eyes filled with recognition as they narrowed on the Elf King. "I remember you from our house. What are you doing here? You're one of them, aren't you?" he asked shaking his head as his hand came up to cover his mouth. "You're working with the one who kidnapped us. Tell me I'm wrong! Tell me you aren't one of those things!" He shoved a finger at Trik and his words were filled with such vehemence that Cassie was sure they might just form a blade and stab Trik in the chest.

"No, Mr. Tate," Trik said in a steely voice, "I would never work with him regardless of whether or not I am of his race. And you will have your justice for what he's done to you and your wife. That I swear."

"Please, someone tell us what is going on?" Mr. Tate insisted as he suddenly deflated like a popped balloon. As he turned to sit back down, he noticed Tony for the first time. "And who the hell are you?"

Tony held up his hands. "I'm just your run of the mill human. Unfortunately, dealing with Trik's kind is part of the family business."

Mr. Tate shook his head. "This just gets more and more outrageous."

"Please, Dad," Cassie began, "listen. This is a very long story."

"And I don't think now is the best time to tell it,"

Trik interrupted. "Tarron still has Elora."

Elora, *Elora?*' Mrs. Tate turned to Cassie. "What does she have to do with any of this?"

"Again, it's a long story," Trik responded. "Time is of the essence."

"Hmm," came the voice of the Voodoo priestess again, who, without anyone noticing, had risen and a placed a pot of tea on the cast iron cookstove. "It seems yo chosen ain't da only one who needed to be learning 'bout patience. You see, Triktaptic, yo battle will find you soon enough. Dat dark elf running round out there in dat swamp no longer concern you."

"He does concern me as long as he has Elora," Trik spat.

"No sir, no sir. You couldn't find him now even if you wanted to. Thanks to me and my mistress, he gonna be wandering out there in dat swamp for a good while. His reckoning be coming through da hands of a light elf sho enough—"

"Cush," Trik breathed. His head tilted back as he pinched the bridge of his nose, realization suddenly dawning on him. Cassie could tell the weight of his position and the responsibility he carried was heavy on his shoulders. Now that her parents were safe and she was able to focus on other things, she found that she desperately wanted to bare some of that load with her mate.

"You bet yo quiver on it, dat's right. Now why don't you and your lovely Chosen have a sit down and tell these nice people what need be telling, whilst we all have some of Chamani's hot tea," the priestess said as she placed four small china cups, which seemed to have been conjured out of nowhere, onto the table.

Trik stood for a moment, thinking about what the old woman had said. Though he didn't trust her sweet southern hospitality act for one second, she had given Cassie back her parents. So far, she hadn't shown any indication that she was going to betray them. He believed what she had said about Tarron and Lorsan upsetting the balance of power, and he believed that the Voodoo goddess didn't want either of those two taking over the human realm. Further, he knew that the priestess held great power here in the swamp. Much like he, and at one time Lorsan, could do in the elfin realm; she could control the thoughts of someone wandering in her domain though it was a practice he didn't like to use. She could make them think that they were wandering in circles, keeping them lost for hours, or that they were being attacked by savage swamp beasts. Many things were possible for one such as Chamani and her queen.

Trik wouldn't deny that the thought of giving up his need to destroy Tarron felt as though his arms had been cut off leaving him feeling useless. But, he understood what Chamani was saying. Tarron was really Cush's problem to deal with. He had stolen Cush's Chosen after all. It was only right that Cush be the one to destroy Tarron. Trik had no right to deny the warrior that honor. Furthermore, Trik didn't like the idea of leaving Cassie and her parents, especially not in their current position in Chamani's hut. They were as vulnerable as chicks out of the henhouse and beyond the cover of trees giving the hawk an unobscured view. A few minutes alone with the priestess and Cassie might be selling their firstborn to Chamani for a magical talisman. Who knew what that cunning old woman is capable of?

"We will let Cassie's parents recover their strength. Then we will be on our way," Trik finally said.

"Good, good, Mr. Dark Elf, you do just dat. Take yo time. My house is your house. If you'll need me, I'll be out back doing a little mixing. The job of a humble housewife is never done, you see?" And she cackled her all too familiar cackle as she shambled out the door.

Cassie, who had poured them all some tea, sat back down beside her parents. Trik and Tony took the remaining seats at the table.

"Who is that woman?" Mr. Tate asked, staring after Chamani.

"*That* is a very dangerous Voodoo priestess," replied Trik. "She and her family have haunted this particular swamp for many years. Don't let her silver tongue fool you for a second."

Trik, away from the sight of Cassie's parents, touched her leg under the table so that they could speak to each other's thoughts. *Be careful what you say, Beautiful. Too much information too quickly could be overwhelming. You have a choice to make. We either tell them about the elfin realm or I make them forget. There is no way to get around either of those options. They've heard Chamani speak and there is no telling what Tarron said to them while he had them in captivity. And we need to get out of here as quickly as we can. Seeing that there is no glass in the windows, we need to find a mirror if possible. I don't think your parents have the strength to trudge through the swamp to get back to the motel.*

"We're going back there to wait for Cush, Elora, and Oakley?" she asked. Trik felt her confusion over the decision with her parents. She wasn't ready to address it just then, but he knew that she was aware that she would have to make a choice, and quickly.

"Yes, Cush will know to go back to the original meeting place. And I want to be close if he happens to need me."

"Voodoo what? You can't seriously believe that any of this is real?" Mrs. Tate asked them both. "I mean, that lunatic who captured us kept rambling on about Cassie being his *chosen*—whatever that means—and elf kings and revenge, and he babbled like crazy. I just thought he was insane. And I figured the old woman is just filled with superstition like a lot of the people in this area."

"Superstitions are often shrouded in truth," Tony pointed out.

Trik nodded. "True enough. And Tarron may well indeed be insane, but I'm afraid the things he said are very real, and Chamani is far more than superstitious, she is the real deal," responded Trik. "Tarron, the man who captured you, is not a man at all. He's an elf—a dark elf to be more precise—as am I or at least I was for a very long time."

Mr. Tate made a gurgling sound deep in his throat. "An elf? You mean like with pointy ears and a bow and arrow? Right and I'm a snow fairy. This is just too much. There is no way I can believe any of this nonsense. My family and I are leaving and getting as far from this place as possible. Cassie get away from that man."

Trik tensed at the command Mr. Tate had given his Chosen, his wife. Father or not, there was no way in hell Cassie would be leaving without him.

"Mr. Tate," Tony said quietly, "it is never advised to come between a male and his Chosen. They take possessive and protective to a whole new level."

Trik started to stand when her father began to rise from his chair, but Cassie put a hand on his arm. Her touch was gentle but her words were firm.

"Dad, wait," she said. "Trik is telling the truth. Show him, please," she said looking at Trik with eyes so full of love that it still made him feel unworthy of her.

Trik stood. In a shimmer, where once there was a handsome man with dark hair, now stood…something else. His dark hair lengthened and turned even darker—so dark that it appeared to have a purple sheen—his eyes turned silver and began to gleam, and, if possible, he seemed to grow taller and more muscular.

"Oh," Mrs. Tate gasped. Mr. Tate's jaw dropped open as though a hinge that controlled it had broken.

"I know it is hard for you to believe, but elves are very real. We are powerful immortal beings. And though we have our own realm in which we live, many of us often travel to this realm, for various reasons—some good, some bad."

"But all of them can be a tad unreasonable at times," Tony smirked at Trik.

"You aren't helping," Cassie snapped.

Tony shrugged. "I'm just making sure the humans have all the facts."

"I see," Mr. Tate said quietly after some time.

"But what does that have to do with us?" asked Mrs. Tate, "or Cassie?"

"Well, apparently Tarron believed that Cassie was his Chosen. All elves have what is called a Chosen, someone that we are fated to be with, someone the Forest Lords, our gods, have chosen specifically for us. It turns out that Tarron's Chosen was actually Cassie's great great-grandmother, on your side I believe, Mrs. Tate.

"But he threw that love away long ago. And, in his own twisted way, he thought he could recapture that through Cassie, who apparently bears a striking resemble to her great great-grandmother." Trik carefully avoided telling them anything about his own Chosen. The Tates had had enough of a shock for one day. They didn't need to hear that their daughter had run off and gotten married without them knowing. For some reason he had a feeling that wouldn't go over near as well as *elves are real.*

"And he thought he could get to Cassie through us," breathed her father. "I'm so sorry, little one," Mr. Tate said to Cassie.

"Don't be, Dad. I'm the one who should be sorry. All this happened because of me." She was in tears again. She stood and hugged them both in turn. "Trik, we need to get them out of here," Cassie said.

"Agreed." He looked around the small shack. Sitting on a counter, with various untoward things resting atop it, was a small rectangular mirror. Trik picked it up by the edges and dumped its contents out on the counter. He brought it over to the table and laid it down, face up.

"Mr. and Mrs. Tate, do you remember how you got here?"

"No, not really," responded Mrs. Tate. "That crazy," she paused before finally stuttering, "*e-e-elf* just burst into our home and attacked us. He knocked us out and we woke up here."

"Well, I'm about to show you. Please take Cassie's hand and don't let go. I'm taking you home." And with that, Trik reached out and took Cassie's other hand. *"We will take them home for now and then go back to the motel. You tell them whatever you want to for now. Once everything is said and done, then you must make the ultimate decision. I've sent a message to Rin to let him know we are coming."*

Cassie simply squeezed his hand acknowledging that she'd heard his words in her mind.

Once they'd all grabbed hands linking the four of them, Trik, with his free hand, touched the mirror and was instantly pulled through it with the others following. Trik kept his eyes and ears open for any attacks from dark elves that had been monitoring the portals for Lorsan, but to his surprise their passage was smooth. Suddenly they were one by one stepping through the hall mirror in Cassie's home in Oklahoma City. Rin was waiting for them a few feet from the mirror. To Trik and Cassie he looked like an elfin warrior, but he knew the Tate's were seeing his human glamour.

"Why is there a strange man standing in our house?" Mr. Tate asked calmly. Cassie was impressed with her father's collectedness despite all of the strangeness.

"This is Rin," Trik answered. "He is one of our most trusted warriors. He's been watching your home to make sure Lorsan didn't set a trap for us. He will continue to stay here as your protector until Lorsan has been dealt with."

"Is that really necessary?" her dad asked. "I am capable of defending myself."

Cassie didn't point out that he'd been captured by Tarron. She didn't figure he would appreciate that. So instead she said, "Yes, it's necessary. I would feel better knowing he is here. He could be a big help if dark elves show up." She glanced at Rin. "Right?"

Rin winked at her and then looked at her dad. "I've totally got your back."

"See, he's got your back," Cassie said as she tried to bite back her laughter. Trik wanted to tell her to just let it out; appropriate or not, he loved hearing her laugh. What were they trying to save if not moments like that—moments of laughter, joy, and love in the midst of struggle?

Trik noticed that Tony was chuckling at the warrior, which he knew would help Cassie not feel so bad about laughing. He gave the human an appreciative nod. He'd been a quiet, but at times like that, helpful presence, and he wanted him to know that he was thankful.

Cassie looked back at her parents. Though she'd let go of her mother's hand, Trik kept her other hand in his holding it tightly, letting her know he was there supporting her, and waiting to catch her should she need to fall.

"I know this is a lot," she began as she brushed some stray hair that had fallen from her ponytail back from her face. "And there is more to explain but I can't do it right now. I need you both to trust me. Can you do that?"

Trik wanted to just tell them to deal with it and take Cassie back with him to wait on the others, but he knew that it was important to his Chosen to make sure things were alright between her and her parents. Humans were so weird.

"I heard that," Cassie's voice murmured into his head. She was getting better at being able to focus on their bond and whatever was going on around them.

"I don't suppose we really have a choice, but we also know Elora needs you," Mrs. Tate pointed out. "You're eighteen, an adult for all intents and purposes. We trust you. Bring back Elora and yourself as well. And please just," —her hand gently brushed a tear from her face as she looked at her daughter— "just be safe."

"I don't suppose we really have a choice," Mrs. Tate pointed out. "You're eighteen, an adult for all intents and purposes. But please just" —her hand gently brushed a tear from her face as she looked at her daughter— "just be safe."

Mr. Tate took a step toward Trik and it took everything in him not to step in front of Cassie. Instinct often took over before rational thought could kick in.

"You will keep her safe." It was not a question.

Trik somehow kept the smirk off his face. As if he needed his Chosen's father to threaten him to keep her safe. The need to keep Cassie safe was ingrained into every cell in his body. It was a part of his very essence. He could no more allow something to happen to her than he could force his heart to stop beating. But he didn't say all of that to Mr. Tate. Instead he simply nodded and added, "Always."

Cush might have thought he was losing his mind had the Voodoo queen not just told him to listen for his Chosen's soul. He might believe he was imagining her voice in his head because he wanted to hear it so badly. But that wasn't the case. The fact was that he had heard her! Her voice, her sweet voice, had been a balm to his aching soul. He wanted to wake up, to be conscious for the interaction, but his soul rejected the idea.

We can see her if you remain in slumber. The words were as clear as if he was sitting across from his own soul having a conversation just as he might with Oakley.

"Elora?" Cush called out in his mind. He and his soul were in one accord as they sought her and it made their effort even stronger. *"Tell me you are alright."*

"I am her soul."

"Yes," his soul answered her. *"You are mine. Tell us you both are okay."*

"She has been in a deep sleep. A spell has been cast on her but it was unable to touch me because I have united with my other half. I have tried to reach her but was unable to wake her. The spell that kept her asleep is weakening. But the other spell is not. It holds her in its grip, wrapping her mind in lies that she cannot see past. She does not know our mate, though she knows something is missing. She is in pain because of the separation."

Cush was sick over the thought of Elora being enthralled to the point that she couldn't remember him. He was even more upset that someone had tampered with her mind. Who knows the kind of damage they could have done to her, short term and long term? The Voodoo queen had spoken of a spell and he had a feeling that she was a part of it. Someone had summoned her and bargained a price for his Chosen. Too bad she would never receive payment because Cush was going to crush whoever was stupid enough to take another's mate, his Chosen.

"Do you know where she is? I can feel her. She seems close." Cush's words were becoming more and more urgent now that he knew some of the circumstances of Elora's disappearance.

"We are in the very land that you are. I am not sure how far we are from you. I feel you, which made it easier for me to reach out to you. I have been calling for you for some time now."

Cush felt the anguish of his soul. He felt as though he had failed her because they had not heard her. *"I am sorry you have had to endure so much for so long,"* his soul practically whispered.

"We are not weaklings. We appreciate your protection and desire to shelter us, but we do not back down from a fight because you aren't there. Do not blame yourself. Come for us now. You are our warrior. You are the one who will vindicate us. Fight for us and do not listen to the lies that will shoot forth from Elora's mouth like piercing arrows. She knows not what she says and she needs you to shed light into the darkness that has surrounded her." She paused and Cush could tell she had more to say so he waited. *"Hurry,"* his Chosen's soul said hastily. *"She is waking and he will be able to fill her head with more lies. He will attempt to strengthen the false bond."*

"Who is he?" Cush and his soul asked at the same time.

"He is the deceiver. The stealer. The defector of his own kind. Tarron of the dark elves. He has attempted to escape with us but the holder of these lands will not allow it. She controls all that happens here. Her will is supreme. She wishes you to destroy Tarron, but I do not know what her desire is once that is done. Be careful, mate."

Cush felt her slipping away from him and he wanted to call out to her to stop. He wanted to order her to stay with him where she belonged, but he knew that Elora needed her soul with her to keep from slipping further into the spell Tarron had bargained for. So, reluctantly, he let her go. As soon as he no longer felt her presence, his soul urged him to wake up. He didn't mention that he hadn't needed the prompting. He was already shaking off the sleep.

Cush's eyes popped open to find Oakley staring at him with hawk-like eyes. His gaze was steady and determined, as though he was an equation that Oakley was trying to figure out.

"Did you take something, like some elf

enlightenment pipe?" the human asked.

Cush stood up more quickly than Oakley could track and he heard him gasp. He forgot sometimes that humans, even half elves like Oakley who hadn't been exposed to them, had never seen just how different their species were.

"Elora is in this very swamp," he said ignoring the question he'd been asked. "I've spoken with her soul."

"Okay, that's not weird or anything," Oakley muttered as he stood up to his feet and brushed his clothes off.

Cush turned in a slow circle with his eyes closed. He was desperately seeking for the bond that predestined her as his Chosen. He reached for her pain, knowing she was feeling the separation just as badly as he was. Oakley started to speak again but Cush's hand shot up stopping him before he could even speak the first word.

Her scent hit him like a freight train and he fought the impulse to fall to his knees in thanks to the Forest Lords. He did shoot up a thank you but then turned and grabbed Oakley's arm.

"You're going to have to attempt to keep up," he growled as he began running in the direction of his Chosen. Her scent was no longer the only thing he could sense. He was beginning to feel her. The further they ran, the more he realized that the Voodoo queen had to have something to do with him being able to sense Elora. She was not nearly as close as his senses were telling him.

Cush kept looking back to make sure Oakley was at least still in view. He had known that there was no way he could keep pace with Cush but then he was doing better than a full human. He figured he must be getting some help from his dark elf blood. On and on he ran, somehow finding the exact spots to place his feet so that he remained on land in the marshy surroundings. He heard a curse behind him and started to slow but then Oakley yelled, "I'm good. Keep going. I'm right behind you. Okay, well not righ ..."

Oakley's voice faded as Cush pushed on. As he ran he asked the Forest Lords to show Oakley the way to his location so that he would not end up lost, and he would trust that they had heard him and would answer.

Just as he was rounding a huge tree that plunged deep into the water, he saw them. They were still a good ways off, but Cush's superior elven eyesight had no difficulty spotting them. Tarron was sitting on the ground with Elora's head in his lap. He was stroking her hair as though he had a right to touch her.

"Be smart, warrior. Fools rush in and rarely come out." The Voodoo queen's voice reverberated in his head and though her advice was good, he didn't like that she could get in his mind.

She was right. He had to be smart. Though he was seeing red because another male had his hands on his Chosen, he could not just bulldoze his way to their location and expect to defeat Tarron without hurting Elora. She was right in his line of fire and he wouldn't risk hurting her.

Cush ran through every battle plan he'd ever put together, weighing each outcome with the probable success. Of course, in those battle plans he had a complete army behind him. About that time he heard Oakley panting as he came up behind him. So, all he had was Oakley. That's about as helpful as having wet matches when you need to start a fire.

"Why. Are. We stopping?" Oakley asked stopping

to pant in between his words.

Cush pointed in the direction of Elora and Tarron. Oakley squinted his eyes and after several seconds he said, "Ahh, okay, now I see them. So again why are we stopping? Why aren't we kicking ass and taking names?"

"First of all, we already know their names and second we need a plan."

Oakley scoffed. "I've got a plan. We kill the bad guy and rescue the damsel."

Cush turned his head to look back at the human. "No offense, but your plan is not a very good one."

"Fine, then you tell me what *your* plan is, oh mighty elf soldier."

He turned back to look at his mate and the dark elf. As he continued to watch the moron touch Elora, he formulated something that he wouldn't necessarily say was a plan, but it was what they had.

"You're going to walk up and act surprised to see your sister. This will distract Tarron. Then I will make my move. And it's elf *warrior*."

Oakley raised his hand. "Question, what is going to be my reason for just happening to be in a swamp, let alone a swamp where my sister just happens to be? And who cares—warrior, soldier— they both fight in battles."

"You can tell him that you made Trik tell you what happened to your sister and you took off on your own in hopes of finding her. And it matters because in my time we were called warriors." Cush shrugged his large shoulders as if it should have been obvious.

Oakley stood staring in the direction that Cush had indicated that his sister and Tarron were resting. After several minutes, he finally turned back to the warrior. "Okay, fine. We'll do it your way. But if anything goes wrong and the whole thing falls apart, I'm totally blaming your warrior posterior."

Cush's brow rose at the remark. "Posterior?"

"It's all I had," Oakley admitted.

"I suppose we all have to work with what our Creator gave us," Cush chuckled as he slapped Oakley on the shoulder. "Now, let's get closer and then we will split up. You will go right and come around to their front. I will go left and come up behind them."

"Just make sure Elora and I are out of your line of fire. I don't feel like getting some elf taser to the face."

Cush pushed his Chosen's brother forward. "Then don't give me a reason to use my power on you."

They continued forward in silence with Oakley shadowing Cush's every step. When he was finally able to see his sister and Tarron, Cush heard him mutter under his breath.

"Why is he touching her like that? And why is she letting him? The Elora I know would be going ape shit on him," Oakley said as he glared daggers at the dark elf.

"She's under some sort of spell. It's dark magic and Tarron bargained for it. It will not be easily broken." Cush knew the kind of magic that could screw with the bond of a Chosen and her mate. And as bad as he hated to admit it, that kind of magic was powerful.

Oakley dropped his arms to his side and shook out his hands. Then he rolled his head from side to side and raised and dropped his shoulders. He looked at Cush and narrowed his eyes. "I'm ready."

"Perhaps you would like to stretch or do a warm up before battle?"

"Ha, ha," Oakley retorted dryly. "Let's just do this."

Cush pointed in the direction he wanted Oakley to go and then watched as he moved as quietly as he could around to the furthest side of the place Tarron had camped out. Once Oakley was in position to move forward, Cush took off quickly and quietly around to the left. He stopped once he was directly behind the two. He was about fifty feet away and he could still hear Elora's breathing. His fists clenched together as he fought his natural instinct to charge in and take her. Instead he made a silent motion to Oakley to indicate he was ready for him to make his move. Now Cush just had to hope that Tarron wouldn't kill the human on sight.

Oakley saw the hand motion from Cush and took several deep breaths. "It's go time, Oak," he muttered to himself. He couldn't deny that he was scared. What idiot wouldn't be when going up against a deranged dark elf? But he felt courage rise up inside of him when he thought of his sister. He looked through the trees and moss that kept him from being seen and saw her prone form. She looked so helpless. Elora, who was usually so bold and courageous, was lying in the arms of her enemy as if she wanted to be there.

Oakley wanted to shout at her to get up, but according to the elf warrior, she wouldn't respond to that because she was under some sort of magic. He would have thought that Elora being half dark elf might have given her some sort of protection against other dark magic, but apparently that's not how it works in real life. Only in the movies does magic have such laws. In real life it was more unpredictable and complicated.

Oakley's eyes snapped up when he saw Cush make the motion again, and he realized he'd just been standing there. With one more fortifying deep breath, he took a step forward. His feet carried him of their own accord as he kept his eyes on Tarron and his sister. He'd only gone ten or so feet when the dark elf's head snapped up and his swirling eyes landed on Oakley. He hissed at him as though he were a cat who'd had its tail stomped on, which only confused Oakley because he didn't think that hissing was much of a dark elf thing to do. Then again, he was only half dark elf so what the hell did he know? Maybe dark elves went around hissing at anything they perceived as a threat, or maybe it was some weird dark elf greeting. Should he hiss back? He quickly dismissed that idea when Tarron slowly began to rise, gently placing Elora on the ground, until he was in a crouch. That, Oakley understood. A crouch was one of those things that predators did, all predators. There was no mistaking that position. It was pretty much the universal body language for *I'm about to eat you for lunch.*

His fight or flight instincts were screaming at him. RUN! But he stood fast. He wouldn't abandon his sister, no matter how many times the weird, crazy dark elf hissed at him.

"Have you come to die then?" Tarron asked, his voice raspy as though he'd been yelling. His head bobbed back and forth and Oakley was sure at any moment a forked tongue was going to flick out at him.

"I heard through the grapevine that you had my sister" —he motioned to Elora— "and being the caring brother that I am, I decided to come check on her."

"How did you find us? Who sent you?" Tarron's eyes narrowed to barely opened slits. Oakley wondered how he could even see him clearly, maybe he couldn't.

He took a step closer and Tarron lunged forward,

gnashing his teeth together. "DO NOT!" he snarled.

Okay, Oakley thought, he can see just fine. "Nobody sent me. Trik actually forbid me to come but I don't abandon my family. Elora is my sister and I needed to know she was safe. Is she?" he asked. "Is she safe with you?"

Tarron seemed offended by the question and he stepped back as though he'd been slapped. "Of course, she's safe. She's mine, my Chosen. I could never hurt her."

"Uh-hu, we'll see about that," Oakley began. "I'm not sure I believe you because I happen to know that a different guy has claimed her as his Chosen, and" —he held up a finger to stop the dark elf from interrupting— "this guy didn't put a dark Voodoo spell on her. So you see," —he shrugged as his lips pursed— "I'm finding it really hard to mesh what you're saying with the facts."

"How do you know what the facts are? You are a mere half elf and the magic in you is weak."

Oakley chuckled. He didn't know where his brave act was coming from but he decided to just go with it. "That may be, but I know another fact," he said and then went silent staring at Tarron. He knew the dark elf would ask, the villains always do.

"What fact?"

And there it is. Oakley smiled to himself. "The fact that you're about to get your evil ass handed to you, courtesy of your friendly neighborhood light elf warrior."

Chapter 13

"Humans never cease to amaze me. They are resilient in turmoil, brave when expected to turn tail and run, and humorous at the oddest moments. But then, I supposed there were times that if you couldn't laugh, the only other option would be to give up. I am not a fan of giving up, especially, where my Chosen is concerned." ~Cush

For the first time in his long life, Cush wanted to do what he'd seen humans do and smack his palm against his forehead. He didn't understand where Oakley's sudden brazenness had come from; he just hoped it didn't get him blown to bits by Tarron's magic. Cush was moving before the last word left his unlikely comrade's mouth. He cleared several fallen trees with barely any effort and moved silently across the bog. He was fifteen feet from Elora when Tarron turned and threw his hand out.

Cush rolled to his right, barely missing the bolt of power the dark elf had shot at him. He landed on the balls of his feet, ready to move again if need be. But Tarron didn't strike again. He simply stared at Cush.

"I believe you have something of great importance to me in your care," Cush said formally. "I ask that you return it. On your honor as a warrior, give her back to me." He didn't add that it had been several centuries since Tarron had been a warrior. He wasn't trying to insult him just yet. First, he would attempt to appeal to his ego and pride. If that didn't work, then he would use brute force.

"She is mine," Tarron spat at him.

Cush clenched his jaw as he refrained from arguing. It was pointless to argue with a madman and the longer he stood in Tarron's presence the more he could sense the taint of black magic permeating him. Whatever it was, it was driving the dark elf mad. That was something that would not bode well for Elora. He needed to get her out of Tarron's hands—the quicker, the better.

"Maybe that is what you believe, but you know that your Chosen perished long ago. There is no way that Elora could be yours. Hear me, Tarron, if there is any good left in you, don't keep up this farce. She will never really love you. It is only the spell that keeps her from running from you. Is that really the kind of love you want?"

"Do not speak of love to me!" Tarron turned, fully facing Cush so that Oakley was at his back. He obviously didn't perceive the half elf as a threat. "You do not understand what love is, what it can do to a man. I'd be doing you a favor by keeping her. All she will do is bring you misery and ultimately destroy everything you once were."

"Maybe," Cush agreed. "But I think it should be my choice as to whether or not I want to give her the opportunity to destroy me."

"You are a fool."

Cush laughed. "Perhaps, but I am her fool. Give her to me. Please." He felt bile rise up in his throat at the politeness he forced himself to use.

Both of their heads snapped down when they saw movement. Elora slowly pushed herself up until she was no longer lying down. She attempted to tame the dark mane on her head but gave up after a few seconds. After several minutes of silence, a voice came from behind Tarron.

"Hey sis, how's the view of the swampland from down there in the sludge?" Oakley asked, his voice light and playful as though two elves weren't about to attempt to kill each other.

"Oakley?" Elora asked as she looked around the dark elf. The sound of her voice sent warmth pouring into Cush, and some of the pain he'd been experiencing began to lessen.

"The one and only," her brother responded.

"What are you doing here?"

"I could ask you the same thing. The last time I saw you we were in Las Vegas getting ready to bust up Lorsan's operations. So tell me, baby sis, how'd you end up in this glamourous marsh with its plethora of plant life and beasts that want to eat us?"

"I, I don't know. I think, but then I can't." She stumbled over her words. Elora began to stand up and, when she faltered, Cush attempted to move to help her but Tarron shot a warning bolt of magic at him. The red ball of power landed at his feet.

Elora whipped around to see the object of Tarron's attack. Their eyes met and Cush felt a different sort of bolt shoot through him. He could practically hear her soul calling to him. He needed to get to her to hold her.

Her brow narrowed as she looked at him. "Who are you?"

Knowing that she was under a dark spell didn't stop the sting of the question. For his own mate to look at him with no recognition in her eyes was a pain he'd never experienced.

"He isn't anyone of consequence, love." Tarron's voice was like a record being scratched as it played, irritating beyond the realm of sanity.

"She didn't ask you," Cush said as calmly as he could. He looked back at Elora and his countenance softened immediately. "I am Nedhudir, a warrior of the elfin race." He figured too much information too quickly might be dangerous to her mind.

"Did your parents hate you? That's a terrible name."

Cush's lips twitched as a smile threatened to stretch across it. Okay, so maybe her mind wasn't as delicate as he first thought. "You said something similar to that the first time you asked me about my name."

Her brow wrinkled as she frowned. "The first time?"

"This is not our first encounter, Little Raven. We have met before. And you do not belong with him." Cush took a step forward but stopped when Tarron moved closer to Elora. "Do you remember anything? Anything at all?" He knew he was grasping at straws, but Cush wasn't sure what else to do. As long as she stood between him and Tarron, she was in danger. He couldn't take any action until she was safely out of the line of fire. So he figured he might as well attempt to jog her memory.

She began to climb to her feet. Her legs were shaky and Cush cursed Tarron for being the one to help her up. Seeing his hands on her did nothing to help him keep his control.

"I don't understand what's going on," Elora admitted. "My mind tells me I'm supposed to be with Tarron. It tells me that I belong to him."

Cush growled. "What does your heart tell you?

What is your soul screaming at you? Do you really think you *feel* anything for that man?" He pointed to Tarron. "Think about who you are, Elora. Is he really what you would pick for yourself?"

Elora turned to look at Tarron. "I, I don't. . ." She looked back at him and her mouth opened and closed several times. The next word from her mouth nearly shattered his already broken heart. "Cush." It was nearly imperceptible and to a human it would have been, but Cush wasn't human. His elf hearing picked it up just fine.

"Yes," he nodded reassuringly. "That's what you call me."

"Elora, don't listen to his lies. He simply wants to confuse you," Tarron barked at her as he reached for her. He wrapped his hand around her forearm and pulled her closer to him.

Elora's eyes squeezed tightly closed and she reached up to grab her head with her free hand. "I remember things, but they don't seem real. It's like I'm watching someone else's life." Her head snapped up and her eyes latched onto his. "Cush, you and I." She motioned between them.

Cush nodded, his heart thudding painfully in his chest as he waited for her to have the revelation she needed that would drive her back to his arms.

"Why?" Her eyes narrowed. "Why me? We shouldn't have ever been together."

"You remember?" Cush asked hopefully.

"I remember," she told him as a single tear ran down her cheek. "I remember all the reasons we should never have been."

It was enough he decided. His patience was worn thin. He was ready to have his Chosen back by his side, safe, and no longer being touched by a dark elf who was tainted by the Voodoo queen. He was ready for her mind to be clear and not full of lies. "Elora," Cush pleaded with her as she looked between him and Tarron. She looked so lost, so confused, and it broke his heart. "Look at me, Little Raven. Look at me and focus only on me."

She turned her head and met his gaze. He could tell she was truly beginning to question what she thought she knew. The anguish that swirled in her eyes nearly drove him to his knees. He needed to kill something or someone. He needed to make everything okay, to make her feel safe and protected, but how was he supposed to fight something he couldn't see? The spell that held her in its thrall had wrapped itself around her mind and twisted her emotions. Her soul wanted him, he could see it, but her mind was telling her that Tarron was her mate.

"He's my kind," she told him. Her voice was unsteady, as though she didn't really believe what she was saying. "I'm a dark elf; he's a dark elf. It makes sense. You and I," —she motioned between them again— "we don't make sense. We never made sense. In the beginning you didn't even want us. So now you have an out."

Her memory was obviously returning, but she wasn't seeing things with her own eyes. The spell was coloring her thoughts. Cush's blood was boiling inside of him as her words hit him one after another like bullets being fired from a machine gun. And just like those bullets could, her words ripped him apart. She was right to some degree, but not about everything. In the beginning, he hadn't realized how much he would need her and want her. He'd been a fool but it hadn't taken him very long to figure it out. Once he'd realized just how amazing she was, he had grabbed onto her with both hands and he refused to let go.

"I think she's made her choice, warrior," Tarron chuckled as he looked at Cush. The words Cush could have ignored, but that damn chuckle had broken the final thread that had been holding him in check.

"Oakley, now!" he yelled as he lunged forward and pushed Elora out of the way. He tried to be gentle, but he was counting on Oakley to catch her and take care of her. He could tend to her after he'd eliminated the fool who'd attempted to take her from him.

Once Elora was out of the way, Cush was in front of the dark elf, with less than a foot between them. Cush didn't even think about what he was doing as his fist flew and connected with Tarron's face. He could have used magic, but he needed to feel flesh beneath his hands. He needed to feel his opponent being broken. Tarron stumbled back from the impact but Cush wasn't done, not by a long shot. He threw punch after punch, each one connecting with its target. Every ounce of rage that he'd kept tamped down had risen to the surface and was now pouring out of him from his fists. Cush didn't even feel any pain as he connected over and over. He punched Tarron in the stomach and heard the crunch of ribs. He followed this up with a right hook and heard the snap of the dark elf's jaw. The sounds of his prey being destroyed only egged him on. Tarron thought he could just take what did not belong to him. He'd tried to take Cassie but instead had ensnared Elora and, though she wasn't who he'd originally sought, the dark elf had become fixated on her. He was a bigger fool than Cush gave him credit for because he honestly thought he would get away with his schemes.

"Stop him, Oakley! He's going to kill him!"

Elora's scream barely registered with him. Her appalled tone made him want to rip Tarron limb from limb. How dare she attempt to protect the snake who'd slithered his way into her mind and played with her emotions! Cush tried to remember that she wasn't in control of herself, but it didn't make it sting any less that she was attempting to shield another man.

Tarron attempted to fight back but his movements were clumsy and slow. Cush grabbed him by his throat and slammed him into a tree causing the trunk to crack. He stared up at the beaten male and was disgusted by what he saw. The sound of Elora screaming at him to release the elf only disgusted him more.

Cush turned to look at his Chosen. Oakley was restraining her as she attempted to get closer to them. He reached down deep for every ounce of self-control, but it didn't stay his tongue. "You think you want him. But you belong with me." His eyes narrowed as he held her stare. "Your soul knows it, but your mind has forgotten. I assure you, you will get over this." The crack echoed across the room as Cush quickly twisted his wrist breaking Tarron's neck. Cush watched the body fall to the ground as Elora's screams played in the background. He didn't turn around to look at her. He wasn't sure he could handle watching his female mourn for another man, spell or no spell. Cush's body vibrated with the rage that hadn't yet been burned out. Killing Tarron hadn't been enough. Images of the dark elf's hands on his mate rushed through his mind and he felt bile rise up in his throat.

"CUSH!"

It wasn't his name that finally drew him from his

dark thoughts. It was the utter desperation in Oakley's voice that had him turning with inhuman speed. His eyes landed on Elora who moments ago had been standing, pleading, and cursing him. Cush felt his stomach roll and his heart stutter. The air rushed from his lungs as though he'd been kicked in the gut, and his foot stumbled back under the imaginary force.

"What's wrong with her? Dammit, Cush, what the hell happened!" Oakley continued to yell but his words were not important.

Nothing was important, nothing but her. The world around him faded away and his vision narrowed in on her. His Chosen's still form lie prone, half of her on Oakley's lap and the other half on the floor of the swamp. He didn't remember moving as he knelt beside them and took her body from her brother.

"ANSWER ME!" Oakley continued to shout.

But he couldn't answer the boy. He was sure if he opened his mouth the only thing that would come out would be a tortured cry that echoed the cry of his soul. In that moment, there was no part of Cush that wasn't in utter agony. He was attempting to hold himself together, though all he wanted to do was cave in under the despair that was swallowing him. He couldn't help Elora if he lost it. Cush leaned down close to her mouth. It was faint, but he felt her warm breath on his cheek. She was still alive, but for how long, he didn't know.

"Don't you dare leave me, not again," he growled at her through their bond as his hand turned her face toward him. Dirt smeared her cheek and clung to her clothes. Her skin was cool and her lips were growing paler. And still she was the most beautiful thing he'd ever seen.

Cush didn't understand it. She'd been fine, other

than her memory being jacked up. Only a few moments ago, she'd been perfectly okay. What had changed?

"You've been successful, warrior." A cool voice spoke from behind him. The elf looked up to see Oakley staring at something, or rather someone, just over Cush's right shoulder.

"Oakley," Cush said softly. When he didn't respond he snapped his fingers in his face finally gaining the boy's attention. "Here, hold onto her." He carefully laid Elora's body back in her brother's lap. He stroked her cheek gently before finally standing slowly and turning to face the interloper.

He wasn't surprised to see the old woman standing there. Her attire, and the many trinkets hanging from her body, revealed her quite clearly as a servant of the Voodoo queen that ruled this swamp. The queen had already come to him once and explained her plan; it only made sense that either she or one of her priestesses would check up on him.

"But then my queen not be thinkin you be havin any trouble."

"Who are you and why are you here?" Cush asked, attempting to keep his voice even and calm.

"I am Chamani. I am a part of this here land. You and yours be guests and guests must play by de rules."

"Do the rules include this?" Cush said, pointing at Elora lying motionless on the ground. Cush took a step toward the old woman. "Your queen," he nearly spat the word at the priestess, "did not mention that when I killed Tarron it would affect Elora. Is that part of the rules, to not share all of the information?"

"Would it have changed your actions? Would you not be killing the man who put de spell on her?"

"He didn't put the spell on her on his own, He had

help. Perhaps, that one also needs killing," Cush threatened as his eyes narrowed.

"My queen not be answering to you. She need to keep de balance. You played yo part in de plan. Whatever else happens not be her concern."

"BULLSHIT!" Cush roared. He very rarely lost his cool, but then he'd never faced the possible death of his Chosen until now. "It is her concern now." He held out his hand and out of nowhere a bow materialized in it along with a silvery arrow. He nocked the arrow and aimed it at the old woman. "Will she protect you, Chamani? Will your queen, whom you have served so faithfully, keep my arrow from piercing your heart?"

"If dat is to be my fate, den so be it."

The old woman didn't seem phased in the least at the possibility of dying. *So be it*, Cush thought as he let the arrow fly.

Lorsan's breath froze in his lungs as he felt his gut clench and his heart stutter. His soul screamed within him, screamed for his mate. She was gone—that was the only thing he knew that could cause this kind of pain.

His knees hit the ground just as he came face to face with his Chosen. He clutched a travel bag in each hand, one containing the Book of the Elves. Ilyrana's eyes were gleaming and she had a smug look on her face. His mouth dropped open and he blinked several times to make sure his eyes didn't fool him.

"How are you here?" he asked, his voice breathless

with the pain he was feeling.

"What do you mean?"

"I mean I just felt…it felt like…like I had lost you."

She laughed. She actually laughed. "You must have been mistaken love, as you can see I'm perfectly fine. So since I answered your question, perhaps you can answer mine, just where are you running off to, my love?"

For a moment he wasn't sure what to think, but her question reminded him of his current situation. "The Forest Lords," he gasped. "They were here. They told me my fate was set and that I could do nothing to change it. I won't go down without a big damn fight."

"Fate?" His mate practically spat the question at him. "Since when do you believe in fate? Haven't you always told me that we make our own destiny?"

"Regardless, if I'm going to die it will be by my choosing and definitely not at the hands of the humans attempting to break down my door. We have to go. Now!" The dark elf queen could see panic in her Chosen's eyes.

"Lorsan, listen to me." She placed both hands upon his shoulders. Then she said the only words that could distract him from making his escape. "Calm down. I've done it, my king. Our troubles are over. I've found an elder. I know the secrets of the book," she whispered, almost desperately, lowering her head and looking directly into his eyes. "Some of them anyway. The rest he will give up, once he's been properly…persuaded."

"You…you found one. Who?"

"Vyshaan."

"Vyshaan? I…I…haven't seen him in years," Lorsan responded. "Where? How?"

"He's been right here under our noses this whole time," she almost giggled, "hiding out at Rezer's place. The light elves led me right to him, just like I thought they would.

That devil, Rezer, hiding an elder. I couldn't believe it at first. By the way, we will need to take care of that elf soon, my love. He has some very powerful secrets. Secrets that could hurt us if we don't attend to them."

"What secrets?" Lorsan asked, a look of disbelief on his face.

"Nothing we can't handle, now that I know how to decipher the Book. Come, love." She took his arm and guided him back into his office. "We have much to do."

A muffled noise reached the office. Apparently there was some commotion down on the casino floor.

"Yes, yes, very much to do," Lorsan said distractedly. Already her old Chosen was returning to himself. If he'd heard the commotion going on downstairs, he made no note of it. A broad grin was beginning to spread across his face. He tossed one of the bags aside haphazardly. The other he placed on his desk, unzipped it, and then gently pulled out the ancient text. He placed it softly on the desk and then looked up at his Chosen, his beautiful Chosen, that had somehow pulled off a miracle.

"Ilyrana, my beautiful, powerful, lovely queen, you have been so faithful all these years, ruling by my side, but this—this is your most outstanding accomplishment. You are truly a worthy dark elf queen."

The beautiful dark elf giggled lightly. "Lorsan, you flatter me." If he didn't know any better, he'd thought she might actually have blushed. That was something he hadn't seen in a very, very long time. He could tease her about that later. Like she said, they had work to do.

"Where is Vyshaan now?" he asked suddenly curious as to why she hadn't brought the elder with her.

Just then more noises came from outside the office. Several people could be heard shouting. It seemed that the commotion had not been contained to the casino floor.

"Damn those accursed humans," Lorsan muttered. "Sometimes I wonder why I even bothered to try and enslave them. They are so taxing."

"He's in one of the holding cells," Ilyrana continued, ignoring her mate's comments and answering his original question. "And so are the light elf king and queen. I didn't want to risk dragging Vyshaan through the casino. He is just as powerful as we remember. It took all my strength and five of my best elves to subdue him. He won't be easy to break, but I think we are more than up to the task." She gave a light chuckle, enthralling him with her sensual smile. "I was able to get a few bits of information from him before he passed out," she continued. "Sit, lover. Let me show you what I've learned."

He dropped into the chair behind his desk and she went and stood beside him.

"Now," she said, opening the book to a random page, "Vyshaan told me the key to deciphering the stories comes from a very complex code based on our own ancient Elvish alphabet. You see these large curly letters at the end of each paragraph? Each of these corresponds with a letter of our alphabet."

"Of course, of course," he whispered peering closely at the book. "But which letters of our alphabet correspond to which letters of the book?" He leaned down, staring, unblinkingly at the letters on the page before him.

Ilyriana moved behind him and began rubbing his shoulders as he studied the pages.

"Well that is the most vexing thing," Ilyrana said lightly, as if she wasn't actually in the least bit vexed. "You see, Vyshaan told me that only an elf that was pure of intentions could decipher the code. Even knowing how the code was deciphered, an elf with evil intent will be unable to determine the corresponding letters." Standing behind Lorsan, she began to massage her Chosen's arms and shoulders even deeper, attempting to relax him. "This is because the Forest Lords designed the corresponding letters to continually shift from one to another. A letter in our alphabet, say the letter ξ, for example, might mean 'R' in the human alphabet one minute and 'T' the next minute. Ingenious really."

"Ingenious?" Lorsan roared. "This is terrible!" The dark elf pounded the table in frustration. How are we supposed to decipher the book if the meanings of the letters keep changing?"

Ilyrana walked around to the front of the desk.

"Well that's the thing, Lorsan. *We* aren't going to be able to decipher the book."

"What are you talking about?" he said, voice and eyebrows both raised. Lorsan attempted to stand but found his body welded to the chair. His upper body seemed permanently affixed to the back of his comfortable leather chair. He thrashed about but couldn't break the magical hold.

"What the?" he growled. "What have you done, Ilyrana?"

"Ilyrana? You think that witch is pure in her

intentions? As if—" Then a bright light began to radiate from the figure before him. In a twinkling of an eye, where before stood his beautiful Ilyrana, now stood, shimmering in all her glory, Syndra, the light elf queen.

"How did you do this?" Venom laced the king's words. "Why couldn't I sense you? I should have...I should have been able to see through your glamour."

Syndra leaned across the desk, placing her face mere inches away from the dark elf as he struggled against the invisible bonds.

"Power," she whispered. "Your pure, unadulterated lust for power has been your downfall at last, you miserable excuse for an elfin king.

You see, I wasn't lying to you, Lorsan. Vyshaan really did give me the key to deciphering the book, and it really does take someone who doesn't want to use the book for evil. When your Chosen and her dark elves took us by surprise, they probably would have gotten the better of us, but Vyshaan...well let's just say he knew which side he had a better chance with, and it wasn't yours."

"**Y**ou can be as loud as you like, former king, either way you will be coming with me." Ilyrana's hand shot out at the same moment's Syndra's did, and the room was lit with a light so bright that everyone had to close their eyes. But just as fast as the light had appeared, the room was plunged into darkness.

Syndra heard grunts and shouts echo throughout the room, just before she felt a hand on her waist.

"Back to back, my queen," Tamsin shouted.

"Of course. You think this is my first battle?" She and Tamsin stood facing outward, backs pressed against each other. She glanced at Lisa who was standing next to the elder. "Stay close to him." Lisa nodded and took a step closer to Vyshaan. Syndra began chanting quickly, waving her hands in front of her. A sphere the size of a Volkswagen enveloped them only an instant before the first bolt of darkness struck it and bounced harmlessly away. Again and again the dark elves sent powerful dark pulses flying toward the light elves. Syndra grunted with the effort to hold against their onslaught. Meanwhile, Tamsin sent beams of light into the darkness, aiming for the sources of the dark pulses. Most went wide, but occasionally a grunt and a splash of light revealed a dark elf falling to the floor, indicating he'd found his mark.

"Concentrate your fire!" Ilyrana's voice rang out in the darkness. "To me, my dark elves!" And she shot a huge dark beam at Syndra's shield. She bore down with all her might. The dark elves followed her lead. They each shot their own bolts at the spot where Ilyrana was aiming, focusing their power, attempting to break the light elf's defenses.

Syndra growled in frustration; the strategy was working. Sweat poured from her brow and her eyes were squeezed shut tightly. Despite her efforts, despite the strength she was receiving by being connected to Tamsin, she was starting to fade. She felt him attempt to push more of his power into her, but he too was waning.

"Hang in there, beloved," Tamsin panted. "You can do this."

Tamsin attempted to shoot a bolt into Ilyrana, but one of her dark elves threw his own shield up in front of her just in time. Syndra knew it wouldn't be as strong as her own, but it held against the bolt just the same.

"I can't, dammit," she grunted. Her teeth were clenched together so tight that it was a miracle they weren't crushed under the pressure. "There's just too many of them." She sank to her knees, but still she held the shield in place.

"We've almost got them," Ilyrana shrieked. "Keep firing! Keep—"

But her words caught in her throat. She gasped. Syndra watched with renewed hope as the dark elf queen dropped her beam and put her hands on her stomach. Suddenly, she began to glow, seemingly from the inside. Brighter and brighter she began pulsing glowing light. A scream, raw and primal, bellowed out of her. The sound of it testified of deep pain and anguish. Ilyrana's eyes were wild, bulging from her sockets. The light elf queen couldn't believe what she was seeing as her enemy began to thrash around the room searching desperately for her attacker. The dark elves around her fell back, obviously as confused as she was. They had all taken notice and had ceased attacking Syndra's shield.

Ilyrana began to hover a few inches from the ground. She flailed her legs but they could find no purchase. Dark purple light, intermingled with the bright white, began to shoot from her eyes, mouth, and throat. The elves around her could only watch in horrid fascination. She began to grow hotter. Syndra could tell that the elves around her could feel the heat radiating from their queen's body, and they began to back away farther. Though it appeared she was still attempting to scream, no sound came from her now, as if a painter had captured her on his canvas catching his muse at the peak of her torment. Finally, after Syndra was sure the onlookers thought they could watch the spectacle no longer, there was a loud pop, as if a fuse had blown, a strong smell of ozone, and Ilyrana simply dissolved in a wafting pile of ash on the floor. The room, once filled with the shouts and reverberations of battle, was as silent as a tomb. Syndra thought it was fitting, since it would be the final resting place of the dark elf queen.

The lights in the room came back on just as suddenly as they'd blanked out. Syndra dropped her shield. She, like everyone else, looked around the room to see who or what had done this.

To her surprise—and based on the shocked faces of others, their surprise as well—there, standing across the room directly behind where Ilyrana had been, was Vyshaan. Purple black smoke was slowly dissipating from his left hand and pulsing white light was fading from his right. No one spoke a word. The dark elves, those that hadn't fallen at the hands of Tamsin's powerful attacks, stood motionless, their mouths agape, too shocked to even flee.

Vyshaan began to walk slowly toward the center of the room, where Tamsin was helping Syndra back to her feet.

"That was some fireworks display," Syndra said, her breath coming in gasps. She looked around for her human friend and found her in the same spot appearing as shocked as everyone else.

"Why would you help us?" Tamsin asked.

Vyshaan stared at them. At first, Syndra thought the elder was not going to answer her mate. Tamsin held on to her hand, communicating to her to be ready in case Vyshaan decided to attack.

"I've spent too many long years in hiding. I want to see my own realm again. And I want to walk there a free elf. I won't look over my shoulder any longer. I've heard the rumors about our new king. I've heard that Triktaptic is a changed elf, that he is a benevolent and wise king. I will judge this for myself. Either he will pardon my past transgressions against my people, or he will slay me. Either way, I hide no longer.

Your Chosen said that she could face our new king with a clear conscious. Knowing her past as I do, that is a very bold statement. A statement that takes a huge amount of faith in this new king. Syndra and I haven't always seen eye to eye, that is sure. But if she trusts Triktaptic, then I would be a fool not to as well."

Syndra, now back to her original form and the battle that destroyed Ilyrana now a memory, continued to stare at the struggling dark elf king. She could hear loud noises outside the office mixed with shouts of men and women. Someone began pounding on the door. Lorsan's eyes went wild with fear.

"Wait, no! You can't leave me here," he begged her.

"Power," the light elf queen said again. She placed a finger gently on the book and slid it slowly back across the desk toward her. She reached down and picked it up, shutting it leisurely.

The shouts outside were getting louder. The pounding was getting more intense as someone began kicking the door. Syndra thought she heard the door frame splinter and nearly laughed when the dark elf king jumped and squeaked like the pathetic rat he was.

"There is one more thing that you have forgotten, Lorsan. You should never, ever, ignore your Creators."

Then Syndra reached into her robes and pulled out a clear vial of bright red liquid. To those unaware it would appear to be an innocent fine wine, but this drink was anything but innocent.

"Well, well, look what I have here, the last little bit of Rapture. I bet there are some people out there who would do anything to get their hands on this." And with that she sat the vial on the desk in front of him.

"You..." The dark elf was foaming at the mouth, using all of his power to attempt to break Syndra's restraints, but to no avail.

"Toodles. Oh and by the way, just to be clear. You were correct. Your Chosen is dead," she said, giving Lorsan a mock little wave with her fingers before striding nonchalantly over to the mirror on the wall and stepping gingerly through it and disappearing from his sight.

Chapter 14

"I am not gone, not really. I will return to you. Every time you see a raven, I will return to you. Every time you see the bright lights of the city, I will return to you. Every memory that you have of me brings me back to you. So you see, my love, I am not gone, not really." ~Elora

"Cush!" Oakley screamed just as the arrow flew from the bow. Everything seemed to happen in slow motion as Cush waited for the arrow to hit its mark. He waited to watch the old woman clutch at her chest watching her life blood leak out. The old woman, who like her queen, had meddled in the affairs of the elves. She'd played her magic where it was not welcome and therefore would suffer the consequences.

"You are in my domain, warrior." The voice of the Voodoo queen reverberated off of the trees around them. It surrounded them and seemed to block out the noise of anything else. "You cannot come into my domain and kill my servants."

He watched as the arrow he'd just launched fell lamely to the ground at the feet of Chamani. He met her stare.

She shrugged. "If it be makin you feel better, I wouldn't be holdin a grudge if you kilt me. I have lived a very long life. Your race be makin me work hard as of late. First, I be havin to take care of da king and now I be havin to tend ta you. Rest be a nice thought."

"Does Tarron's death have anything to do with

what's happened to Elora?" Cush asked the empty air. He couldn't see the queen but he could feel her cold presence. If the Voodoo queen was joining their little meeting then the old woman, who he guessed was a follower of the queen, was the least of his worries. A voice spoke in his head.

"The spell connected them. They were no longer two separate beings, though not one as you and she are one. They were still connected. In order to guarantee that the spell works, it connects not only their lives but their deaths as well. The only reason your female is not dead is because of the bond between you. She holds on because of you, Cush of the light elves. You must mean a great deal to her. She fights the pull of death even now though it is futile."

Cush's ears began to ring as everything around him began to fade. It had been for nothing. He had lost his mate regardless of the fact that he'd rescued her from her abductor. She'd been lost to him from the moment she wandered off in the casino. Ever since then, he'd been chasing a dead woman. He turned back to Oakley who held the girl in his lap as her life force rapidly faded away.

Slowly, his feet carried him back to her and he dropped to his knees beside her. His little raven, so brave and fierce, was now quiet and broken. He'd only known her a short time and yet they'd been through so much together. She had challenged him in that short time. She'd made him a better man and he'd been unable to protect her. Elora had given herself to him, throwing everything she knew out the window and jumping headlong into his world, ready to stand at his side. But instead of standing beside him, she now lay before him still as stone but for a very faint rise and fall of her chest.

He took her hand in his and brushed her dark hair back from her face. *"How am I supposed to go back to the life I had before you?"* Cush felt his hand tightening on hers and had to make a conscious effort to relax his hold so that he wouldn't hurt her. He'd never felt such pain, such utter despair in his long life. His chest grew tighter and tighter and he was finding it hard to breathe. In the end, Tarron had been right about one thing. Elora, through no fault of her own, had brought him misery, and he would never be the same.

It wasn't supposed to be like this. He'd never dreamed that he'd find his Chosen and, once he had, he never imagined losing her. But here he was, in a damn swamp of all places, watching the life seep out of her body. There was so much he wanted to experience with her, so many places he wanted to show her. Instead of a future with her, all he could see now was a black, endless void before him.

"I never took you for the type to roll over and give up like a dead cockroach."

Elora's voice was weak in his mind, but it was there. *"Come back to me,"* he ordered her. He knew she didn't particularly like being ordered around, but at that moment, all he wanted was to see her open her eyes and tell him off.

"I wish I could. Everyone has a time, Cush. This happens to be mine."

"NO, I don't accept that. You are mine and I'm not ready to give you up."

A soft laugh filled his head and for an instant it warmed the coldness growing inside of him.

"Ready or not, warrior, we can't appoint our own time of death," she so helpfully pointed out.

"When did you become so philosophical?" he practically growled at her.

"I guess dying has had that effect on me."

"You are not going to die. I won't allow it. Now save your strength because you're going to need it."

"Cush," she began but he interrupted her.

"Would you give up on me? Would you sit there and watch me take my last breath?"

He could feel her indignation and he knew he had her. *"Of course not."*

"Then dammit, Elora, don't ask that of me. Don't ask me to let you go."

"I just don't want you to be even more disappointed when it doesn't work."

He laughed out loud but it was not a humorous sound. *"You think I'm disappointed? Babe, I'm a whole hell of a lot more than disappointed. We are not done, Elora, not by a long shot."*

"What happened to Little Raven?" she asked.

"You have to earn that title by fighting for your life, by fighting for us. When you open your eyes and tell me you aren't leaving me, then I will gladly call you that."

Cush felt her pull away from him. She was mad. He almost found the situation funny. His Chosen was dying, and she was ticked off at him for telling her that he wouldn't call her by his pet name unless she fought to live. Okay, so maybe that was a dick move, but if it made her angry enough to not give up, then he'd do it again.

Cush stood and turned back around to face the priestess who still stood there watching him with curiosity.

"Your bond be a strong one."

He bit his tongue to keep from saying, thank you

captain obvious, instead he asked a question that had only one acceptable answer. "Can she be saved?"

"That is up to you," she answered cryptically.

Okay, not the answer he was expecting.

Cush heard a curse behind him and turned to find Oakley setting his sister down gently before standing and marching toward the priestess. He tried to grab the boy but Oakley ripped his arm from Cush and pointed at Chamani.

"Who the hell are you? What gives you the right to determine if a person lives or dies? I don't give a crap if you serve the devil himself. You have no right!"

"Perhaps not, but I serve one wit power enough to give herself de right." Chamani remained calm despite the human bearing down on her.

"That's crap. By your thinking, I should be able to determine a person's end if I hold a gun, which would make me powerful. Where is the justice in that?"

"Justice does not play a part in my plan, boy." The voodoo queen's voice boomed shaking the trees and ground around them. "I keep the balance, and if other lives are lost while that happens, that is no concern of mine. I needed the warrior to complete a task; he has done that task. The fate of his female was never my concern; she was a tool."

"A tool?" Cush said in a voice that was entirely too calm. He could feel his blood begin to heat in his veins as his anger burned to a new level. "You may play your games with others but I am no mere human. I am no pawn to be moved as you see fit. I serve those even greater than you. I serve a king who bows before the Forest Lord, our creators, and because of that I am more powerful than even you."

The Voodoo queen's laugh sounded as though she

was holding on to sanity by a thin thread. He imagined that to depend on the worship of finicky humans would make anyone insane. She would be nothing without her followers and she knew it. Her tricks and games were a way to make her feel powerful. Cush was not going to play—not anymore. He'd killed Tarron because it needed to be done, not because the queen wanted him to. And he would not let Elora die just because she said it was what was going to happen.

"I've told you before this is my domain. There is none who can contest my will."

Cush felt their presence before they appeared and he dropped to one knee. He lowered his head and waited to hear the voices of his creator. He knew they would come if he called on them. Regardless of the fact that this was the queen's domain, she wasn't all powerful or omniscient. She was limited and her power paled in comparison to the Forest Lords.

"Child of ours, warrior of the elfin race, we have heard your cry. Speak your heart."

"You are not welcome here!" The Voodoo queen yelled and she sounded afraid for the first time.

"SILENCE," the Forest Lords boomed. "You have meddled enough in the lives of our children. We have given you your domain and set your boundaries in place, and you have crossed them. You will pay for that indulgence."

When they said no more, Cush took it to mean that they were waiting for him to speak.

"The spell that was cast over my Chosen is taking her life. I humbly ask that if it is not her time, tell me how to save her. Please." Cush waited, hoping that he would hear the answer he need to hear.

Finally, after several tense moments, they spoke.

"Elora, daughter of Lisa and Steal, half human, half elf and Chosen of Nedhudir, it is not your time."

"Can you save her?" Cush asked.

"She can be saved, but it will take faith on your part, and action. We will guide your feet, but you must guide your will."

"Will you leave me be?" the Voodoo queen asked in a much more subdued voice.

"You will suffer the consequences of your actions. Whether those consequences destroy you is up to you." And just as suddenly as they appeared the Forest Lords were gone.

Cush stood and turned to pick up Elora. Once he was standing with her in his arms, he motioned with his head for Oakley to follow.

"Good luck, warrior," Chamani said in a voice that held no ill will.

"I don't need luck, priestess. My creators are on my side. If they stand for me, then none can stand against me. Not even your queen." Without another word he took off at a jog that he knew Oakley would be able to keep up with.

"Do you know where we're going?" Elora's brother asked as they put the priestess farther and farther behind them.

"We need to get back to the motel."

"How do you know that?"

"It just feels right." Cush didn't understand it himself, but he didn't question it.

"You do know how girly you just sounded, right?" Oakley chuckled.

"Oakley."

"Yeah?"

"Shut-up."

"Just save my sister and I'll never say another smart ass thing to you."

It was Cush's turn to laugh. "I'd like to say I believe you, but your track record doesn't serve you very well."

"What are we going to do once we get to the motel?" Oakley asked, ignoring Cush's comment.

"Save my Chosen."

"Well, that's a relief. I was hoping we weren't going back there to take a swim in that luxurious pool," he huffed. "I meant *how*, Cush. How are we going to save her?"

"All of the details of the plan haven't come together just yet."

"That's reassuring."

"Oakley?"

"Whaaaat," he drew out.

"Stop talking."

"That's just a nicer way of saying shut-up."

"Perhaps. Would you rather I threaten your life if you utter another word?" Cush knew Elora would want him to be nicer to her brother, but nice just wasn't on his list of important things at that moment.

"Calm down, G.I. Joe. I was just stating a fact. I'm a little stressed, that tends to happen when my sister is dying."

"Please be stressed in silence."

"I'll get right on that."

Tamsin, Vyshaan, and Lisa hopped up from their

seats on the hotel bed when Syndra came striding through the mirror on the back of the bathroom door with *The Book of the Elves* clutched in her arms. Tamsin muttered a silent prayer of thanks to the Forest Lords. Apparently, their plan had worked. He had no doubt in his mate's abilities, but it took a massive leap of faith to allow her to go into Lorsan's office, alone, disguised as Ilyrana. But, as they had all decided, it was the only way they could safely get the book away from the dark elf king without another dangerous battle, this one taking place in very close proximity to the humans.

"Any problems?" he asked.

"Worked like a charm," Syndra responded. "Lorsan had no idea. I left him tied to his chair with a mob of bloodthirsty humans beating down his door."

"Do you think that was wise?" asked Tamsin. What if Lorsan gets free and takes his frustrations out on the humans?

"I don't think he will. There was no way he could escape from the spell I placed on him, especially after it had been infused with power from the Book."

"So you were really able to do it? You cast the spell on him without him even knowing it?"

"I simply looked over his shoulder and read the words silently. I felt him lock into place and he didn't even realize it.

A twinge of jealousy washed over Tamsin as he imagined his lover leaning over Lorsan's shoulders. He quickly squashed it, recognizing his mate's cunning and bravery, and understood that she had done what she needed to for the greater good.

And I guess we have you to thank for that," she said turning to Vyshaan.

"Thanks is not necessary," said the elder. "It was

the least I could do. Now let's get this book to our new king, shall we?"

"Good idea," commented Tamsin. "Trik phoned earlier. He should be here any second. He and Cassie located her parents. They were a bit shaken up, but otherwise unharmed."

"Great, let's get outside. This place is a dump," said Syndra as she turned up her pert little nose and glanced around the room. "It's worse than Lorsan's dungeon."

"The conditions didn't seem to be bothering you when you were necking with your elf," responded Lisa in a deadpan manner.

"Don't' get me started. Despite the lack of cleanliness in this place, there is a perfectly serviceable bed right there. We could pick up where we left off," Syndra cooed as she stepped to Tamsin and placed her hands around his neck.

"I do not need any more images in my head that can't be burned out. I'm out," breathed Lisa, who walked out the door with all three elves, chuckling, in tow. Tamsin, the last one out, shut the door behind him and breathed in the humid swamp air, which seemed as fresh as a mountain morning compared to the stuffiness of the hotel room. Syndra placed the Book on a dilapidated picnic table that was standing sentinel by the empty hotel pool. They each sat down and Vyshaan began to explain everything he knew about the book.

Lorsan, huffing and puffing, stepped through the

very bathroom mirror that the former light elf queen had only moments before. He crept to the hotel window and carefully looked outside seeing the three elves and the human pouring over the Book—*his* Book. It took everything in him not to storm out of the room and attack them. But he knew such an action would only ensure his death. He must be careful now. Without Ilyrana at his side, he knew just how vulnerable he was. Syndra showing up in his office wearing the face of his mate was a testament to that. His mind flashed back to his office as he watched his nemesis walk through the mirror without so much as a glance back.

Lorsan screamed at the back of Syndra as she lightly skipped through the mirror with *The Book of the Elves* in her hands and the declaration that his mate was dead. Just then the door exploded and his office was filled with angry humans. They saw the Rapture on his desk. Like a school of piranhas, they descended on the vial. They were no longer forming words. The only sounds escaping them were primal screams and guttural utterances. He felt as though a pack of zombies had descended and the vial was like a fresh beating heart to them. Lorsan strained against his bonds, but still they held fast. The first human to make it to the desk, a burly man covered in tattoos, leapt toward the vial. He was stopped just inches away as two more humans, a man and a woman, came crashing down on his back. They slammed into the desk, knocking the vial over. It rolled backward, falling off the desk and landing under Lorsan's feet. The swarm of humans came over the desk, engulfing him. His chair fell backward and he sat, back to the floor, facing the ceiling. The humans were biting, clawing, and scratching; each trying to hurt the other while also attempting to make it to the Rapture.

Lorsan felt the pain of many punches and kicks raining down on him. He threw up a protection spell around his body, much like Syndra had earlier—though his was darker and less powerful. Just then he heard a tinkle of glass breaking. A human had inadvertently stepped on the vial. The last drop of Rapture was now running across his hand-scraped hardwood floors. If possible, the humans' fury increased. Some howled, pummeling the clumsy fool who had stepped on the vial. Others dropped to their knees pushing each other out of the way as they tried to lap the precious liquid with their tongues. Still others kicked at Lorsan's protective shield, trying to get to the elf. Somehow they seemed to understand that he was the source of all their problems.

All of a sudden, Lorsan felt his power returning. He should have realized when he threw up his protective shield that whatever magic Syndra cast on him was fading. Apparently, the Book's power extended only so far. When she went through the portal, transporting herself almost fifteen hundred miles away, her spell began to weaken. He strained outward and felt the magical bonds holding him break apart. He was free. With a surge of renewed power, he sent a shockwave out from his body, the force of it throwing the humans away from him—some landing hard on his office furniture, some bouncing hard off the office walls. He roared and jumped onto this desk, surveying the destruction the humans had caused.

They were cowering now, scrambling backward to get away—running, crawling, and toppling toward the exit.

"I should kill you all for this," he screamed at them. But he did not. He had bigger fish to fry right now. He leapt from his desk, soaring across the room, and plunged through the mirror calling on the magic of the portals to trace the last occupant to enter through that mirror. Syndra thought she'd bested him, but like her mate, she was a fool.

Trik, Cassie, and Tony emerged from the hotel room that he and Cassie shared, after having teleported back from the Tate's house. Mr. and Mrs. Tate had not wanted to let their daughter leave, but in the end they'd given up, realizing that their daughter was no longer a child. Trik walked over to the window and pulled the drapes aside to look out. He hoped he would find Cush standing there with Elora and Oakley in tow, but that isn't what he saw. What he did see was just as reassuring. Four figures sat at a picnic table near the pool. He was taken aback by two things simultaneously. First, that one of the individuals was holding up *The Book of the Elves*, reading to the others as a kindergarten teacher might read *The Hungry Little Caterpillar* to her students. And second, that the teacher in question was none other than the elder Vyshaan himself. Any other time, Trik might have slain the elder on site, or at least attempted to. But as Tamsin, Syndra, and Lisa seemed to be hanging on his every word, it seemed a bit rash to exact judgment on the elder without at least asking a few questions first.

He took Cassie's hand and pulled her toward the door. Then he glanced over at Tony. "It looks like the kicks just keep on coming."

Cassie frowned at him. "Who's doing the kicking

and who's getting kicked?"

Trik just winked at her and lead her from the room.

"I hate it when he winks like that instead of answering," Tony huffed as he followed them. "It usually means whatever he knows is about to bust you in the gut and knock the air out of you."

Cassie laughed. "I'm glad I'm not the only one who gets annoyed with him."

"I'm right here you know," Trik pointed out.

"We know," Tony and Cassie said at the same time.

"Vyshaan," Trik said quietly, staring at the elder as he approached the table. Everyone jumped to their feet, startled. Apparently they had all been so enthralled at what Vyshaan had been teaching them, they'd forgotten all about their surroundings. It must have been interesting in order for Tamsin to not be aware of what was going on around him.

"Hold, Trik," came Tamsin's steady voice. "Vyshaan has something to say before you pass judgment on him. And Syndra and I would also speak on his behalf."

"What? What positive thing could you and your queen have to say about this...this...coward?"

"He helped Syndra, Lisa, and I escape Lorsan's casino," replied Tamsin.

"And he helped us get *this*," Syndra interjected, raising *The Book of the Elves*. "And is teaching us how to decipher it."

"And just why would you do that?" Trik spat at Vyshaan.

"Trik, I understand why you would feel the way you do about me. I admit that I abandoned my people in their time of need. Not just when I began working with Lorsan but also when Lorsan blew his castle to hell. I didn't want to deal with the aftermath, and I didn't know how to face you after I'd heard you had returned as our King. So, yes, you are right. I was a coward. I fled, when I should have been fighting for my people. It was the elders' job to protect them. And I failed them. For that, I do deserve death.

But, Trik, I'm not the only one who has abandoned my people. You yourself have not always been blameless. You were the right and true king. But you threw that destiny away so you could serve your own dark nature."

Trik growled in frustration. "Don't you try and turn this back on me. I've faced the Forest Lords for what I've done. They passed their judgment and showed me mercy."

"And now I'm simply asking you to do the same for me," replied Vyshaan. "The Forest Lords aren't here. You must be their instrument of mercy."

"And how do I know that you are sincere? How do I know that you aren't doing all this just to save your own skin? I can't read your intentions or your heart. How do I know you aren't lying?"

Vyshaan breathed deeply. "I'm not."

"Perhaps, I can help in that regard," Syndra spoke up, interrupting the intense conversation. "Am I not mistaken in noticing that we are a couple of elves short? Where is your trusty warrior, Cush, and his Chosen?"

"Good question," Lisa spoke up. "I was told my daughter would be here and that Cush was coming for her."

"She is here. But she seems to be in the company of a different companion than Cush. Cush and Oakley are here, and I only know that for sure because of that vehicle" —he pointed to the yellow Jeep Wrangler— "and the footprints around it that lead toward the swamp. Few have a foot that large and it is not a modern shoe. It is definitely the boot print of an elvish warrior. I asked him to wait for us, but I am not surprised that he didn't. If my Chosen was out there without me, I wouldn't be waiting to find her either. So, they are out there—somewhere." Trik made a sweeping motion with his hand toward the swamp. "He will get her back, but he alone must do this. It is a battle he must fight."

Lisa looked as if she was going to be sick. "And no one thought to tell me this before now?" The blood had drained from her face and she was pale as death.

Trik clenched his jaw. "It wouldn't have done any good. There was nothing you could have done. You don't need to be upset with Tamsin and Syndra. They were obeying an order from their King. If you want to blame anyone, you can be pissed off at me."

"I understand what you are saying, but that doesn't change the fact that my daughter is apparently in danger, and now my son as well. Whether or not I could have done something to help is irrelevant. I am a mother and I will always feel the need to fight for my child, rational or not. Is she going to be okay?" Lisa stepped away from the table turning to the vast swamp forest.

"Cush will take care of her," Cassie told her friend's mother as she took her hand. "He won't stop until she's safe."

Lisa nodded, but her face had not regained any of its color and her eyes were wide as she chewed on her bottom lip, still staring into the forest.

"You know how protective our males are, Lisa. I know you will worry, but if anyone can save her, it is Cush," Tamsin added.

"That may be so," Syndra said. "But you know that a Chosen can be both a benefit and a distraction on the battlefield. Cush and Elora are just now figuring out their bond. She cannot lend him strength as a Chosen should. She will only cloud his judgment and make him vulnerable."

"I have no doubt that Cush is capable but Elora is not herself," Cassie blurted out, drawing the attention of everyone present. She glanced at Lisa who had swung back around to look at the group. Cassie continued as her best friend's mom listened. "According to the priestess, she is under a powerful compulsion spell. Who knows what she will do? She might even try to protect Tarron and hurt Cush."

"Trik, I strongly advise that you send Cush some help. This swamp, plus the addition of Elora, could be enough to turn the tide of battle in favor of Tarron. It is your duty as king and our duty as his friends to help him," Syndra said in a voice that reminded them all that she was a queen regardless of whether or not she wore a crown.

"Not to mention, Oakley was with Cush. Elora's brother is out there, Trik. She will never forgive me if anything happens to him," Cassie pleaded.

Trik was silent for several moments. "And if I go into the swamp, what about him?" Trik asked, pointing to Vyshaan.

"There is no need for you to go. Let Tamsin and I take him into the swamp to find Cush. If he helps us again, we can trust that he has changed his ways. If he betrays us, well…" Syndra suggested.

"No," Trik responded. "It's too dangerous. Chamani and her mistress are causing too much turmoil in this land. I should be the one to go."

"You cannot," chimed in Tamsin. "There is something that is much more important. Something that has been lost to our kind for far too long. This," he said tapping the Book, "must be protected at all costs. You are the only one powerful enough to keep it safe."

"Tamsin is right," continued Syndra. "And we cannot take it into the swamp. That would be foolish. The Voodoo queen might want you to stay in power, but I doubt she would have any qualms about taking the book for herself in an attempt to keep our people weak. There is just too much that could happen out there. Besides, if anyone has the ancient knowledge necessary to challenge Chamani and her mistress, it's an elder. It is only right that Vyshaan go. If nothing else, perhaps, simply just to make amends for what he has done."

Trik breathed deeply. "As always, you speak wisdom, light elf queen. It will be done as you say. You and Tamsin take Vyshaan and go. However, you must not interfere with Cush unless all seems hopeless. He may not appreciate your help, well-meaning though it might be. And don't take your eyes off of him," he commanded, pointing toward the elder. "I hope you are right about him."

Lisa raised her hand gaining the attention of the group. "Love that you guys are making a plan to get my children out safely, but I'm not just standing around waiting. I'm going with them," she motioned to Tamsin and Syndra.

"I don't suppose my ordering you to stay would make a difference?" Trik asked.

"If it would make you feel better, you're welcome to order away. But when it comes to my kids there is no force on earth that can keep me from them. Until you have children, there is no way you can understand. Your life no longer has anything to do with your own safety, your own happiness, or your own health. Everything you are, everything you have, and everything you will do is for them—for their safety, their health, their happiness, and their future. So no, your orders will do nothing to keep me from going after them."

Trik nodded. "How can I attempt to dissuade you after a speech like that?" He turned back to Vyshaan and his face lost all emotion. "Do not betray us. I would hate to have to use the skills I acquired as an assassin, but I will if necessary."

"I will not fail you, my king," said Vyshaan bowing low. Trik did not miss the formality that the elder used when he bowed. His arm was across his chest and the possessive words, *my king,* was another way to indicate that he was declaring his loyalty to Trik. He watched without another word, as the four headed into the dark swamp. He truly hoped he was doing the right thing in sending them into the spider's trap. Like a web weaved for its victims, the swamp stretched out before them, waiting for the unaware or the foolish to stumble into it. His people were neither, but neither were they invincible.

"Forest Lords protect them," he muttered under his breath. He felt Cassie's hand slip into his and felt his soul reaching for hers. He looked down at her and saw the faith in her eyes that was always there.

"They will be fine," she told him gently. "You have to learn to delegate. You aren't a lone assassin anymore."

He leaned down and pressed a tender kiss to her forehead. "No, I am not, nor will I ever be alone again. And you, my queen, as usual, are right. They will be fine. No other outcome is acceptable."

Chapter 15

"We will face many battles in our lives. Some of those battles will be within ourselves, some will be with those we love, and some will be with our adversaries. Regardless of the battle, what matters isn't how it ends, but how we handle ourselves while in the midst of it. Does our character under fire reveal a person worthy of respect despite the outcome? Do we fight for justice or revenge? If we are on the side of good, does our attitude in all situations reflect it? Battles will come, and even if we lose, if our character stands true, then we have still won." ~Triktapic, King of the Elfin Race

Cush heard the footsteps long before he saw who they belonged to. He knew some of them weren't human. But there was at least one that stepped with the heavy footfalls of a human. A few of them were definitely his kind. Coming to a quick stop, he turned and looked at Oakley. "We are about to have company."

Oakley's eyes widened. "Friend or foe?"

"Not sure," he answered as he narrowed his eyes looking through the trees and hanging moss.

"How do you know someone is coming? I don't hear anything."

Cush adjusted Elora in his arms and wrestled with the need to keep her with him or hand her to Oakley so his hands would be free if he needed to protect them. "Elf hearing, remember?"

"Ugh, another cool power I get to miss out on being half elf," Oakley grumbled as he looked in the same direction that Cush was gazing.

"Haven't we already discussed this?" Cush asked. "Some humans that are half elf do have powers, but as I said before, that is rare, and their powers are not as strong as in a full blood."

Oakley snorted. "That's just my luck. I would be one of those without the power. My dad was a freaking dark elf and I didn't get jack from his heritage."

"That has yet to be seen, Oakley," Cush argued. "Our superior senses and magical powers aren't the only thing unique about us. We have half a soul until we meet our other half. Perhaps, you too will have a Chosen."

The human shrugged. "Maybe."

Cush turned his attention back to the approaching visitors. "I don't understand. I can hear them getting closer but I still can't see them. I should be able to see them by now."

"Perhaps, you are getting old." Tamsin's voice carried through the trees.

Cush's head whipped around toward the voice, but still he didn't see his former king. "Is your mate with you?" He figured Syndra must be with him if they were invisible; it was one of her talents.

"Of course, I am with him. Who would protect him if I didn't come?" Syndra asked as she, Tamsin, Lisa, and another male elf materialized before them.

Cush glanced at Tamsin and then at the other male. He recognized him right away. "Vyshaan," he said in acknowledgement.

Lisa started toward her son but Oakley held up his hand. "I'm fine, Mom. Elora is the one you need to be checking on."

Cush watched as she changed course and headed for the girl in his arms. He took a step back, his natural instinct to protect his Chosen kicking in. Lisa paused; her eyes narrowing on him. "I won't hurt her, Cush. I know she is yours, but she was mine first. I just need to see her." She waited, watching him.

Cush looked down at Elora and could practically hear her telling him to get a grip. His lips twitched as he thought about how she would admonish him if she were able. Finally, he looked back up at her mother and gave a slight nod. Lisa rushed forward and brushed the hair from Elora's face.

"She's breathing," she told him unnecessarily. She looked up at him; her eyes glistened with unshed tears. "Is she going to be okay?"

"I need to get Elora to *The Book of the Elves*."

Syndra walked up to him, approaching slowly. He was pretty sure he wouldn't attack the light elf queen, but after his reaction to Lisa, he could understand Syndra's caution.

"Easy, warrior, I only want to assess her," she said gently as she stepped up next to Elora's mother. Syndra placed a hand over his Chosen's heart and her palm began to glow. Suddenly Syndra hissed and jerked her hand back. "This is no natural injury; it is the dark magic that is killing her. My power is useless for her."

Lisa frowned. "What does that mean?"

"It means she needs more power than I have," Syndra explained. "I am powerful, but I am not so prideful that I cannot admit when my power is not sufficient."

Cush nodded. "The priestess of this swamp claimed that there was nothing that could be done, but

I can't accept that. There has to be something in that book that could help her."

"We have the book," Tamsin informed him.

"Is it with you?" Oakley asked.

They all shook their heads. "We left it with Trik. We didn't want to take a risk of losing it in the swamp. And by losing it I don't mean dropping it into an alligator's mouth." Syndra gave him a pointed look.

Cush understood. They didn't want to bring something as powerful as *The Book of the Elves* into the Voodoo queen's territory. Like a shiny new toy, the book's power would call to the queen and she would answer it eagerly.

"I can help her, with the book," Vyshaan clarified. "I'm not saying that I can save her for sure, but there is magic in the book that we have not used in a very long time."

Cush didn't know if he should trust the elder, but he didn't have time to give it thought. "Let's just get back to the motel and go from there." Without another word he took off at a run. He heard Oakley curse before he heard his footsteps behind him. He knew the others were following close behind.

They hadn't ran more than a mile when Cush felt his feet growing heavy until finally he could no longer lift them. Frustration and rage rolled through him as he shouted, "You have been warned! What part of the words from the Forest Lords did you not understand?"

"What's happening?" Lisa asked.

Cush glanced behind him seeing that the others had caught up but were also immobilized where they stood.

"The Voodoo queen can't seem to leave well enough alone," Cush answered.

"The game has changed," her voice rang out. "A new piece is now in play. How can I possibly ignore such information about a book that is known throughout the supernatural world? And here it has practically fallen into my lap. I will worry about the consequences after I have the book. The power I will obtain from it will be enough to rival your creators."

Syndra laughed and the sound was dark, promising violence. "You are a fool if you believe such nonsense."

"You dare to address me with such insolence?"

"I will dare to do a lot worse than that if you don't release us. My patience for stupid supernatural beings has been pushed to the very edge today. So unless you feel like playing Russian roulette and seeing just who is more powerful, I suggest you heed my warning." Syndra held her arms loosely next to her sides. She looked relaxed, but Cush knew how quickly the queen could move. She wouldn't be caught unaware.

The Voodoo queen laughed and the sound surrounded them. "It's cute that you actually think you are a match for me."

Syndra let out a tired sigh. She looked over at her mate. "When will they ever learn? I don't just speak to hear myself talk."

Tamsin shrugged. "You have to leave some alive for them to spread word of your power, love. Decimating all of your enemies doesn't allow for gossip."

"True," Syndra nodded. "But some of them get on my nerves so badly that I just can't keep from silencing them for good."

"Are you going to take action, former queen, or are you just going to keep talking?"

"Bloody hell, I am so done," Syndra growled. She

closed her eyes as she held her arms out, with her palms up. She began chanting in the old language of their people and Cush knew they were all about to witness the awesomeness that was Syndra. For whatever reason, the Forest Lords favored her, and when she called out for their strength, they always answered.

The ground around them began to shake and the wind whipped around them. Cush stumbled as his feet were suddenly released and he reached out to brace himself on a tree to keep from toppling over with Elora in his arms. When he looked back he wasn't surprised to find Syndra glowing as her power continued to build. Thunder boomed overhead and clouds began to gather over them as her voice grew louder. Cush looked past Syndra to her mate. Tamsin was making a motion with his hand and he realized that he was telling them all to get down. The group dropped to the ground just as a flash of light exploded blinding them all. A pulse of power shot out from where Syndra stood and a deafening sound roared around them. And then there was nothing. The wind had stopped, the thunder was silenced, and the light was gone.

Oakley's voice was what finally broke the silence and had everyone opening their eyes and standing back up. "Remind me to never, ever, ever piss her off." He motioned to Syndra as he turned in a circle taking in the devastation.

Cush didn't know how far the radius of damage extended but from what he could see for the better part of a mile every tree, bush, and plant had been leveled to the ground. Like rows of dominos being toppled over, the forest had collapsed. Cush had to agree with Oakley's statement. He hoped he never faced the wrath of Tamsin's Chosen.

"I could have taken her." Syndra's voice drew everyone's attention. She was glaring daggers at Vyshaan.

He bowed his head. "I have no doubt of that. I was merely backing you up."

Tamsin looked from the elder to his Chosen. "You shared your power?"

"I simply gave hers a little jolt."

"Little?" Lisa asked. "I'd say that's a whole hell of a lot more than a little."

"Did you kill her?" Oakley asked.

Syndra shook her head. "No, one just doesn't kill an evil goddess so easily. But I sent her back to the fiery pit where she was before her people called on her. The Voodoo queen is a demon. Her power comes from the belief of those who summon her. She has been in this realm for a very long time. So I and…" —she glanced at Vyshaan— "and apparently him, sent her back to square one. She will have to be summoned again in order to come back to the earthly realm."

"Did she really think you couldn't beat her?" Lisa asked.

Syndra laced her fingers together and turned them outward, cracking her knuckles. She leaned her head side to side, stretching out her neck. "I'm sure she knew, but those who crave power are prideful and that pride serves as a blindfold keeping them from seeing the truth that is staring them in the face."

"Syndra, Vyshaan, thank you for dealing with our adversary," Cush told them, though he was sincere, his voice was emotionless. "But I can delay no longer. I must get her help." He motioned with his head to his Chosen. He didn't ask them to join him, nor did he care if they did. He was focused on one thing—saving his mate.

Together, Trik, Cassie, and Tony, sat at the table studying the fabled Book. For so long the book had been right under Cassie's nose hidden at her best friend's shop. But she wouldn't have known its importance if she'd have found it back then. That was before Cassie even knew anything about elves or magic or any of the other strange stuff she'd seen. That time seemed a world away now. The book was beautiful to be sure, written in stylized ancient elvish script. Even though she was a human, she could still feel the power emanating from the book. Trik sat beside her muttering to himself. Delicately he turned the ancient pages, each one bringing a look of wonder to his handsome face. Tony sat across from them, staring at Trik with interest.

"What is it, Trik?" Cassie asked her Chosen.

"It's just. It's in here. Everything. Everything is in here. Everything that has happened to our people and everything that will happen. And I can read it. I don't know how, but I can. None, other than elders, are supposed to be able to decipher it, but I can see it clearly somehow."

"The Forest Lords," Cassie said. "They've given you a gift, Trik. They wanted you to have the book."

"But why me? Why now?"

"Why not now?" Tony interrupted. "You are the recently restored king of the elves, the true king. Who else in the world would they give it to?"

"No, that's not what I mean," Trik responded.

"The Book has been hidden for ages, yes. But ages past, the Book was always given to the elves in a time of great need, to aid them in their survival. I don't see why I would need the book now."

"Hm, there must still be something for you to do," Cassie suggested. "Something we've missed in all our running around."

"Well I don't—"

Cassie let out a shriek, interrupting Trik as she was yanked backward off the bench. She flew through the air and landed hard. Rocks and grit dug into her hip. She opened her eyes and tilted her head back until she could see who it was that towered over her. She stared up at one very haggard looking dark elf. His disheveled appearance was matched only by the hatred plastered across his face. Bleeding from several cuts and scrapes along his hands and face, his breath coming in rasps, he reached down and yanked Cassie up by her hair. Her scalp stung and she was pretty sure if he held her any tighter he would rip her hair from its roots. Wrapping his left arm around her neck, he held her fast. The dark elf raised his right hand, which was glowing with black malice, to her face. The spell was only inches from her skin. Trik was up in a flash, facing her attacker— Lorsan.

"Don't come any closer, assassin," Lorsan hissed, holding the waiting spell even closer to Cassie's face. She bit her tongue to keep from whimpering and enraging Trik even more. "You know I'll do it."

Trik let out a low, dark chuckle. "You are a dead elf."

"Like my Chosen?" he said, bitterness dripping with every word. "We shall see." He paused, and when he spoke again Cassie could hear the longing in the dark elf king's voice.

"Why did it have to happen like this, Trik?" he said. "We had such a good thing, you and I. You were always so good at what you did. And I *know* you enjoyed your work. You may have all these other simpletons fooled, ready to follow you off a cliff, but I know the *real* Trik. The real Trik is a killer, plain and simple, ruthless, heartless, and malicious. You were never meant to be king, Trik. You were always meant to be an assassin."

Cassie watched as Trik stood, rooted to the spot, considering Lorsan's words. She could tell the minute that Lorsan's words began to affect him. As though a veil suddenly fell over his face, all the evil things he'd done seemed to wash over him. Cassie knew he was thinking about all the people he'd hurt and killed and all the lies he'd told. Trik had told her once that he could see the faces of those he'd wronged, and that there were so many of them that they began to run together. He even saw Elora's father, Steal. He had died like a warrior. He hadn't begged; he'd simply asked Trik one time to show him mercy so that he could be there for his kids and his Chosen. When Trik denied him, Steal had simply nodded and awaited for the blade to pierce his heart. Did Trik even consider the consequences before he took the dark elf's life? Even after Elora's father had mentioned them, did he even consider that he would leave two children fatherless? He knew the answer to that question.

"Don't listen to him, Trik," screamed Cassie. She had to get through to him to keep the memories from drowning him. Even though they were not touching, she could see all his thoughts written on his face. Even after all they'd been through, all the good he'd done, he still couldn't let go of his past. "You're not that person anymore."

"Shut up!" spat Lorsan, tightening his arm like a noose around her neck.

Cassie continued to struggle, but she could no longer speak. Lorsan was cutting off her airway.

"You should let her go now," Trik said through gritted teeth. Cassie saw him clench and unclench his jaw as he inched ever so slowly toward her and Lorsan.

"Is this really what you want, Trik? This human? How many humans have you killed? You used to brag about how easy they were. About how you loved toying with them, especially the females. How many have you put under your spell, Triktapic, and taken your pleasure from them, only to slip a dagger into them when they least expected it?"

Cassie had stopped fighting the elf. She hung limp in Lorsan's arms, attempting to stifle the whimpers that kept slipping through her lips. She knew any sign of pain from her and it would only cause Trik to lose focus. She saw his hands fisted at his sides. His entire body shook as he stalked closer to Lorsan. His eyes narrowed on them. He was a predator in every sense of the word and he had his prey in his sight. He was waiting for the perfect moment to attack. She knew first hand just how patient a hunter her elf king could be.

"You want this human, Trik? I can give you *every* human. It can be like old times again. Now that we have the book it can be so much better. With you by my side and the book in my hands, we can conquer this realm by next week."

The last few words Lorsan spoke were drowned out by a booming noise that had all of them ducking. A flash of light lit up the darkened sky and a gush of wind slammed into them, nearly knocking them all to the ground.

Cassie had no clue what was happening, but she used the distraction to her advantage. In the next instant, Lorsan let out a howl that could have awoken the entire swamp. His grip had loosened enough that Cassie was able to lower her chin under his arm. She clamped her teeth down on Lorsan's forearm biting as hard as she could. He jerked his arm away and she fell to the ground. The bolt he had been holding went flying outward. At precisely the same time Trik had made his move lunging toward them. The dark power Lorsan had been holding hit Trik square in the chest. There was an explosion of darkness that temporarily blinded Cassie. When she could see again, Lorsan was nowhere to be found and Trik lay on his back staring at the sky, black smoke wafting from his chest.

She heard an ear piercing scream, not even realizing it was coming from her own mouth, as she saw Trik lying on the ground. He was still, too still. She ran to him and threw herself on top of him; huge tears cascaded down her cheeks showering his face.

"Trik, Trik, are you okay?" The words stumbled out of her mouth as her lips trembled. Trik was silent. His eyes closed. He looked as though he was sleeping. She cradled her love's face, but he remained motionless. Cassie placed her ear against his chest but she detected no breath.

"No, no, no, Trik," Cassie sobbed, holding Trik's face. Her thumb ran across his lips and images of his kisses filled her mind. They were all she would have because he wouldn't be kissing her again. Every memory she had of him would be all that was left and it wasn't enough. Their time together had been much too brief. She felt robbed of her future. Lorsan had taken many things from her, but now he'd taken the one thing that she couldn't live without. "Triktapic, you can't do this. You can't leave me, not now."

Suddenly a thought hit her like a bolt of lightning as she recalled the things Lorsan had reminded Trik of. *He's going to die thinking I believed all those ugly things that Lorsan was saying about him,* Cassie thought. *But I don't, Trik, I promise. I know the man you have become. I love you.* Truer words had never come from her lips. She loved him with every fiber of her being. Her soul had found its other half when she'd bumped into Trik in that office at her father's workplace. Cassie had never even realized that there was a hole inside of her until Trik was there to fill it. Her chest constricted and her stomach rolled with nausea. It was becoming increasingly harder to breathe and she gasped for air. Cassie wasn't sure why she was bothering to try to suck in air It wasn't as if she wanted to go on if Trik was not going to be by her side. She could feel her soul reaching for him and, when his didn't respond, Cassie felt a fresh flood of grief pour over her. This wasn't how it was supposed to end. Trik was supposed to have handed Lorsan his backside on a platter. He was supposed to stand victorious over the enemy. Evil was not supposed to prevail. Her fist pounded on his chest as a cry rose from her throat.

"Noooooooooo!" She pounded his chest again. "Not like this! Dammit, Triktapic, I love you. Do you hear me? I. Love. You. I don't want to do this without you—live this life. You're supposed to be with me. Please, please don't go." Her rant ended in a soft whisper as her head fell forward pressing against his forehead. Cassie's head swam and her vision blurred.

The agony of losing him was wrapping around her leaving her breathless. Before blackness overcame her, she heard these words in her head.

I'm none of those things anymore, A'maelamin, because of you.

Trik's voice broke through the fog that was beginning to fill her head. She opened her eyes and found she was staring directly into his shining silver ones.

"No matter what Lorsan said, I simply looked at you, Cassandra. You are my light. You are what rescued me from that life. Without you I am nothing, and with you I am everything." Trik pressed his lips to hers, his hand wrapping possessively around the back of her neck. It was quick, but filled with promise. When he pulled back, his eyes were swirling with passion and need. Trik closed his eyes briefly and then opened them back again, seeming to have gained control of himself. "And as much as I want to continue this conversation, right now we still have work to do. But rest assured, beautiful, we will pick up where we are leaving off."

Cursing the insolent human girl, Lorsan ran to the picnic table and snatched up *The Book of the Elves*. A quick glance toward the swamp and his feet stumbled as he saw the result of the power that had hit them only a few moments ago. He continued forward and it took effort to pull his gaze away from the destruction. He didn't have time to wonder at its cause. Pain in his forearm helped distract him from the swamp, and he glanced down and saw that his arm bled from where she'd taken a chunk out of it. He should filet her for that little stunt. But he didn't have the time right then. He wasn't going to wait around to see how much damage his bolt of dark magic had done to Trik. How lucky it was that his spasm at feeling the girl bite him had sent the magic directly into the impudent King. He probably would have missed the shot under ordinary circumstances. Lorsan was quite certain that blow would have killed any other elf on the planet. But Trik wasn't just any other elf. Lorsan could stop to finish the job, but if Trik wasn't severely weakened, Lorsan knew that he would have no chance in a fight against the King. Not today, anyway. But later, after he'd had time to study the Book properly, after he'd increased his own magical power to a level Trik couldn't even dream of, well…then he would be back for his former servant.

Slowed slightly by the lingering injuries from his bout with the humans in his office, Lorsan still moved like a feline predator. In a flash he was speeding across the parking lot, book in hand, headed back to the motel room, back to the mirror.

Crack.

As he stepped across the threshold, his face encountered Tony's fist. Lorsan had been in such a hurry that he hadn't seen the human hiding just inside the room.

With a primal scream, Tony put everything he had into that punch. He knew that he was no match for Lorsan, but he had to do something. Though he'd been shocked by the wind and pulse of magic that had knocked him on his butt, his head had been clear enough for him to think to take advantage of the distraction. He'd jumped to his feet and made a run for the open door of the room he assumed Lorsan had emerged from. Just as he'd turned around to lean around the edge of the doorway to make sure he hadn't been seen, Tony saw Cassie clamp down on Lorsan's arm and had to hold back a shout of praise for her quick thinking. He saw the bolt of dark magic hit Trik in the chest and saw Cassie running to him across the parking lot. Finally, he saw Lorsan snatch up the book and head directly for the room in which he was hiding. When the dark elf king paused, his head turned toward the swamp, Tony had turned to see what had caught his attention. He was pretty sure his jaw had hit the ground when he saw the destroyed forest. The land had been leveled. Like a bad wreck, he had a hard time pulling his eyes away, but the sound of footsteps had him turning back to Lorsan who was once again making a beeline for the room where he hid.

He could have let Lorsan speed right on by, never revealing his presence. He could have followed the dark elf king, pledging to work for him once again. Lorsan might have been angry that he had sided with Trik, but Tony knew Lorsan's greed. The dark elf king would take him back if he came back groveling. Anything would have been safer than what he did. But as he watched the dark elf speeding toward him—knowing that he would disappear into the portals, lying in wait until he could come back stronger—Tony knew that he must do something. So he closed his eyes and he swung his fist as hard as he could.

Lorsan staggered backward. Tony guessed that it probably wasn't from any pain, but more because of surprise. He knew that it probably hadn't crossed Lorsan's mind to worry about the human who had once worked for him. Tony hadn't even been a blip on his radar.

He shook his head and looked around, locating Tony.

"Well, well, if it isn't my old employee," Lorsan chuckled. "Finally grown a spine, I see. But I'm afraid your bravery is misplaced. You didn't think you'd actually betray me and get away with it. And now you've saved me the trouble of actually having to hunt you down. I really must thank you for that."

Lorsan stepped into the room, grabbed Tony by his throat, and flung him down on the motel floor. His back hit with a thud knocking the wind out of him.

"Such a waste. You were the only human I could ever tolerate for longer than a few minutes. Oh well, Vegas is full of pretty boys that can run a casino. I'll find another one. And now, Tony, this is goodbye."

Tony watched as Lorsan raised his hand with sparks of dark power building around him. He drug himself to his knees and looked up at the elf. He stared directly into Lorsan's eyes. There was a time when he would have been cowering, groveling, begging the dark elf to spare his life. Actually, he'd had to do that a few times in the past, but no longer. He, too, was not the person he once was. He'd chosen to do what was right. He'd chosen to make a stand, and he was finally proud of who he was, even if he wasn't going to be that person much longer.

Then something strange happened. The power in Lorsan's hand fizzled. The elf's eyes grew wide and a red liquid dripped from his mouth. He made a strange gurgling noise and then toppled, face down, right in front of Tony, a black dagger protruding from his back. He looked at the body of the dark elf king and then up at his attacker. His head tilted to the side as he rubbed his jaw. "That was sort of anticlimactic."

"Not exactly how I wanted that to happen," said Trik, standing over the elf's body. He reached a hand out to help Tony up. "But anticlimactic" —he pointed over his shoulder toward the forest that had been devastated— "wouldn't be what I'd call that."

Tony's brow lowered as he looked past the king. "What the hell happened?"

Trik turned and headed for the door. "If I was guessing, I'd say someone pissed off Syndra. That sort of damage has her signature written all over it." He stepped out of the room and grunted as Cassie came running up and threw herself into his arms.

Cassie pressed her face into Trik's chest, feeling his warmth seep into her skin. She listened to his heartbeat, letting it reassure her that he was alive and no longer lying lifeless on the ground. "Don't ever do that to me again," she said as she leaned back enough to look up at him.

"Don't attempt to save your life? Um, sorry beautiful but that's not a promise I can make."

"No, you quiver carrying butthead, I mean don't ever nearly die."

"I wasn't dying," Trik brushed her lips with his thumb causing her to tremble. "I was resting my eyes."

She heard Tony's laugh though he tried to cover it with a cough.

"You picked a really bad time to take a nap." She pressed herself closer to him and closed her eyes when she felt his lips against her hair. She could have stood there, wrapped in his embrace forever, but life was not that kind.

"I would love that as well," Trik whispered having picked up on her thoughts. "Unfortunately, we need to investigate what has leveled an entire forest. And I imagine it has something to do with that group of people that are running like a pack of wolves are nipping at their heels."

His words had Cassie whipping around. Her eyes immediately zeroed in on the large form that held a limp body in his arms. Her breath was knocked from her lungs for the second time in less than an hour as she saw someone she loved looking much too lifeless.

"Trik," she whispered his name like a prayer. Her feet were moving before he could respond to her plea. All she could see was her best friend being carried by her mate. She didn't care about those running around them, nor did she care about the leveled trees behind them. All she cared about was making sure Elora was going to be okay. She figured she must still be alive since they were running, and as relieving as that thought was, the one on its tail end crushed it. Even if she was alive, the question then became, for how long?

Chapter 16

"Sometimes beauty comes in the strangest form. One might think that for something to be beautiful then it must be pleasing to the eye, nose, skin, or ears. But beauty comes in another form. It is found in the soul. And as her soul rises up to meet mine, I see a beauty that nothing can rival."
~ Cush

Cush had never seen a more relieving sight than that of a human holding a book. It wasn't just any book; it was the book that he was praying had the knowledge to save his Chosen. That book had been written by the Forest Lords, through the hands of his people. He had to believe he wasn't hoping in vain.

Though the run from the edge of the forest to where Trik, Cassie, and Tony stood was less than a mile, it felt as though it took hours to get there. When he finally stood before them, holding Elora tightly against his chest, he glanced at Tony and then looked back at Trik.

"I killed Tarron, but the spell she was under had linked their lives together. The only thing keeping her alive now is her bond with me. Please allow Vyshaan to look through *The Book of the Elves* to see if there is any way to save her." Cush heard Cassie's sharp intake of breath but did not have the time or patience to care that she too would be hurting over Elora's state.

Trik took the book from Tony and held it out to the elder who stood with the others behind him. Cush started to head toward the opened door behind Trik but the king stopped him. "That room wouldn't be the best place to take her." Trik turned toward another door and held his hand out. Light shot from his palm slamming into the door knocking it open. "That one would be a better choice."

Cush didn't question him. He turned to the other door and headed toward it. Once inside, he laid Elora down on the large bed and sat down beside her, his hand clasped to hers. He looked up at the elder who stood on the other side of the bed holding the book. He was already flipping through the pages.

Cush heard Trik ask for the details on what had taken place in the swamp, but he tuned out the other voices as they answered him. All of his attention was focused on the woman before him.

Syndra listened as Tamsin filled Triktapic in on the events in the forest but her eyes were on Elora's still form. Lisa was standing at the end of the bed biting her nails with Oakley next to her. His arm was wrapped around her shoulders pulling her close to him as he offered her quiet support. Syndra had known Lisa for a very long time and had watched her kids grow up. In some ways she felt like they were her own family. There was no doubt in her mind that she would protect all of them with her own life, and she would do whatever she could to save Lisa's daughter. Whether it would be enough was yet to be seen, but she damn well wasn't going to stand there doing nothing. She stepped up beside Vyshaan.

"Anything?" she asked him.

He didn't answer for several minutes but then he stopped on a page and said, "Possibly."

Vyshaan touched the page with a long, tapered finger and Syndra's eyes widened as the words on the page began to change. When every word was done moving around, she realized that he had changed the language. The words on the page were in English, where moments before they had been in an ancient tongue that only the elders could read. Most of the book was that way, though there were a few pages that were readable by any elf. The page they were looking at most definitely hadn't been one of those pages.

Her eyes scanned the page greedily as she hurried to find out why he thought this particular magic would be able to help Elora. By the time she'd reached the last word, hope had taken root in her heart. It was a small amount, but it was hope nonetheless.

"I'll be honest, Vyshaan." Syndra looked up at him. "I had hoped that we'd never work together again, but right now I am glad that you are here."

He nodded. "I understand, and truthfully, I am glad I am here. Perhaps, this will start me on the road to redemption."

"Something tells me this will move you a long way down that path," she agreed. "Now, let's do this."

She felt Tamsin's hand on her shoulder and his power flowing into her. Syndra was powerful, but part of that power was from her mate. They were stronger together because they could share their magic and Tamsin was extremely generous with his power.

Vyshaan held the hand that wasn't holding the book out over Elora's still form. Syndra did the same, with both of her hands out. Their palms were facing down as magic began to flow from them.

"Cush," —Syndra looked away from Elora briefly to address the warrior— "call to her soul. Merge yours with hers. It will strengthen your bond." He nodded and she turned her attention back to her task.

The words that had been on the page began to fill her mind and she chanted them. Her voice blended with Vyshaan's and everything around her faded away. All of Syndra's concentration was on pulling magic from the well inside of her. Heat radiated across her hands and up her arms but she paid no attention to the uncomfortable sensation. Syndra wasn't going to be able to do this with power alone. She needed Elora to use her own will to fight the spell. Syndra was fighting against the spell, trying to break its hold. She didn't know if it would be enough. She had no idea how she would face her friend if she was unable to save her daughter. She prayed it wouldn't come to that. Tamsin stepped closer to her, his breath on her neck as he wrapped his arm around her waist; his power continued to flow into her.

"Whatever the outcome, we will face it together, as we have always done." His voice was a calm presence in her tempestuous mind. She was so thankful that she had Tamsin. They had lived several lifetimes full of joy, pain, sorrow, and love. Through all of it they had been side by side supporting one another. She wanted that for Elora and Cush. Lisa had been robbed of that life when Steal was taken. She had been overjoyed that Elora would get to have what she did not. For Lisa to have to watch her child lose that future was more than Syndra could bear. She prayed that would not happen.

Cush closed his eyes and let his soul take over. *Call to her*, he told it. He held his breath as he waited, hoping against hope that she would answer.

· *I feel her*, his soul said. *She hears me but she cannot answer. Something is preventing her from doing so.* Cush knew it had to be the dark spell's lingering effects. She was drifting further and further from him and he didn't have a clue how to hold onto her.

He could hear the chanting from the elder and Syndra but their voices sounded far away. His whole world was lying on the bed, in an old rundown motel room, dying because of the selfish and greedy man. He wished he could resurrect Tarron and kill him again and then repeat the process all over. Dying one time was too kind for the dark elf; he deserved much more suffering.

He thought back to the fight between him and Tarron and felt his gut churn as he remembered hearing Elora crying out on behalf of the male who had captured her. Selfish as it was, Cush didn't want her to die when her last words had been for another male. If she was taken from him, he wanted to be the last name she spoke. He knew that she didn't really want Tarron, but it still hurt to hear her concern for another.

It can't end like this, he thought to himself. They needed more time. *He* needed more time. *By the grace of the Forest Lords, please let this spell work. Please.*

Lisa's eyes blurred as tears filled them. Her daughter was grown, maybe only eighteen, but grown nonetheless. She'd been through more trials than most would ever go through in a lifetime. Despite this, Lisa still saw her as the baby she'd held in her arms the day she was born. The awe and wonder of seeing a little life that was a part of her had been beyond overwhelming. She had stared down at her daughter, so new and vibrant, and pictured the life that was ahead of her. Never in a million years had she thought it would come to an end so quickly. No parent should ever have to watch their child slip away. It went against the order of things. It was supposed to be her dying first. Lisa should be the one slipping away. She was the parent and that's just the way it was. But there she was, watching the body before her take shallow breaths as the life continued to drain from her body. She watched this and couldn't do a damned thing about it.

The chanting stopped, pulling Lisa from her thoughts as she turned to look at Syndra. The light elf queen's eyes were on her daughter. Her jaw clenched tightly as she waited. Lisa was afraid to look back at Elora. She was afraid she wouldn't see what she was hoping for. It was almost as if not looking kept hope alive. But after what seemed like an hour, Syndra turned and met her eyes. The despair she saw in them took her breath away.

Grief crashed down on her like a turbulent storm and drove Lisa to her knees. She heard Oakley call to her but she couldn't decipher his words. The only thing she knew was that a piece of her had just died. A life that she and her love had created had been ripped away from her before its time. Elora's life had only begun. There was a whole, incredible journey before her and, like a thief, death had stolen her before she could even take a step toward it.

When she'd loss Steal, Lisa had been sure that she would never be happy again. But the light that shined from Elora and Oakley had kept the darkness of his death at bay. Now one of those lights was gone. That pain was so very different than the pain of losing her mate. It was a pain that was drenched in failure. As the parent it was her job to protect Elora and she had failed. She didn't know if there was any coming back from the pit she was falling into. Elora, her daughter—fierce yet kind, strong but vulnerable, dry and yet so very humorous—was gone.

The sudden emptiness robbed him of his breath. Cush's eyes snapped open as he heard Lisa's cry, and he fell to Elora's chest. There was no rise and fall, not even a shallow one. She was still, completely and utterly still.

Cush couldn't move. He could only stare at his Chosen, willing her to breathe, silently begging her to sit up and snap at him for no reason, but nothing happened. She was gone. She had left him to face eternity without her.

Cush leaned forward until his forehead rested on her stomach. He didn't feel her fingers in his hair or hear her heartbeat speed up the way it did when he touched her. There was no soft sigh from her beautiful lips or whispered words of love. He would only experience those things in the recesses of his mind. Every future touch, taste, scent, or smile would happen only in his thoughts from the memories that would haunt him.

His shoulders began to shake as those very memories bombarded him.

"The one time a guy lies on top of me and he isn't even interested." He heard the words in his head and felt his eyes widen. Realization rushed in—his touch, her thoughts, his mind. Cush nearly shoved her away from him in his hurry to stand.

He leaned closer to try and hear what she was mumbling and nearly laughed when he finally deciphered it.

Over and over Elora muttered, "Goth girls don't cry, goth girls don't cry."

She jerked her arm back with a frustrated growl. "No worries, I won't force you to marry me. I'll get over you."

"So you're telling me that you don't want me, but nobody else can have me either?" she asked

"Are you trying to tell me you don't carry a quiver?" He leaned down next to her ear and whispered, "No, Little Raven, I don't carry a quiver. I wield a sword."

"But now you see how freaking amazing I am and you just can't see yourself without me?"

"I didn't ask to be your Chosen either! I didn't ask to feel this way about you. I didn't ask to feel empty when you leave the room. I didn't ask to feel the breath be ripped from my chest when you look at me. I didn't invite the freaking fluttering butterflies with their flapping and swooning into my stomach, and I didn't ask to want you with an intensity that—frankly—can't be healthy. So you can take your little temper tantrum and shove it up your ass, Cush. BECAUSE I DIDN'T WANT THIS EITHER!"

"I won't let you go, Elora. There is no breaking up, or divorces, or whatever other silly things you humans do when you tire of your mate."

"No worries, love. I kill my men when I'm done with them."

"Okay, okay," he chuckled, "then I'm done running and you are mine. For eternity, Elora, you are mine."

The memories kept coming, one after another: his refusal to admit he wanted her, her rant putting him in his place, their first kiss, their first declaration of love.

They threatened to suffocate him but he couldn't turn them off. They were all he had left and with each recollection he felt as though a knife was being stabbed into his heart and twisted until the muscle was completely shredded.

With his head still against her stomach, he slipped one arm underneath her and wrapped the other around her waist pulling her closer to him. His tears flowed freely absorbing into her shirt as one by one they fell. Cush felt his soul cry out only to be returned with silence, and it brought on a fresh wave of grief. The world around him was gone. He was drowning in a sea of despair without the hope of rescue because the only one who could save him was gone.

Cassie stood with wide, tear filled eyes as she watched Cush wrap himself around Elora. She had started toward the bed but Trik had stopped her. *"He won't let her go. And he will most likely become violent with anyone who tries to touch her. You will have to say your goodbye from a distance."*

Cassie didn't like it, but she understood. She understood because she knew Trik would be the same way if it was her lying in that bed. So she stood at the foot of the bed and cried for the friend she'd lost. She cried for the future, they had always planned together, being taken from them both. She cried for Cush and the anguish she knew he was in. But most of all she cried because the world had been robbed of this incredible person who brought laughter and love and passion to everyone and in everything she did. The world would never get the chance to experience the enigma that was Elora: the half human, half dark elf, but wholly wonderful person. Moments ago she'd still been breathing, there'd still been hope, but now, now she was still.

"I didn't get to tell her about her father," Trik said softly. Cassie immediately felt guilt fill him.

"She wouldn't have held it against you," Cassie reassured and she knew it was true.

"Still, I needed to apologize not because I expected forgiveness but because she deserved it."

Elora deserved many things, and death was not one of them. Cassie clenched her teeth attempting to hold herself together. She didn't want to fall apart with Lisa there. Elora's mom was already grief stricken. She didn't want to add to that with her own sadness. She leaned against Trik and let his silent presence give her strength, and she was thankful that he was so strong because she had never before felt so very weak.

"You know he will not leave her on his own," Syndra told her mate. They stood in the furthest corner of the room watching Cush. Her own heart was breaking as well, but Syndra didn't have the luxury of breaking down. Someone had to take charge and it fell to her and Tamsin. Trik was needed by his Chosen, Oakley and Lisa were in no state to think clearly, Tony wouldn't last two seconds against an enraged elf warrior, and Vyshaan seemed to be in shock over the fact that the spell had not worked. They were the only ones who had a chance in hell of getting Cush away from Elora so that they could tend to her.

"I don't understand it," Tamsin said keeping his voice soft.

"Understand what?"

"Trik and Tony killed Lorsan, Cush killed Tarron,

no more Rapture will be produced, Cassie's parents are safe, all of these challenges have been conquered, and yet this is the result." He motioned toward Elora. "I know in war there are casualties, warriors die. That's just part of it. But this, a young woman with so much ahead of her, this should not have happened."

Syndra wrapped an arm around him and leaned against him. "I agree, but it has and now we must figure out some way to live with it." To some she might sound cold, but Tamsin knew her. She knew that he understood her need to be doing something, to be moving toward a goal. And in grief, moving forward meant beginning the healing process. It wouldn't happen overnight, or in a week, a month, or even a year, but if they could accept that Elora was gone, then at least they could begin moving in the right direction.

"I don't know that Nedhudir will be able to accept that." Tamsin was focused on the warrior that he'd known for millennia. She looked up at him and she could see the warrior's pain reflected in her mate's eyes.

Before Syndra could respond she, along with everyone else, fell to her knees. The once warm, stagnant air was now cool and vibrant as it filled the room. The grief that was nearly suffocating began to lift, and in its wake, comfort and compassion seeped in.

Syndra couldn't move, but she wasn't afraid, not anymore.

Cush lifted his head as warmth flowed over him. He was surprised to see that everyone in the room save him were on the floor on their knees with their heads bowed. They didn't seem to notice the light that was emanating off of the three beings standing on the opposite side of the bed where Syndra and Vyshaan had been.

Keeping Elora's hand in his, he started to slide off of his chair to kneel.

"Stay where you are, warrior," one of the Forest Lords told him gently.

Cush returned to his seat and bowed his head. "Have you come to take her soul?" His voice was calm, though on the inside he was anything but.

"We told you once before that it was not Elora's time. The dark spell that was cast over her should have been destroyed when our daughter Syndra cast out the demon that inhabited these lands. However, it was not, because, Chamani, the demon's conduit lived on. We have reached out our hands and taken the life of the one who took the life of one of ours. Our wrath has been satisfied and so we have come to return that which was taken."

Cush watched in complete awe as the Forest Lords leaned over his Chosen. She was bathed in their light; her once pale skin glowed with the signs of life. They each laid a hand on her head and spoke as one. "Wake, daughter. There is more work for you to do. Wake and be healed."

As suddenly as they had been there, they were gone, taking their light with them, but they left something much more beautiful behind.

The breath rushed out of Cush as he felt Elora's hand squeeze his own. Her chest began to rise and fall as the life the Forest Lords had given her brought his Chosen back to him.

"Cush." The sound of her voice filled every empty place inside of him. He felt her soul reach for his and he lost it.

Cush buried his face in the space between her neck and shoulder as fresh tears flooded his eyes. He felt her fingers glide through his hair as she pulled him closer. His arms wrapped around her and though he tried to be gentle he held her tightly to him. He could hear the chaos going on around them, but still he held on keeping her sheltered by his larger form.

"You were gone," he told her through their bond because he didn't have the control to speak out loud.

"I'm here now," she said gently.

"You were gone," he repeated because the grief was still so near. *"And I was alone."*

"You are mine, Nedhudir, and I am yours. We will never be alone again, not in life nor in death."

His body shook with adrenaline as reality crashed into him. His Chosen, Elora, his little raven, was alive.

Chapter 17

"Life is so fragile. Yet if you treat it like a breakable trinket, placing it on the shelf for safekeeping, you might as well have thrown it against the wall and shattered it, because either way you will have ceased to have lived."
~Cassandra

"**M**arry me." Cush's voice filled the mostly dark room. The only light was from the candles that he'd lit when they had entered. Elora had known something was up when her warrior had brought her into the romantic atmosphere with that mysterious smirk plastered on his usually stoic face.

A month had passed since she had laid on a bed in a dirty, run down motel room and died while Cush held her. Elora didn't remember anything during the time she had been lying there lifeless, but she remembered everything before. There had been many late night discussions as she tried to come to terms with how she had acted and felt while under the dark spell. Through his memories she had felt how painful it had been for him, and Elora felt like she needed to fix it somehow. Yet he kept telling her that there was nothing to fix because nothing was broken.

"And I will say it again if I need to," he told her having picked up on her thoughts. "Let it go, Little Raven." Cush lifted her chin to look up at him. "It was a trial that we endured. It is a part of our past. I'm talking about our future. Marry me."

"Are you asking or tell me?"

"Yes."

"Will you always be this demanding?"

"Yes," he answered again.

"That could get annoying," Elora said as her eyes narrowed on him.

Suddenly she was on her back with a very large light elf warrior hovering over her. His broad shoulders blocked out anything beyond him and he was all she could see. Cush's eyes held a fierce emotion that she'd only seen when he looked at her.

"I won't live without you. We belong together and I want all of you. I want to give you all of me. You have been raised human and I know your custom is to marry your mate before you become one. Don't make me wait any longer, Little Raven. End my torture and marry me, please." His deep, rich voice glided over her like the softest silk, wrapping her in his spell. How could she deny him, not that she wanted to, but honestly what woman could say no to that?

Elora continued to search his gaze. She had no doubt that Cush loved her and she loved him. She had no doubt that she wanted to be with him for the rest of her life, no matter how long that it was. "What about my dark side?"

His lips kicked up in a crooked smile, making him look even more dangerous as his hand glided up the outside of her thigh to her hip and then to her waist where it stilled. His fingers tightened, gripping her possessively. "I told you before, I'm happy to indulge whatever you need. When I say you are mine, I mean all of you, dark side included."

"Okay then," she said as she ran a finger down his strong jaw.

Cush's brow rose as hope beamed back at her. "Okay then, as in yes?"

Elora nodded but stilled as soon as his lips pressed to hers. The world around her melted away as he became her only reality. She didn't hear the knock at the door, nor did she care if the whole world was watching. All that mattered to Elora in that moment was the man who had captured her heart and showed her just how amazing it was to be needed, wanted, cared for, and chosen. Though she had been destined for him and him for her, he'd chosen her as well. Cush had made it clear time and time again that he would choose her above all others, protect her, love her, sacrifice for her, and shelter her.

"Either she said yes, you're trying to convince her, or you lost a Jolly Rancher down her throat." Syndra's voice managed to penetrate their little bubble. "If it's the first, get your butts up and let's get this over with and then you can pick up where you left off."

As Elora's brain began to work again the she elf's words sunk in. "What is she talking about?" she asked as she pulled back to look up at him.

"I told you I don't want to wait any longer," Cush answered, the familiar determined edge filled his tone.

"The reverend Tamsin will be presiding over the ceremony. Let's go, chop chop." Syndra clapped her hands attempting to hurry them along.

Cush pulled Elora to her feet. She knew the dumbstruck look on her face had to be comical, but truth be told that's exactly how she felt—dumb and struck.

"Wait," —she held up her hand attempting to push Cush back— "you're telling me that we are going to get married now? Like this?" She motioned to herself. She was wearing her signature black and purple get up: black skinny jeans, black combat boots, and a black fitted tee with a purple raven on the front.

"Oh, for quiver's sakes," Syndra huffed as she walked over to her and muttered something under her breath and waved a hand in front of Elora. "It's not like you're going to have it on for very long, not with the way he was pawing at you just a moment ago."

Elora looked down at the transformation she had undergone. She now wore a black fitted corset and long flowing black skirt.

"I didn't figure you'd want white," Syndra smirked.

"Now can we go?" Cush asked as he reached for the still raised hand. He pulled her toward him and Elora stumbled a bit before righting herself and walking beside him. Was she really going to marry Cush right then? She'd said yes, but she'd also figured that they'd have a few months to plan it or something.

"Are you feeling overwhelmed?" Cush spoke to her mind.

"What if I said yes?"

"I'd say soon enough you will be too distracted to care." He sent her a roguish wink as he looked down at her, not pausing his stride in the least. He finally stopped before a door and she realized it was her favorite room in the entire castle. Cassie called it the temple of doom. But to Elora it was peaceful. With its deep purple walls, black candelabras, and velvet black furniture, it was the perfect oasis. It was just a sitting room, or maybe more like a small library because of the shelves that lined one wall. The floor consisted of black obsidian tiles. Each alternating tile beset with a carving of a raven in flight. Cush had done it for her. One of the many ways he tried to meet her needs.

Elora could hear the murmur of voices behind the closed door. Her palms began to sweat and her heart beat a little harder in her chest.

"If this really is too much, we can wait," Cush finally spoke as he turned to face her. His tall form towered over her, making her feel small but in no way insignificant. In fact she felt covered, sheltered, and safe. Elora tilted her head back to look up at him. She planned to marry him, so why not today? It wasn't like there was anyone else better for her, nor would she ever want anyone else. Her mind jumped to what else being married to Cush meant—not just being tied to him for the rest her life—but to the intimate parts. Was she ready for that?

"I will wait for as long as you need. Marry me, Elora, but don't worry about whether or not we will make love. If you aren't ready, that's okay. I want you. Make no mistake, my desire is strong, but I will wait." He brushed his fingers across her lips as he whispered again. "Marry me."

She knew he was sincere. He wouldn't pressure her into anything. "Let's just handle one thing at a time," she said as she smiled up at him. "I know that I want to marry you. So, let's focus on that." Elora let out a deep breath suddenly feeling lighter. She'd made the right decision. She belonged with Cush.

The door opened in front of them without their help and Syndra squeezed passed. "I give it a couple hours tops, and you'll be begging him."

"Syndra, you aren't helping," Cush rumbled.

She shrugged as she entered the room. "Who said I was trying to help you two? I'm trying to do the rest of us a favor. The tension between you two is wound so tight that you're bound to snap at any moment, and I personally don't want to be scarred for life if you finally go at it in the halls."

"Syndra, behave yourself and get up here so you can be a witness." Cassie's voice carried from behind the former light elf queen.

Syndra rolled her eyes. "Good grief, give the girl a crown and she takes the whole damn kingdom," she muttered as she gave Elora a wink and then turned and walked toward Cassie without a backwards glance.

Cush began to lead her again. Elora's attention was drawn to, first, the people gathered and then the room itself. Only a few were present, for which she was very grateful. Cassie, Trik, Lisa, Tony, Rin, Oakley, Syndra and, of course, Tamsin all stood in a half circle by the one window in the room. It was a stained glassed depiction of a tall tree, bare of all its leaves with ravens resting on some of the branches. The glass had purple, blue, and black hues to it with a touch of yellow from the moon and stars that were a part of the scene. A single, tall candle sat on the sill, causing the glass to glow.

When they'd finally reached the small group, Elora glanced over at her mom. They had always been close, but after her brush with death, her relationship with her mom was deeper. Lisa had shared all about Steal and her life before he died. She talked about what it was like to live in the elfin realm and about how she and Syndra had become such good friends. It was like she was getting to know her mom for the first time. And realizing they were a lot more alike than Elora realized. She let go of Cush's hand and walked over to her mom wrapping her in a hug. "Thank you for being my mom," Elora whispered to her.

She felt her mom squeeze her a little tighter before

letting go. "It is a privilege and honor, sweet girl." Lisa gave her a warm, approving smile and added, "Love the outfit."

"Wouldn't expect anything less," Cassie agreed. As she held her arms open for a hug, Elora grabbed her arm and jerked her into an embrace. "I'm so glad you didn't die for good. I would have missed the crap out of you," Cassie muttered causing both of them to laugh.

Elora pulled back to look at her. She bit her tongue to staunch the tears that threatened to fall. "I love you too, Cass." Her voice was thick with emotion that she swallowed down as she stepped away from Cassie and looked at the man her best friend had fallen in love with.

Elora had liked Trik from the start, but after the conversation she'd had with him a week after the swamp catastrophe, she liked him all the more. Triktapic, king of the entire elfin race, came to her and knelt at her feet. At first Elora had thought it was a joke, Trik had a wicked sense of humor, but Cassie had been standing in the doorway of the room with a face full of worry.

"What's going on, Cassie?" Elora asked her friend while looking down at the kneeling king.

"There is no easy way to say this." Trik's voice sounded as though he was in pain. "I am the one responsible for the death of your father." He paused but began speaking again before Elora could stop him. "I won't make excuses for what I did. All I can do is say that I am so, so very sorry." He looked up at her and to her utter shock there was a sheen of wetness in his eyes.

Elora wasn't sure what to do so she patted his shoulder and said, "Stand up, Trik." He rose to his feet gracefully and met her eyes. "I knew about it, but I also know that you were a different person then. I know that since that time you have changed in many ways, and you have been broken by your past, only to then be built back up a better and more honorable man. If you need to hear it, then I will tell you. I forgive you."

His eyes widened and after a few heartbeats he let out a slow sigh. "Thank you."

Trik's hand on her shoulder brought her back from the memory. "I'm happy for you, Elora. And I too am glad that you didn't die for good."

She grinned up at him and then hugged him. "Thank you."

Trik pulled back until just his hands were on her shoulders. He glanced over Elora's shoulder and then looked back down at her. "Your future husband is looking at me like he wants to stab me with that sword he's always bragging about. It might be a good idea for you to go hug him."

Elora rolled her eyes. "Literally about to marry him and he still feels the need to mark his territory." She walked back over to her waiting warrior. "Quit glaring at Trik before he decides to whip out his quiver and arrows and shoot you."

Cush's lips twitched as he looked at her with a mischievous gleam. "Would you tend my wounds?"

"Yes, I'd cauterize them with a hot poker. Now are we doing this or what?"

"We are definitely doing this."

Tamsin cleared his throat and Elora looked up at him. "Do you come of your own free will, Elora Scott?"

"Do I look tied up to you?" she asked with a smirk.

"Not yet," Cassie coughed but the words were not lost.

Cush chuckled and the sound sent shivers down

Elora's back.

Tamsin smiled patiently at her.

"Yes, I come of my own free will," she finally answered when she realized he wasn't going to continue until she did.

Tamsin nodded and then looked at Cush. "You have the rings?"

Cush nodded as Elora's head whipped up to look at him. He'd gotten them rings? Just how long had he been planning this?

Cush squeezed the hand he still held in his. *"Long enough,"* he answered her unspoken question.

Tamsin began to speak as Cush turned to face her and took both of her hands in his. Once again the world faded away and it was only them. She didn't register most of what was said and yet managed to somehow speak the right words when it was time. Elora wondered if her face reflected even a portion of the adoration she saw in Cush's face as he stared at her. Then he began to speak and tears began to blur her vision of him.

"I am honored to be your mate, your husband. I promise to cherish you." His hands left hers as he spoke and cupped her face as he took a step closer to her. "I promise to protect you and provide for you. I pledge to you my heart, my body, my affection, and my love. All of it is yours alone. I take you into my keeping, a precious treasure, and I forsake all others."

Elora couldn't speak. No air would leave her lungs as his thumbs caressed her cheeks where he held her. She was captivated by his words and the emotions flooding into her through his thoughts.

"Elora, do you take Cush to be your husband, your mate?" Tamsin's asked.

Elora's hands clenched in Cush's shirt where she held it fisted against his chest. She hadn't even realized she'd grabbed onto him. She was finding it hard to form her own words when his were saturating her thoughts. "I don't know how I'm supposed to top that," she said looking up into his intense gaze.

Cush gave her a crooked smile. "You don't have to top it, just say yes." His warm breath blew against her face as he spoke.

"Yes," she whispered. "With every fiber of my being, yes."

"The rings now," Tamsin said and Cush released her face as he reached into his pocket and pulled out two platinum rings. One was a band that looked as though three strands of rope had been braided together and then wrapped into a circle. The other was a thin band with a black gem positioned on the top, with two smaller purple gems on either side. Her warrior had good taste in jewelry, she grinned to herself.

Cush's hands were steady as he reached for her hand and placed the larger ring in her palm. Elora wrapped her fist around it, afraid of dropping it while he took her other hand and slipped the ring with the three gems onto her left ring finger.

"With this ring, I thee wed."

It was her turn next. Elora's hands were not steady. She shook like a junky as she took his larger hand in hers and began to slip the ring onto his finger. "With this ring, I thee wed," she repeated as she stared at the ring wrapped lovingly around his finger. A symbol for all to see that he was spoken for.

"You may kiss your bride."

Tamsin had barely gotten the words out when Cush had her wrapped in his strong arms, his lips moving against hers. There was clapping and maybe some whistles but neither of them heard it clearly. They were too lost in one another.

Somehow they made it back to their room. She was in Cush's arms the whole way, and her lips roamed over his and his jaw and neck as he walked. She heard a door open and close and then felt a soft mattress beneath her. His body covered hers and it was as if they'd never left the room. Just as Syndra had said, they were picking back up right where they'd left off before they'd gotten married.

"We're married," Elora breathed suddenly as Cush's mouth did wicked things to her neck and collar bone. She gasped and gripped his shoulders catching a glimpse of her new ring. "By the way, totally good job on my ring." Elora was pretty sure he heard her despite the breathlessness of her voice. He grunted something but his mouth seemed quite content to remain busy on other things besides talking.

"You're in control, Little Raven, you tell me when to stop and I will."

Elora was surprised to hear his voice sounding so gruff in her mind. It was filled with the passion that he was showing her through his touch and kiss, and frankly, it was doing tantalizing things to her. She wanted to throw herself at him, and, well, she wasn't even going to entertain the ideas her dark elf side wanted. So, instead of overthinking it, Elora relaxed into her husband's care. He had said she was in control and she trusted him to stop if she got to that point.

"Let me take care of you, beautiful," he whispered to her. *"It is my privilege to love you."*

Elora let out a shaky breath. The room grew dim as the candles around them began to burn out but still he loved her, never pausing in his pursuit of her. He talked to her, laughed with her, and made her his sole focus.

Hours later they lay wrapped in each other's arms, the sheets tangled around their bodies, and all of the candles had long gone out. Cush had kept his word, slowing down when she asked him to. She never once told him to stop, but she'd been nervous, and a tad self-conscious. But passion had eventually overshadowed all of that and the need to be a part of him had won over the fear and insecurities.

"I love you, Elora," Cush whispered against her hair as his fingertips trailed along her bare spine.

"Of that I have no doubt," she teased but then looked up at him, resting her chin on his chest. "I love you back," she said meeting his eyes. They laid there quietly, staring at one another both overwhelmed by what the night had brought and excited about what the future held. Whatever it was, they would face it together.

"I can't believe my best friend is married," Cassie said as she sat on their bed while Trik brushed her hair as he did every night before they went to bed.

"We've been married for a while now, beautiful," Trik said from behind her.

Cassie rolled her eyes. "You know who I mean."

"If you mean your best *girl* friend, then yes. But since I am your best friend, I was a little confused as to why you'd still be surprised."

"Glad to see that being king of an entire race

hasn't made you humble," she said dryly.

"I'm confident. You can be humble and confident at the same time," he pointed out as the brush was replaced by his fingers. The gentle tug against her strands was sensual and he knew what it did to her.

"Don't try to distract me," she scolded and attempted to move out of his reach but he was much faster than her. His arms wrapped around her waist from behind as he rested his chin on her shoulder next to her ear.

"I don't want to talk about Elora and Cush. I want to talk about us."

Cassie turned her head so she could see him from the corner of her eye. "What about us?"

"Are you happy?" He paused and turned her more toward him. "I mean here, in this realm."

Cassie's brow bunched together as she attempted to understand why he was asking her such a silly question. "Of course, I'm happy. I wouldn't be here if I wasn't."

"I know, but I just don't want you to feel like we have to stay here. If you want to live in the human realm with your family, we can."

"Trik, we've had this conversation before. You are needed here and I belong with you so the simple answer is we live in the elfin realm and visit my parents when we can. I promise you that if I—at any point—become unhappy, you will be the first to know."

Trik stared at her for a few minutes longer before leaning forward and placing a soft kiss to her lips. "Thank you."

"Now can we talk about Elora?" Cassie asked attempting to hide her smile.

"No, now you will tend to your mate." Trik tugged

her down until she was splayed across his chest.

"Tend to my mate?" Cassie asked laughing as he smacked her bottom.

"Most definitely," he purred as he rubbed his face into her long locks. "I'm very deprived this evening. I had to go and watch my warrior get hitched to that dark little ball of trouble you call a friend and then I had to wait while you and Syndra chatted about throwing her an after wedding shower and then—"

Cassie placed a finger over his lips effectively halting his rant. "You poor, poor neglected quiver boy."

"Finally, we're getting somewhere," he said around her finger. "You understand that I have a neglected quiver."

Cassie threw her head back and laughed. "You will be the death of me, Triktapic," she teased.

"Hmm," Trik moaned into her neck. "But what a sweet death it will be."

Epilogue

"Often people think that a second chance means you did something bad on your first try. What they don't realize is that sometimes a second chance is just a different kind of good than the first chance. I like the idea of a different kind of good and I'd like to believe that just maybe my different kind of good is coming." ~Lisa Scott

6 months later…

"**A** little birdy told me that you turned Tony down, again." Syndra stepped out of the mirror and into Lisa's storeroom, like she'd done a thousand times before. And like a thousand times before, Lisa gave her a glare that said, stay out of my business. Syndra wondered if she'd ever realize that glares didn't work on her.

"He's practically a kid," Lisa said as she flipped the page on the clipboard she was holding.

"All you have to do is wait a decade and he'll be your age," Syndra pointed out.

Lisa snorted. "And then a decade later he would be older and then several decades later he would die and I would not. Been there, done that. I don't do reruns."

"Apparently you don't do anyone," Syndra muttered under her breath, but loud enough that her friend would hear.

Lisa dropped the clipboard on the counter with a loud clap and crossed her arms in front of her. "Did you come for a reason or were you just hoping I'd poison your tea and put Tamsin out of his misery?"

Syndra laughed. "Wow, you are prickly." She walked casually around the storeroom ignoring Lisa's scowl. "Why exactly are you prickly like a cactus these days? Oh and," —she tapped her lips with a finger as she turned back to face her— "why can't you come to dinner tomorrow? Elora said that you canceled, again."

"I'm busy," Lisa huffed. "If you didn't know, I sort of run a business when I'm not in your realm. I still have a life out here apart from the rest of you."

"Hmm, hmm, I see. Okay, so that still doesn't answer why you're cancelling dinner? You have six other nights to, as you call it, run your business."

Lisa stared at her eyes wide like a cornered rabbit. Syndra could have backed off, but she cared too much for her longtime friend to let it lie. "Or, perhaps, your business can't change his plans to a different night?"

"Why are you so obsessed with me having a love life? First Tony, and now you think I have some mystery guy on the side. Maybe I just need a break, Syndra."

Syndra shook her head. "I'm not buying it. You've never needed a break from me before." Lisa didn't respond and when she picked up her clipboard again, Syndra knew that she wouldn't get any further with her.

"Okay, fine, new topic," she said as she leaned against the wall. "Elora and Cassie told me that you are making them get their GEDs. I'll have you know that anytime you do something that ticks them off I get an earful for days. It's annoying."

Lisa grinned and eyed her. "So it's annoying for them to bug you repeatedly about something that you don't want to talk about?"

"Touché," Syndra conceded. "Fine, I'll leave you

to your business. But you better be at dinner next week or I shall be very put out."

Lisa saluted her but didn't look up from her clipboard. Syndra let out a sigh as she walked back over to the mirror. She glanced back one more time wondering, not for the first time, if she should ask Trik to put his spy experience to good use.

Lisa let out the breath she'd been holding as soon as Syndra disappeared through the mirror. She set down the clipboard and pen and rubbed her sweaty hands on her jeans. Syndra was like a bloodhound when she got a scent, and at the moment the scent she was chasing just happened to be Lisa and the secret she was keeping.

Truth be told, it really wasn't much of a secret because there was nothing to tell, not yet. At the moment it was just half a dozen handwritten notes left in her mailbox at the store. When she'd gotten the first one, she didn't even recognize the name. It wasn't until the second note that she realized who had left it. And that was when she decided to keep the notes to herself. She'd be lying if she said she didn't hurry to work each day just to see if there was another one waiting on her. A grin formed on her lips as she thought about the last one she'd gotten.

She walked over to her desk and opened the middle drawer and picked up the first piece of black folded paper in a stack. Her hands shook, just like the first time she'd opened it, as she unfolded it. And just like the first time she read it, her heart started galloping in her chest.

I remember you. You took my breath away then,
And a century later you still do.

Dinner, Wednesday, 7:00 p.m.

Yours,
R

From the author:

Thank you so very much for going on this journey with me and the characters from the Elfin Sereis. This is the last book in this series, though there will be a Novella about Lisa, Elora's mother. So be looking for that! I hope that you enjoyed your journey with Cassie and Elora.